"David Stout's mystery/suspense novels grow increasingly impressive. THE DOG HERMIT . . . surpasses in range, depth, and insight even *Carolina Skeletons.* . . . [A] seamless storyteller growing steadily more confident of his talent and skills."

—*Buffalo News*

▲▼▲

"You'll like David Stout. You'll love THE DOG HERMIT. . . . The suspense bubbles quietly, gently as the author draws tension from his characters in a seamless weaving of all parts of his story to a sweeping conclusion."

—*Mystery News*

▲▼▲

"The tension builds until you want to scream. [A] great novel. . . . A book to read if you want to sit up all night."

—*The Armchair Detective*

more . . .

▲▼▲

"An emotion-packed story . . . action down to the wire."

—*Chattanooga Times*

▲▼▲

"A gripping novel."

—*Library Journal*

▲▼▲

"Intriguing characters and surprises that keep coming."

—*Mansfield News Journal* (OH)

▲▼▲

"A canny, breathless ending. This is one of the best of the season."

—*SSC Booknews*

▲▼▲

BOOKS BY DAVID STOUT

The Dog Hermit
Night of the Ice Storm
Hell Gate (with Ruth Furie)
Carolina Skeletons

DAVID STOUT

The DOG HERMIT

THE MYSTERIOUS PRESS

Published by Warner Books

A Time Warner Company

Astute readers will notice that there is no Bessemer in upstate New York, no Hill and Deer counties, no city of Long Creek, along New York's Southern Tier. They exist in my imagination, as do the characters and events in this novel.

If you purchase this book without a cover you should be aware that this book may have been stolen property and reported as "unsold and destroyed" to the publisher. In such case neither the author nor the publisher has received any payment for this "stripped book."

MYSTERIOUS PRESS EDITION

The Mysterious Press name and logo are registered trademarks
of Warner Books, Inc.

 Mysterious Press books are published by
Warner Books, Inc.
1271 Avenue of the Americas
New York, NY 10020

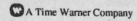 A Time Warner Company

Printed in the United States of America

Originally published in hardcover by The Mysterious Press.
First Printed in Paperback: February, 1995

10 9 8 7 6 5 4 3 2 1

For Ruth Furie, who carries the light

One

■ ■ ■

The thick, strong hands of the mechanic steered the four-wheel-drive pickup off the road, into the tiny clearing barely big enough for the truck. The metallic slam of the door broke the hush of the deep woods. As he stood next to the truck, he heard other sounds: snow collapsing from the upper branches of the evergreens onto the lower boughs, then tumbling all the way to the bottom and landing on the ground with loud *plops*.

He had caught the weather just right. There was enough snow left in the woods for him to drag the heavy sled without much trouble, enough to drag the sled back to the truck with its heavy load. He knew the sled was strong enough. It had been used for ice fishing.

If he had judged his time right, and the weatherman was right, the snow would be gone by tomorrow—along with his tracks, if that mattered.

Not quite winter. The ground was not cold enough to keep the snow for long, and it was still soft enough to dig in. And it was in between hunting seasons: Small-game hunting had

1

just ended, and deer season would not start for another ten days. That meant he might be the only person to be in this part of the woods all day, which was fine with him.

He let down the back of the truck and set the sled on a level spot of ground. Then he hauled out the two tanks (green for oxygen, red for acetylene), the cutting torch, and the hoses and arranged them on the sled, buckling them down with the straps he'd fastened to the sled. Safety mask (check), work gloves (check), and he was on his way.

He had to walk a few hundred yards through the trees, down a gradual slope to the dump site. Things were exactly as they had been on his last visit. A shopping cart lay on its side, among old cans and an ancient rusted stove. And there was the other metal thing that had caught his eye while he was doing his own after-dark dumping. Yes, it was as he remembered. It would work; he was sure of it. But it lay under some other waste metal that was either too heavy or too sharp for the man to clear.

He put on his mask and gloves and in no time was running the flame around the metal he needed to cut away. The man was an expert with the torch, and he worked quickly and efficiently. The snow around him hissed from the sparks.

He still had plenty of daylight by the time he freed what he had come for. Puffing from the strain and taking care to avoid the hot metal, he horsed the object onto his sled, strapped it down, and resecured the tanks, torch, and hoses.

Done.

He took out a candy bar, started to eat, let himself relax. His hair was wet from sweat.

The man was tired but pleased when he got back to the pickup. Some of the snow had melted just in the short time he'd been gone, and the only tracks in what was left were his own. Warm weather must be on the way.

He was sweating heavily. But after he put his gear onto the truck (along with the object he'd come for), he was surprised to feel a slight chill on his skin.

"Make up your mind," he said to the graying sky.

The man made sure the big metal thing wouldn't roll in the back of the pickup. Then he drove back to the shop. He encountered no one on the road in the woods and only a couple of cars on the main road.

Just before he got to the shop, he stopped to buy a cold six-pack. Then he went to the shop, where he and his partner dragged the metal thing inside.

"What do you think?" said the man who had dragged the thing out of the woods.

"I think it'll work."

"Damn right. Let's get started."

So the two men set about with torches, drills, screwdrivers, nuts, and bolts to fashion the thing for its intended use. It took a couple of hours, but they didn't mind. They had the six-pack for company (the beer went fast, and one of them went to fetch more), and they worked easily together. They were brothers.

Two

■ ■ ■

Jamie was tired, and he floated in and out of sleep on the front seat next to Tony. He hadn't wanted to put on his pajamas before leaving his father's for the ride home, but his mother had told him over the phone that he had to.

Usually, his father drove him back home after the visits. His father would take him to the door and say hello to his mother. They seemed real friendly to each other after the visits, shaking hands sometimes, and Jamie couldn't understand why they couldn't all be together again if they got along so well.

It just couldn't be—that was what both of them told him. It just couldn't be. Someday he'd understand.

"Damn," Tony said. "Oh, you're awake, huh."

Jamie giggled, because he knew his father had told Tony not to swear in front of him.

"How come you said 'damn,' Tony?"

"Don't tell your dad. I'm counting the snowflakes. See?"

Jamie sat up straight. "Lookit, Tony. Millions and millions and millions."

4

It seemed to Jamie that all the snowflakes God had ever made were flying at the car, dancing like feathers in the headlights. Jamie could tell that Tony was driving more slowly. "Can you see okay?"

"No sweat, pal."

Jamie was happy. Though it had been too cold to ride the pony, his father had taken him to the barn to say hello to it. The pony had been glad to see him and had pranced in the stall. Jamie liked the smell of the pony and had said, "He makes good air."

His father had laughed at that.

Jamie knew it would be a long time before he could ride the pony without his father next to him. He was only five.

"There must be millions and millions of snowflakes. Huh, Tony?"

"Yep."

"Maybe even zillions and zillions."

"You got it, pal."

Jamie watched the snowflakes flying toward the car (like white bats, that's what they were like), until he felt himself getting sleepy again. The last thing he remembered before his eyes closed was Tony patting him on the knee.

"Son of a bitch!"

Tony's swearing woke Jamie up and scared him. Tony almost never talked that bad . . . .

"What is he, crazy?"

"What's the matter, Tony?"

"Nothing, pal. Don't worry."

But just then Tony reached over and checked Jamie's safety belt. He's making sure I'm buckled, Jamie thought. Jamie was afraid.

"Damn. First they give me a detour with no warning, then . . . Jesus!"

Jamie saw the orange cones in the headlights (witches' hats; that's what they were), saw the other lights, coming in through the back window and shining off Tony's face. Tony looked scared.

Alongside the car, there was a big dark shape (a truck, Jamie thought), and it looked close enough for Tony to reach out and touch. The shape pulled ahead, then moved to the side. Jamie heard Tony swear again, saw him pull on the steering wheel, felt the car go bump, bump, bump on the side of the road.

The car stopped, and there was a big bright light shining into Jamie's eyes, and he turned to look at Tony and saw Tony's eyes, which were all shiny and afraid, and two men stood in the big bright light with masks on (all different colors, like for skiing), and the snowflakes blew all around the men, and Jamie could see that they were pointing big shiny guns at Tony, the kind of guns his father used to shoot birds. And Jamie started to cry, because he knew he wasn't dreaming.

"Jesus!"

Jamie heard how scared Tony was. Then he saw one of the colored masks real close to Tony's window, saw the gun barrel pointing at Tony's head. Then the gun barrel wiggled up and down, and Tony opened the window.

Cold air and snowflakes blew in.

"Put your hands on the wheel and hold tight," a mean voice said through the mask.

The door on the other side opened, letting in more cold and snow. Jamie turned and saw the other man, the other mask. The man unbuckled Jamie's seat belt, grabbed him so tightly that Jamie's arms felt pinched. Jamie made fists, swung at the man, got ready to kick.

"Tell the kid to cool it," the other man said. "Do it, or I'll blow your head off."

"Jamie, don't. Don't. Oh, Jesus . . ."

Jamie had never heard Tony afraid before.

"We're taking the kid. You're gonna stay right here. With any luck, you can get loose before you get too cold."

Jamie was out in the cold now, blinking in the light, snowflakes blowing all around him, being held tightly against a man's winter jacket. He saw the other man tying Tony's hands to the steering wheel, saw Tony's face all white and scared.

"You're gonna stay here and take a good long time getting yourself untied, aren't you? Aren't you?" said the man who was tying up Tony.

"Yes. Please. Yes."

"Good. That way, you won't get your brains blown out. We'll be in touch on how to get the kid back. Tell his old man if anyone tries anything, we won't just kill him. We'll diddle him first."

Three

■ ■ ■

Tom Ryan cursed silently as Lyle Glanford stood in the doorway of the newsroom. The publisher of the *Bessemer Gazette* was frowning, and Ryan knew the frown (reflecting puzzlement rather than anger) meant trouble. As Ryan watched, the publisher ran his fingers through his white hair, then headed for Ryan's desk.

Shit, Ryan thought. "Mr. Glanford," he said.

"Ry, do we have anyone over in Hill County?"

"A stringer, you mean?"

"No, not a stringer. I mean, have we sent a staffer over there? To follow that kidnapping over around Long Creek?"

"Oh, uh, not—"

"Well, hell. Seems like we should. People over there look to our Country Edition to know what's happening. Especially those who don't have cable. Hell of a case, don't you think?"

"Hell of a case, yes."

"Who can we send? You're running the city desk today, you tell me."

"Most of the staff has gone home, Mr. Glanford. What

8

with Thanksgiving and all. If we sent someone and they were there over the holiday, technically we'd have to pay overtime. . . ."

"Overtime?"

"For Thanksgiving work, Mr. Glanford."

"Work out something, Ry. You're the editor. Call in a favor."

That won't be enough to pay for the trip, Ryan thought. "The thing is, Mr. Glanford, we thought we were supposed to be cutting back on the travel expenses . . . ."

The publisher shot Ryan a look.

". . . to conserve our resources for big stories like this," Ryan said, recovering instantly. "We'll, I'll get someone over there pronto."

"Good," the publisher said as he stood to go. "Make sure it's someone who knows what he's doing."

"Right." But who? Ryan thought.

Fran Spicer had been tapering off all afternoon, and in a few more minutes he could lock his desk and start his holiday. He would be off not only Thanksgiving but for the next three days, as well. He didn't know exactly what he would do— watch some football, try to keep busy so he didn't mope too much—but he had learned to take each day at a time.

Fran Spicer was a general-assignment reporter. On a big metropolitan daily, a general-assignment reporter was supposed to be a star who could write tragedy, comedy, and everything in between, and do it fast.

But Spicer did not work for a big metro daily. He worked for the *Bessemer Gazette*, the only newspaper in a decaying Great Lakes rust-belt city. There were two kinds of general-assignment reporters on the *Gazette*. There were young ones who hoped to work their way onto beats, then go to a bigger city, and there were the old and tired ones. It had been a while since Fran Spicer was young.

He had spent the afternoon doing busywork—transferring notes from his pad to a computer, which he would never get that friendly with, and sorting out his files.

Spicer sensed a presence behind him.

"Any plans for the holiday, Fran?"

Spicer didn't like Ryan's tone. "Watch some games, I guess."

"The publisher's been paying attention to the outside world again," Ryan said.

"Always a bad sign," Spicer said. Nope, he didn't like the way Ryan was talking.

"He's got a real burr up his ass. About that kidnapping over near Long Creek."

Spicer was relieved: Ryan was going to tell him that the publisher wanted the *Gazette* to run a story on his favorite local charity, the Fund for the Protection of Children, using the kidnapping as a news peg.

"He wants us to send someone," Ryan said.

"Where?"

"To Long Creek. To follow the kidnapping."

"Are you serious, Ry? When?"

"Yesterday."

Spicer knew what was coming next, but he didn't quite believe it. "Me?"

"You. Most of our people have family plans. Plus, you've been around a while. If I send some young smart ass, he's apt to get crapped on by those redneck cops over in Hill County."

Spicer knew there was more.

"And," Ryan went on, "I figured we could work something out on Christmas. You already got off Christmas Day, like I promised earlier. I think I can guarantee you the whole week off, through New Year's."

"You *think*?"

"I can do it."

"When do you want me to leave? And for how long?"

"Tonight. We'll play it by ear. You'd better get going. Looks like snow's on the way."

"What about expenses?"

Ryan frowned. "Cashier's closed by now. Tell you what . . ." The editor took out his wallet and peeled off three twenties. "This'll help a little. Use your credit cards. Keep receipts. They're, uh, getting kind of stingy downstairs."

"I know."

"That's why I figured this could be kind of a personal

arrangement between you and me. You get some extra time off, like I said, and you maybe down-hold it on the expenses.''

Now Spicer understood, and he could have predicted what Ryan said next.

"'Course, technically you're entitled to an extra day's pay at time and a half for working Thanksgiving,'' Ryan said. ''But I thought you could sort of forget that in return for all the Christmas and New Year's time.''

Spicer had to give Ryan credit; he seldom missed a trick.

"Okay with you?" Ryan said.

Spicer thought about it; maybe this Christmas he really would get the time to make things up with the boy. ''Sure. I'll down-hold.''

"I appreciate it, Fran. But that doesn't mean you can't treat yourself to a nice meal tomorrow, if you can find one over there.''

"Right. Thanks.''

Ryan turned to go, then changed his mind. ''You, uh, feel okay, Fran? I mean, up to it and all?''

They both knew what that meant. ''Don't worry,'' Spicer said. ''I've been sober.''

"Oh, I know. I just meant . . .''

"I'll be fine.''

Spicer tucked several blank notepads into his battered briefcase, grabbed his soiled topcoat from the top of his desk. ''I'll stop in the morgue and make copies of the clips we've had.''

"Here they are, Fran. Along with a printout of the latest wire story. Take a few minutes and brush up on the details.''

Spicer sat down at his desk again and began to read the clips. The boy was Jamie Brokaw, five-year-old son of Richard Brokaw and his former wife, Celeste. Brokaw had founded and still controlled a cable-television company and was one of the few wealthy residents of Hill County, deep in a pocket of rural poverty and rusted-out factories along New York State's Southern Tier near the Pennsylvania border. Jamie Brokaw visited his father on weekends.

Sunday night, as the boy was being driven back to his mother by the father's chauffeur, Anthony Musso, the car had been forced off the road by two men in a truck who had first set up a phony detour, complete with the orange cones used by highway crews.

The men had been masked and armed with shotguns. They had tied the chauffeur's hands to the steering wheel while they pulled the boy out of the car and spirited him away. The abductors had said they would be in touch with instructions on securing the child's release.

On Tuesday, a letter had arrived at the home of Richard Brokaw; it was a message spelled out in newspaper headline letters pasted to a sheet of common notebook paper. The message demanded fifty thousand dollars for the child's safe return.

It said that instructions for delivery of the money would follow.

The note said the boy would be killed if the ransom wasn't paid.

The envelope containing the message had been sent from a post office on the outskirts of Hill County, some miles from the community of Long Creek, near where the kidnapping had taken place. Investigators theorized that the crime had been planned sometime in advance. The authorities presumed that the abductors were familiar with the habits of Richard Brokaw—not surprising, since he was one of the richest and best-known residents of rugged Hill County.

Hell, Fran thought. He's probably the only rich guy in the county. No wonder his kid was the target.

The fact that the letter had been sent from so far away only created more trouble for investigators, who had no idea where the boy might be and where the kidnappers might have come from. In any event, because he had been missing more than twenty-four hours, the law now presumed that he might have been taken across state lines—meaning the FBI could enter the case under the so-called Lindbergh Law.

Fran read on, intrigued.

Detectives had refused to comment on whether they had ruled out the possibility that the kidnappers had had help from the inside. That would mean the chauffeur, Fran thought. But if they were suspicious of him, they'd zero in on him and sweat something out of him. Wouldn't they?

"Investigators said they had no reason to suspect that any disagreement between Richard Brokaw and his former wife had led to the kidnapping. The boy had been scheduled to return to his father's house for Thanksgiving. One investigator described the relationship between the former husband and wife as 'cordial, especially where their son's welfare is concerned.' "

The latest story said the kidnapping had drawn dozens of reporters to Long Creek, "once a thriving rail, coal, and steel center but for decades a decaying rust-belt town" that wasn't used to that much attention from the outside world.

Sure, Fran thought. He had lived in the state long enough to know what that meant: Long Creek (and most of Hill County, for that matter) was isolated and didn't care much for strangers. And the cops were reputed to be a bunch of bad-tempered head knockers.

Well, Fran thought, I ought to be able to handle this. Hell, I was a pretty good police reporter once. He put on his coat and headed for the coffee shop. He would get a couple of sandwiches to eat on the way.

One of Ryan's assistants approached. "Don't give me any new problems," Ryan said.

"Relax," said the assistant, a tired-looking middle-ager. "I just need to bounce some schedule changes off you."

"Yeah? Well, there's gonna be some more." Ryan told his assistant about the encounter with the publisher.

"Shit," the assistant said, "we're supposed to pinch pennies. By logic, that means covering a kidnapping a couple of hundred miles away with the wire services. Yes?"

"Yes. Only now, the publisher wants to play newspaper. So we're sending our own reporter."

"Well, who're you gonna send?"

"He's sent already. Spicer."

"Fran Spicer? Jeez, are you sure. . . ?"

"How the hell can I be sure of anything?" Ryan snapped. "I figured Spicer was our best bet to down-hold on the expenses and not screw up too bad. He still owes me, and he remembers. I didn't come down too hard on him the last time he went off the wagon, after all."

The assistant frowned and nodded. "Did you ask Will Shafer?" Shafer was the executive editor.

"Hell, no. He's taking a long holiday. Publisher comes up to me and lays the problem in my lap, I gotta come up with something."

"Hmmm. I just hope Fran doesn't stop someplace on his way there, if you get my drift."

"Yeah, I get your drift. Speaking of that, what do you say we head across the street for a little holiday-eve cheer."

About the only thing that still worked reliably in Spicer's car was the heater. He was thankful for that as he drove into the evening, catching a look now and then at the pink and purple sunset in the mirror. He had driven through traces of snow on the outskirts of Bessemer, and there was no telling if there was more ahead. The weather was likely to deal a lot of surprises this time of year: sixty degrees one day, thirty the next.

What had Ry said about getting a nice meal on Thanksgiving? "If I can find one," Spicer whispered. The sandwiches from the coffee shop had been filling without being satisfying.

The more he thought about it, the more pissed he was at Ryan, and himself. The editor had just assumed that he had no Thanksgiving plans. Well, he didn't—not exactly—but he *had* been looking forward to watching football. He liked to call Mark at halftime and talk about the game. A little father-son chat about football was good. At least his mother didn't try to stand in the way of that, the bitch. Fran was proud: His ten-year-old son had a better head for football than a lot of high school kids.

Up ahead, Spicer saw an exit sign and on a hill to the right a big sign for a gas station. He would stop now; no telling where he'd be able to get gas tomorrow.

He pulled up to a self-service pump, put ten dollars' worth into the tank, went inside to pay the attendant and use the john. Coming out, he saw a bar on the other side of the road not quite a hundred yards away. It was a low, dark structure. The cars out front were tacky-looking (Some are as bad as mine, Spicer thought ruefully). The very shabbiness of the place, especially its pink neon beer sign, was inviting. Spicer could almost taste the first jolt of peppermint schnapps, followed by that first long gulp of cold beer cutting through the sweetness.

Our Father, who art in heaven. Our Father . . .

Just in time, Fran got into the car and drove back onto the highway. He deliberately avoided looking into the rearview mirror.

The next time Fran felt the thirst, he was on the two-lane to Long Creek, just after he'd gotten off the expressway. It came without warning, as it usually did, although Fran thought it might have something to do with having seen the friendly-looking bar earlier in the evening.

With the thirst in his throat, he drove toward Long Creek. Once, he saw a white-tailed deer cross the road. He saw the creature's eyes in his headlights for an instant. Then the vision was gone.

Fran Spicer pressed on, into the gloom. The thirst was still with him, and his palms felt moist in his gloves. I'm getting such a bad case of nerves, I'll be lucky to sleep tonight, he thought.

The more he thought about it, the more he thought Ryan had been a son of a bitch. How many goddamn years had he been at the *Gazette*, and how many good stories had he done out of the courthouse and city hall and the school board? Too many to count. It was the things you couldn't control . . .

Our Father, who art in heaven.

He slowed down when he saw the liquor store by the road. He would be right in Long Creek in another twenty minutes or so. Probably need something to get to sleep with.

The cheap whiskey and port wine were displayed on a front counter.

"Cold out there," Fran said. "Looks like snow."

"You're in luck," the owner said. "Five more minutes and I woulda been closed."

The thirst was galloping now. Fran's heart was beating so fast, he was pretty sure he'd need help getting to sleep. He picked up a bottle of peppermint schnapps and a six-pack of beer. "Get me through the weekend," Fran said, afraid that the owner had noticed the tremble in his voice and in his hands as Fran handed him a twenty.

But the owner, middle-aged and bored, scarcely looked at him as he rang up the purchase and slid the change over the counter.

"Thanks," Fran said. "Have a good holiday."

"You need any cups?" the owner said.

"No." Fran thought that was a snotty thing for him to say, but he didn't feel like telling him off. Why bother?

It had been some years since Fran had been to Long Creek, and the stretch from the interstate was longer than he had remembered. He was getting too old for long drives; his nerves would really be shot by the time he got there.

He had the thirst, all right, but he was pretty sure he could hold out until he got to Long Creek. He would be tired by then. Sure, that would be all right, to have a couple of drinks to help him get to sleep. The sun never came up on a day he couldn't handle a story, especially a good police story, with a little something inside him.

Several minutes passed between the sets of headlights going the other way. Ahead, on the other side of the road, he saw a low concrete building: some kind of shop or garage. He could see a driveway leading around to the back. He slowed down, turned into the driveway, braked sharply.

Fran sat in the dark, his engine still going, as he stared into the oasis of light his high beams dug out of the blackness. He could feel his heart beating faster. The thirst was rising up in his throat. Our Father, who art in heaven.

He switched his lights onto low beam and drove slowly along the narrow driveway. When he reached the end of the building, he saw that the driveway turned sharply, forming a small parking lot at the rear.

Fran Spicer pulled behind the rear of the building, turned off the lights, cut the engine. He was alone in pitch-darkness. It was good that he was out of sight from the road. For God's sake, if he did decide to have something before he got to Long Creek, he had to be out of sight of any cop.

Oh, Jesus. Our Father, who art in heaven.

Fran reached for the bag that held the schnapps and the six-pack. His fingers clawed at the paper, found the schnapps bottle. Could he still change his mind? Our Father . . .

Four

...

"**N**o!" The boy's outburst came from pure anguish.

The man with him chuckled sadistically.

"No, don't!" the boy pleaded.

Another chuckle, softened only a little by compassion.

"No, no, no!" The boy was getting worse by the second.

His father only laughed. "What did I tell you, Brendan. Every time he tries to scramble, he gets sacked."

Will Shafer sipped his beer and nibbled at his second slice of mincemeat pie. The neighbors who had come for dinner were gone. Will was thoroughly enjoying himself, eating leftovers and watching a football game on the big-screen TV in the basement rec room.

"No!"

"Easy, son. You almost knocked your sandwich on the floor." Will was pleased: His son, soon to be twelve, wasn't much of an athlete, especially compared with his youngster sister, Cass, but at least the boy was learning to enjoy some sports.

"Third and fifteen," the boy complained. "Oh, man. . . ."

"Brendan, they need a quarterback with a couple of good legs. What's his name's too old."

"He's not *that* old. Is he? There! Run! See!"

"Fourth and nine. Thirty-three is old for a quarterback."

"That's not as old as you."

"Not by a long shot. But it's old for a quarterback. His future is behind him."

"What's that mean?"

"It means I feel like another beer."

The rec room phone rang but stopped after one ring. That meant Karen had answered it upstairs.

"Will!" Karen shouted.

Will Shafer turned down the TV and picked up the phone. Please, God, don't let it be Lyle Glanford. He had managed to forget all about the paper today. Shafer's relationship with the *Bessemer Gazette*'s publisher had been tense lately.

"Will, it's Tom Ryan. Look, I'm sorry to bother you at home. It's about Fran Spicer."

Damn, Will thought. Fran must have fallen off the wagon again, with a crash. "What is it, Ry?"

"He's hurt real bad, Will. He's in the hospital."

"What happened?"

"Auto accident, Will." Nervous pause. "He was on assignment."

"On assignment? I thought he was taking a long Thanksgiving weekend."

"He was, originally. But I needed, I mean, Mr. Glanford came up to me and . . ."

"Just tell me what happened, Ry. What's Fran's condition?"

"Critical, Will. He's in intensive care, so he's automatically listed as critical. But it sounds really serious."

"Damn. He's in Bessemer General?"

"Uh, no. He's over in Hill County, actually."

"Hill County? On assignment?" Now Will was flabbergasted. "Fill me in, Ry."

Will stuck a finger into one ear to blot out his son's groans and cushion poundings, and pressed the receiver hard to the other ear. Patiently, Will listened to Tom Ryan's account, which was heavy on what the publisher had decreed, or what Tom Ryan thought he had decreed. Ryan even used one of the publisher's favorite verbs, *down-hold*.

"Jeez, Will. I had to send him. There was no one else."

"Okay, Ry. Okay. We'll just have to make sure he's treated okay."

"He's in Long Creek Regional, Will."

"All right. Someone will have to . . ." Will paused, shook his head. "I mean, I'll make a call and see that he has what he needs. Do we know anything about what happened?"

"Took a curve too fast, Will. Sideswiped another car. The driver, a young woman, she was banged up a little. Fran, uh, it seems he was drinking, Will. They found booze in the car."

Will felt very sad. "Okay, Ry. Thanks for calling. I'll get in touch with the hospital to see that Fran has what he needs."

"Uh, Will. One more thing. Should we send flowers?"

Will smiled, but ruefully. "Sure, Ry. I'll approve the bill myself."

Shafer hung up, slumped in his chair. He was all but oblivious to the sounds of the game. He was sad over Fran Spicer and angry at Tom Ryan for sending him to Hill County. The sad truth was that Fran Spicer was the worst-possible choice for such an assignment. A major crime story, especially one that was still developing, required a reporter of resourcefulness and energy and good judgment. Fran had had all those qualities, once.

"But that was a lot of drinks ago," Will said softly.

"What?"

"Nothing, son. Just talking to myself."

The phone rang again. Will went to the foot of the stairs and hollered up. "Karen, can you please get that? I'm not here, okay? I don't feel like talking to anyone right now."

After a few minutes, Karen called down and said she needed to talk to him. Will went up to the kitchen.

"That was Lyle Glanford," she said. "Something about Fran Spicer being hurt real bad?"

"Yes, that's what the first call was about. He was in a wreck over near Long Creek. A bad one."

"Oh, I'm sorry. The publisher wanted to be sure you knew about it. He said you should call him if you had any questions about what he wanted you to do."

"Damn." Will knew what that meant, and what he had to do. He dialed the publisher's home number.

"Will?" the publisher said.

"Lyle, I just heard about Fran. Terrible."

"Yes, it is. What the hell did Ry have in mind, sending him over there?"

A voice in Will wanted to say, Why don't you ask him? He got his job by kissing your ass.

"Will?"

"I'm sure Ry had to make a spur-of-the-moment decision, Lyle."

"Hmph. Well, it's done. Will, we need someone over there to look after him."

Ah yes, Will thought. The paternalistic publisher. And who might that "someone" be?

"Will, we just have to . . . ."

"I understand, Lyle." Will said good-bye and hung up.

Will's job had not been secure lately (at least that was the feeling he had been getting), partly for reasons beyond his control. He knew he might have to leave Bessemer someday, and he knew in his heart that he could cut it in a bigger city, but he wasn't ready to do it now. And he certainly wasn't ready to quit the *Gazette*. There were a lot of reasons; two of the simplest were the new furnace and the braces on his daughter's teeth. Damn, he wouldn't get to say good-bye to her, because she was at a friend's house.

Will went upstairs and packed an overnight bag. An hour later, he was on the highway, heading toward Long Creek. He was on edge, probably from the coffee Karen had made him just before he left. She insisted that he needed a jolt to minimize the danger of falling asleep at the wheel after too much to eat and two or three beers.

His wife was right, Will realized as he drove into the night. Ruefully, he thought that Long Creek had caused him plenty of trouble even before this latest, unexpected event. Long Creek had been a target of several on-again, off-again circulation drives by Will's paper.

Will had long argued that the *Bessemer Gazette* could make real gains in and around Long Creek. The cities nearest to Long Creek were Binghamton and Elmira, and neither paper in those communities had done much to court Long Creek readers. Perhaps that was because both Elmira and Binghamton looked down on Long Creek. Elmira and Binghamton were relatively prosperous, having more or less made the change from economies based on heavy industry to ones founded on services and high-tech products.

Long Creek had never made that adjustment. Some of it was due to a lack of political leadership, and some of it may have had to do with Long Creek's location: stuck in a rocky valley, with not that many good roads in or out in any direction (decades before, the city fathers had staked Long Creek's future on rail transport), and those roads apt to be snowed in from December through March.

In any event, New York State's other major papers had done precious little in Long Creek, whose own community paper was parochial and pathetically boosterish. Time and again, Will had argued with the *Gazette*'s publisher that the paper might as well try to win some Long Creek readers; after all, the Albany papers weren't, and neither were the Rochester papers.

Besides, Will had argued, a dying city like Long Creek, with aging politicians and labor leaders (often, they were the same) and probably more than a little corruption, was a wonderful opportunity for three or four aggressive reporters. The *Gazette* might win some prizes as well as readers.

Depending on his mood and the latest balance sheet, the *Gazette*'s publisher, Lyle Glanford, was more or less persuaded by Will's arguments. Unfortunately, building circulation in an area required patience and commitment, not a stop-and-start effort, and the *Gazette* had never stationed any reporters in Long Creek full-time.

When the *Bessemer Gazette* showed signs of doing well in Long Creek, the publisher seemed to think the circulation had been his idea. "And when things go lousy, it was all my idea," Will said aloud. "What could be fairer than that?"

Five

...

He paused on the hill to look back at the tracks left by his snowshoes and the sled bearing the Christmas tree. His legs were pleasantly warm from the uphill trek, and the air tasted cold and pure. All around him, it was still, and the sun was setting through a gap in the pines over the ridge that lay ahead of him.

Usually, the sunset at this time of year was a faded peach; this evening, there was more orange in it, and he wondered why. He would tell Jo about it. Maybe she was watching the sunset right now. He hoped so; it would be almost gone by the time he got to the cabin.

Happiness filled his chest when he thought of the cabin. Jo would have the fire going just right (she built better fires than he did), and she had been baking bread when he left to find a tree. He had been gone longer than he'd expected, and the bread would be done by now. Just the thought of it made him smile so broadly that the frost on his beard and mustache crinkled. Could there be a better night to eat warm bread by a warm fire? He would sip whiskey (standing in the cold, he could almost smell it, feel it in his throat), would cut some of Jo's bread into pieces to dip in the beef stew that had been simmering all day. Later, he would gently rub Jo's belly, where the baby was growing. They would name it Jason; it would be a boy. He knew it.

He walked again, down a hill through thicker woods. There was a small stream at the bottom, and he would have to find a narrow place to cross before starting up the last rise, to the top of the ridge. From there, he would be able to see the cabin.

It was darker next to the stream, and colder. He held his breath for a moment, listening to the low gurgle of the water over stones beneath the snow and ice. He breathed again, deeply and slowly.

Time to start up the rise. He had promised Jo he would be back while there was still daylight. He looked toward the top of the rise, squinting through the trees.

Flashes of orange along the top of the rise. The orange shimmered and danced. Not the sunset, not the sunset.

Terror filled his heart. He splashed through the stream, one snowshoe breaking through the crust, knife-cold water at his ankle. He scrambled up the rise as fast as he could. The footing was worse in the cold dark of the trees, the snow brittle, cracking under him. He looked toward the top; the orange still flashed. He had to get to where he could see.

A snowshoe caught on a buried branch, and he pitched forward into the snow. He let go of the sled with the Christmas tree, and it slid back down the hill. He got up, stumbled again, and scrambled through the trees. Up, up toward the top of the rise, praying that he wouldn't fall. Got to get to the top, to see, to see.

And then he was standing on the top of the rise, looking across the gently sloping meadow, his eyes telling him what he had known. The orange was from the cabin burning. The color glistened on the snow, brighter now than the dying sun.

Where was Jo? Where was their dog? Through tears, he stared at the flames and smoke. Smoke, there was so much smoke. She must be safe where he couldn't see, behind the smoke. He screamed as loudly as he could, tried to make a sound like Jo's name, but all that came out of his throat was a scream. But she must be able to hear him, must know he was watching. Where was she?

God, don't let this be. Could he still bargain with God? Please, don't take Jo and the dog both. Please.

He ran again, his snowshoes bursting through the crust as he went down the slope toward the flames. He screamed as he tripped and fell. He had to get up, had to get up so he could see. If he kept watching, Jo would appear, waving to him. The dog would be with her. She and the dog could not be in the flames, could not be.

He screamed as loudly as he could, trying to say Jo's name.

In the dark, the big dog snarled, barked, then growled in bewilderment. The hermit sat up in bed, eyes wide, until he could make out the blue-black rectangle of the window against the darkness. The dog snorted, perhaps annoyed with him for disturbing its sleep again.

"Wolf," he whispered.

The dog bounded up on the bed, stretched his body—a hundred-plus pounds of sinew, bone, and muscle—alongside the man's.

"Good Wolf. Good Wolf. Go to sleep."

He felt safe now, with the dog breathing next to him, safe enough to try to sleep again. He closed his eyes. Then he rubbed the sweat from his forehead and cheeks with the back of his hand, feeling the burn scars on his face.

Six

■ ■ ■

Will hated hospitals, and this day he would rather have been almost anywhere. He'd had a fitful sleep at the Long Creek Inn, at the edge of town. Now he dearly wanted to be home.

Like so much else about Long Creek, the hospital was depressing and dark. The hospital smell, a mixture of floor wax, alcohol, and vomit, made his breakfast sit uneasily in his nervous stomach.

"You'll have to put on a gown," the nurse said. "And your visit will be limited to fifteen minutes."

"Fine," Will said. "Can he, uh. . . ?"

"He drifts in and out, if that's what you mean. The crash trauma itself was bad enough, especially the rib piercing the lung. He had a lot of bleeding, some of it internal."

They were outside the intensive-care unit now. The nurse (about Will's age, handsome, businesslike but not unfriendly) handed him a pale orange gown.

"Hold out your arms," the nurse said. "There. It goes on backward, just like a lobster bib. Fifteen minutes."

* * *

Fran Spicer's head was propped on pillows and swathed in clean white bandages. A clear plastic tube ran into his nose, another into one arm. The exposed part of his face was yellow-purple with bruises.

Will sat in a stiff metal chair at the foot of the bed. He glanced at the beds on either side (a man lay in one, a woman in the other, both very old and thin), then looked again at Fran. The eyes were closed, the lids puffed and purplish.

"Ah, Frannie," Will whispered. "It's okay. It's okay. It was our fault, Frannie. Ours."

When Will had started as a reporter at the *Gazette*, back around the time some of his young staff members were in diapers, Fran Spicer was covering Bessemer city hall. Covering it well, too, or at least as well as the publisher would let him. Fran Spicer had shown Will the ropes, had taught him a great deal about city government and the ethnic crazy quilt that defined city politics.

Fran had spent way too much time at a tavern owned by a city councilman, drinking far into the night, long after he had picked up the latest political gossip. Throw in some marriage problems, some unpaid bills, add some more drinking . . .

"Ah, Fran. I'm so sorry. We shouldn't have sent you, old friend. It's not your fault."

The eyes opened slightly, focused on Will, glistened in recognition.

"Hi, Fran. Rest easy, old friend."

The eyes opened wider despite the puffiness. The lips moved.

"It's okay, Fran. Don't try to talk. Just rest."

But the eyes shone brighter through the slits in the puffiness, and the lips moved again.

Will leaned forward, held his breath to hear.

"The story of my life," Fran said softly. "The story of my life." The eyes rolled from one side to the other, then closed.

Will stood up. No point in staying. Fran was out of it. Worse, he sounded like he was giving up.

"Thank you," Will said, shucking the gown and tossing it into the small canvas bin for dirty laundry.

"We've not been able to contact any relatives," the nurse said. "Can you help?"

"Oh boy. Fran, Mr. Spicer, is single. Divorced for several years now. He does have a young son, but he's not old enough to take charge. Say, what are we talking about here?"

"I can't tell you for sure. Is there anyone who can make some decisions, if they become necessary? And before that, there's the paperwork on insurance and all. If he has any."

"He does." Will explained who he was. He said the *Gazette*'s personnel office would be in touch on the insurance information, and that the hospital should call him personally if there were any problems.

Will turned to go, then thought of one more thing. "When he needs clean clothes to go home in, you can let me know. Okay? I imagine the clothes he was wearing when he was brought in . . ."

"Yes, they're a bit soiled." The nurse went into a little room behind the counter, emerged a moment later with a cardboard box. Will opened the top flaps, felt sad all over again at the sight of Fran's threadbare suit lying wadded and dirty.

"This is blood, I guess. These marks."

"Yes. There was a fair amount. He might have come through it better if he'd used his seat belt. He wasn't thrown from the car, but he might have been banged around less if he'd been buckled in."

Will was surprised; he remembered riding with Fran a few times over the years, and he would have sworn that Fran was in the habit of using the seat belt.

Will folded the box flaps down again, but not before the smell of spilled beer hit his face.

"The smell was pretty strong when he was brought in," the nurse said. Will saw that her name tag read H. CASEY.

"Mmmm. He was, he had a problem. No question. He did try hard. Well, thank you. I guess I'll be going."

"Mr. Shafer, you know your friend here is in pretty rough shape. His recovery is far from certain. In fact . . ."

"Spell it out for me."

"A man his age in good health, it would still be tough.

Your friend here, because of the years of alcohol abuse . . . we're dealing with a patient who's much older, in a sense.''

"We're talking about death, then."

"I'm saying it's touch and go, Mr. Shafer. There doesn't seem to be any next of kin to tell."

"So I'm elected." Another thing that goes with the territory, Will thought.

"His chest was crushed. Broken ribs, fluid in the lung. Now, that fluid is very dangerous, given the patient's condition. And the strain on his heart is considerable."

"He could die. I know." Suddenly, Will was not only very sad but very tired. "As I said, the *Gazette*'s personnel office will be in touch. And I'll be around for a day or two. At least."

Seven

■ ■ ■

Jamie was in the dark, but it was not a dream, not a dream! Something was holding his arms and legs. Something. He wanted it to be the blankets and bedspread, tucked in real tight, but he knew it wasn't.

A light! A light went on, but not a light in his room. He was not in his room. He was cold.

"Watch that thing. Hold the light down here so I can get the straps loose. . . ."

Jamie screamed as loudly as he could. It was hard to make loud sounds. His throat hurt from crying, and from the shouting he'd done before they made him be quiet in the long cement room. They had slapped him, hard enough to make him cry, and scared him real bad. He'd stopped hollering, but he hadn't been able to stop crying in the long cement room.

"Shut the fuck up, kid."

Jamie was afraid. He screamed again, praying someone would hear.

Something hit his face, harder than he had ever been hit before, even by his father when he was mad.

"Shut the fuck up, I said!"

"Jesus Christ, you trying to kill him, or what?"

"You shut the fuck up, too."

Kill him! Trying to kill him! Now Jamie was afraid to scream, afraid he would be hit some more. His face hurt all over, his nose more than it ever had. His face had never hurt so much. He had never been so afraid. Now he wanted to go to the bathroom.

Back in the long cement room, they had made him swallow pills. They'd made him sleepy. Each time he came up out of sleep, he thought he might be in his own room again, and that he'd been dreaming about being taken away.

The tight feeling went away from his arms and legs, but now his hair was being pulled. Jamie cried and kicked, but only once, because his hair was pulled even tighter.

"Stop kicking, you little shit."

"Easy."

"Easy, my ass. We gotta get him in there and get the hell out of here. Down on your knees, kid."

In the light, Jamie saw a round black hole.

"Get in, kid."

No! He would not let them put him in there, not in that black hole! Jamie kicked as hard as he could. The hand let go of his hair, but then Jamie felt himself spinning around.

Wet. It was wet underneath him, and everything smelled like rotten leaves. There was a loud water noise. The light was jumping all around.

Jamie felt himself being lifted off the ground by his feet and under his shoulders. He had to pee, and his face still hurt.

"Get his feet in. . . . Just get his feet in. . . . There. . . ."

The hands let go of Jamie's feet, and his feet dropped onto something hard.

"Okay, now shove. . . ."

No! Jamie screamed as loudly as he could. Please, let someone hear! Mommy!

A hand came down real hard on his face, making his nose hurt real bad again. He was afraid of nosebleeds.

"Listen," one man said. "Stop kicking and go all the way in, and you'll be okay. No one's gonna hurt you. Pretend it's a game, like we said back there. No one's gonna hurt you. There's a flashlight in there. And candy bars."

Candy bars.

"Just go in, kid," the other voice said. "Just go in. No one's gonna hurt you."

Jamie felt big strong hands on top of his head, pushing him. Then he was sliding, sliding into the dark. He screamed, and his voice bounced back at him, like from inside a well. Sliding, sliding into the dark, bumping into soft things that crinkled like cellophane. Candy bars.

"All right, close him in," the meaner voice said.

"Right."

Jamie felt something—a bag—being put into his hands. "Here, kid," the other voice whispered. "You won't get hungry. There's candy bars and plenty of bread. Water, too."

"He'll find it, for Chrissake. He won't starve."

Bread and water. His mother and father had told him stories about witches and ghosts and locked-up places where they gave bad people bread and water. But there were always funny things in the stories, happy things at the end, so he wasn't scared when he got sleepy.

He heard a noise by his head, like a garbage can lid going on, and then he was in the darkest dark he could ever remember. He heard other sounds, then the mean voices. He couldn't tell what they were saying. He heard feet. He thought he heard the sound of water.

His nose hurt. He went in his pants. He couldn't help it. Then he started to cry in the dark. He kept his eyes closed as hard as he could, and for a long time. All the while, he cried. If he cried too loudly, the sound banged back into his ears, and he wanted to cry even louder.

He was afraid to open his eyes, because whenever he did there was nothing but dark. There was not even a little light, not even a little. It was all black where he was.

Oh. They said there was a flashlight. He felt with both hands. Oh. He was wrapped in a blanket. No, more than one blanket. He found the flashlight between the blankets. The switch was hard to push.

There. Light. He was in a small round place with shiny metal all around him.

He started to cry again. "Mommy!"

"Take it easy, kid. We're gonna see you're okay. Honest. My bro—"

"Shut the fuck up, you idiot."

"All right. All right."

"Just dig, and we'll get the hell out of here."

The voices were up above. Oh. There was a round hole, just over Jamie's stomach. Like a chimney. That's where the voices came from.

Noises all around. Shovels and dirt. Dirt was being thrown on the metal thing he was in. A little dirt came down the chimney.

"Watch it," said one of the men up above.

"Sorry, kid."

He had thought the long cement room was the worst place in the world. Now he wished he was back there. It had a toilet and a sink and no windows. They had put him in there with blankets and a pillow. And a little fur toy bear. One of the men had given him the bear to play with. Jamie wished he had it now. He had left it in the long cement room.

Jamie didn't know how long he'd been in the cement room. He couldn't even tell night from day, and they'd given him the pills to make him sleep. After they'd given him baloney and cheese and apples.

The toilet stunk in the long cement room. But he wished he was back there, instead of in this round metal place.

"Mommy!"

Oh. The shovel and dirt sounds had stopped. He didn't hear the men anymore. He thought he heard wind in the chimney. And the sound of water.

He lifted his head, but it hit hard on the metal and hurt. He had thought that by lifting his head he might wake up. He might find that he had been having a bad dream, that he really was in his bedroom, after all. Whenever he woke in the night in his bed, he raised his head and looked for the light under the door.

This time when he raised his head, there was only the shiny

light off the metal. He knew it wasn't a dream. His head hurt bad where he had bumped it. It felt like it was bleeding.

"Mom—MY!" he shouted as loudly as he could, so loudly it made his throat more sore. The sound banged back into his ears.

Jamie did something he hadn't done since he was real little: He kicked as hard as he could, up and down. Both big toes and both heels hit real hard. Both his toes hurt real bad and he screamed louder than ever. The sound banged back into his ears.

His toes hurt even worse than when he stubbed them on his dresser at home. He couldn't rub them.

"Mom—MY!"

It was a long time before his toes stopped hurting. When they did, they felt cold.

A long time later, Jamie was too tired to cry anymore. His eyes felt big and sore and his cheeks all wet and puffy. He cried harder than when he was real little and heard his mother and father fighting real bad at night. His throat was sore from crying and screaming, sore because he had to breathe through his mouth because his nose was all full up.

Jamie started to cry again but made himself stop. He made fists and banged down as hard as he could.

He felt something else. Something crinkly, like waxed paper. There was something mushy in his hand. Bread. Wet bread.

He reached down farther. Something hard and round, cold. Wet. A bottle.

Bread and water.

Eight

■■■

Will finished talking to the publisher and hung up, disgusted. He dreaded the next call he would make, but there was no putting it off.

"Good morning," his wife said. "How's it going? Are you coming home soon?"

"Not as soon as I'd like." He told her what Lyle Glanford had said, and the demands he had conveyed without stating them: that it would be good for Will to stay in Long Creek to look after Fran Spicer, and that as long as he was there he should follow the kidnapping case "as the *Gazette*'s representative."

"That bastard," Karen said.

"It's not that he's malicious. Just thoughtless, in the most literal sense. He thinks this is the same as my going to chamber of commerce meetings or United Way luncheons. My time is his time to use." Will paused, trying to keep his anger from poisoning the conversation. "I know plenty of editors, and they all feel sometimes like they're being chopped into little pieces by their publishers. But Lyle may be worse than most."

"His top editor is much better than the paper deserves."

"Thanks. I needed that. His background is all on the business side, so he has no idea of the time and effort involved in covering a major story. And he doesn't care to know."

"Damn him anyhow!"

"Goes with the territory."

"For now," Karen said.

Ah, yes. Neither was in the mood to chew on that last thought. Will could not be sure how long the publisher would want him around. Come to think of it, there were times when Will wasn't sure how long he'd put up with things, regardless of what Lyle Glanford wanted.

"As long as you're there, try to enjoy yourself," Karen said. "You might like playing reporter again."

"I'd like it better if I were ten years younger. And single. Besides, I'm rusty."

"You were a fine reporter. You know damn well you were."

Will thought that over: She was right; he had been a good reporter. "Bless you. Kiss the kids for me."

"You sound tired."

"I'm going to try to pace myself. Fran looks like hell, by the way. It's touch and go. The nurse said that."

They talked for a few more minutes. When Will said goodbye, he thanked the Big Power for giving him such a wife.

He had a big breakfast in the coffee shop, stopped at a stationery store to pick up a notepad and a couple of cheap ballpoints, and headed for the police station. He had called the night before and learned that a briefing was scheduled.

Outside the station, several television news vans were parked. Will saw from the letters on the side that two were from stations a long way from Long Creek. For God's sake, there was a crew from Bessemer. He hoped they wouldn't recognize him.

In the lobby, there was a white poster with an arrow and the words PRESS CONFERENCE. The arrow pointed to a large windowless room, which was already nearly full. Will stumbled over a thick cord on the floor.

"Watch it, buddy!" a cameraman said.

"*You* watch it," Will said.

A microphone on the table squeaked, then tipped over. The noise was magnified electronically as a young policeman tried to adjust it. "Take your seats, please, so we can get started," the policeman said. "I'd like to introduce the Long Creek police chief, Robert Howe. Chief?"

A glistening blue uniform adorned with gold stars and braid and stuffed with a fiftyish man of big belly and red face marched into the room and sat down in front of the mike.

"As you all know—" The mike shrieked and clicked. "As you know, it's now five days since the abduction of Jamie Brokaw. Since that time, the Long Creek Police Department, under my command, has conducted an exhaustive search in and around the city. We have been assisted by the Hill County Sheriff's Department at every stage of this investigation, and I can assure you that there has been total cooperation and coordination between our two agencies. We also have the full cooperation of the FBI, and we are in constant—"

"Excuse me, Chief," a reporter interrupted. "This is all well and good, this stuff about police coordination, but we'd like to know about the kidnapping investigation."

Frozen silence. The chief glared at the questioner, a young man (probably from New York or Philadelphia, Will thought) with plenty of guts and brass but not enough wisdom to keep his mouth shut. Small-town police chiefs, Will knew, usually weren't troubled about maintaining good relations with the press.

"Tell you what," the chief said. "We can do this my way, or we don't have to do it at all. What's it gonna be?"

Dead silence.

"Fine. As I was saying, we have been conducting as thorough an investigation as possible. The FBI has been assisting us, and I would like at this time to introduce Special Agent Gerald Graham from the Pittsburgh office."

Jerry Graham! Will sat up. This had to be the same Jerry Graham he'd known in Bessemer fifteen years ago. More, even. They'd actually gotten to like each other.

Yes, there he was. That's Jerry, Will thought.

Special Agent Gerald Graham walked in, still tall and lean, with the clear blue eyes, curly brown hair still thick but graying over the ears. In his charcoal suit and maroon silk tie, he could have passed for a stockbroker.

Will hid behind the shoulder of the man in front of him. For some reason, he didn't want Graham to spot him right away.

The agent sat down in front of the mike. Will figured the FBI was really running things behind the scenes, that the introduction of the police chief had just been part of a charade.

"Good morning, ladies and gentlemen," Graham began. "I will tell you what I can. No more, no less. And I'll ask that you use some discretion and remember that a little boy's life may be at stake here."

May be at stake, Will thought. What's Jerry saying? What's he thinking? That the boy is dead?

"Now then, just so you can get your facts as straight as possible, let us recap what's happened to date."

Will was certain he detected an underlying contempt in Jerry Graham's voice. Graham never had been a big fan of the press.

The agent summarized the bare facts of the abduction. As he did, he quickly answered a question that had occurred to Will: Was there any possibility of collusion on the part of the chauffeur who had been driving the boy back to his mother? Or that one of the warring parents had taken the boy?

The answers were no. Will wondered about that but had no reason to think Jerry Graham wasn't being straightforward.

Then Jerry Graham touched on the initial ransom note, demanding fifty thousand dollars; Will was familiar with that part of the case because he'd checked the wire service before leaving Bessemer.

"We have reason to believe that there was a high degree of planning," Graham went on. "Naturally, we have been anticipating, hoping, that the kidnappers would follow through on their promise in the initial note—that is, that they would provide instructions for the safe return of Jamie Brokaw."

Chairs squeaked; throats were cleared. Everybody waited.

"Unfortunately, that has not happened. Instead, just this morning, we received a second note."

There was a low muffled noise, not unlike that of a dog

waking from a nap and shaking itself, as the reporters snapped to attention.

"This later note, also spelled out in newspaper lettering, gave a new ransom demand, in the amount of two hundred fifty thousand dollars," Graham went on. "This note says that the boy is alive and well, and that instructions will be forthcoming for delivery of the ransom and release of the boy. That's all I have to tell you. I'll take questions now."

Will had been taking notes furiously. A big story was getting bigger, and he was both embarrassed and amused at the butterflies in his stomach. Could he still write a decent story? If he couldn't, he would be the laughingstock of the office among the young reporters, who were contemptuous of editors anyhow.

Oh, of course he could write a decent story, for God's sake. He had to: The *Bessemer Gazette* couldn't send its executive editor out of town and not get a good story out of him.

"Sir, where was the second letter postmarked?" The reporter was young, sandy-haired, wearing glasses.

"Oh, yes," the agent said. "I forgot to mention that. It had a Deep Well postmark. Deep Well, as I guess most of you know, is fifty miles or so farther away from Long Creek than the post office where the first message was mailed."

I should have thought of that question, Will thought. God, what am I doing here?

"And what do you think that means, sir?" the same reporter persisted. He wore a deliberately mismatched coat and tie. He wore ambition on his face.

"Well, we think it could mean that the kidnappers have taken the child out of this area," Graham said evenly. "That's part of the reason I'm here, after all. Because the victim has been missing more than twenty-four hours, we presume he might have been moved across state lines. In this case, into Pennsylvania."

"Sir, do you think the boy has in fact been moved across state lines? And if he has not been, doesn't that mean the kidnappers will be tried in state court, assuming they are caught, and that your presence here is in a sense unnecessary?" The questioner was a strikingly lovely young woman with flawless skin and rich black hair—a TV reporter, Will assumed.

Graham looked at her with steel in his eyes. "I have no way of knowing the child's whereabouts, therefore I have no opinion. Until the boy is found, wherever that may be, I would like to think I can make a contribution."

The young woman nodded respectfully but was clearly not cowed. Beautiful and tough, Will thought. Network material.

A young man shouted, "Agent Graham, what do you make of this second, much higher ransom demand?"

The agent looked uncomfortable. "I'm not sure what to make of it. It could be that, having succeeded in abducting the boy and eluding capture, the kidnappers are now flushed with success and are thinking, Hey, why not go for a lot more?"

A tall young man stood up. "Isn't that a problem, sir? Theoretically, the kidnappers could escalate their demands out of sight. Would those demands be met?"

While Graham thought about his reply, Will studied the reporter: midtwenties, long hair in studied disarray, a short-sleeve shirt in winter weather to show off his biceps. For a moment, Will hoped the reporter would apply to the *Gazette* someday. So Will could turn him down.

"I'm not dealing in theories," Graham said finally. "Our practice is to place the safe return of the victim above all else. We are waiting for the kidnappers to deliver instructions on the safe return of the boy."

"Sir, if the boy is farther away, does that make him harder to find?" asked a young man with a high voice.

What a stupid goddamned question, Will thought. I'd rather not ask anything than ask one like that.

Will studied Graham's expression. Yes, he still puts on the poker face. The academy must teach them that.

"Every kidnapping is different," Graham said at last. "If the boy is not close by, it does increase the territory we have to search, obviously."

"So the authorities are actively hunting for the boy even as you wait for more instructions from the kidnappers?" the high voice went on.

"Yes."

"Would you care to go into more detail?" the high voice pressed.

"No."

"Sir, do you yourself have children, and, if so, does it affect how you approach this case?"

"Yes. And no."

There was a rumble of laughter at Graham's neat put-down.

"Do you think the boy is still alive, and what do you think the chances are of getting him back alive?"

There, Will thought. The bottom-line question, asked in an insensitive way by a young man with a fashionably dirty raincoat and a sneering mouth. But the essential question nonetheless.

"I have no way of knowing. It is our hope, above all else."

"And are the boy's parents good for the kind of money the kidnappers want?" the questioner pressed on.

The agent looked annoyed. Will didn't blame him. No wonder a lot of people think the press sucks, Will thought.

"The boy's father is a man of means. He is good for that kind of money, as you put it. At this time, I would like to introduce the boy's parents, who have something to say."

A startled murmur ran through the room; no one had said anything about the parents appearing.

A man and woman came through the side door, together and yet not together, or at least not together in the way husbands and wives look together. The man's face seemed stitched tight, so that no quiver of eyelid or lip would betray his emotions. The woman's face was swollen and red, and she wore dark glasses.

The man pulled out a chair for the woman, who nodded slightly, as though accepting a favor from a courteous stranger. Then the man took a seat on the other side of the microphone, so that the FBI agent was sitting between them. Had they planned it that way? Will wondered.

The FBI man slid the microphone toward the woman.

"My name is Celeste Brokaw, and I am the mother of Jamie Brokaw, who is only five years old. . . ."

The woman lapsed into choking, racking sobs. An embarrassed silence seemed to fill the room to overflowing, and Will wished he was somewhere else.

"He is only five years old," the woman repeated. "I don't want him to be afraid; I don't want him to be hurt. I don't want him to be . . ."

There seemed to be no sound or movement in the entire room, save for the mother's keening and her heaving shoulders.

Suddenly, the father grabbed the microphone. "All we want is our son back. Can you understand that, whoever you are? You who have him, do you understand? I have the money. You can have it all. Just give me back my son."

The father slid the mike back to the FBI agent. Then he slumped in his chair, closed his eyes, shook his head as though he couldn't believe such a thing was happening to him.

Will felt soiled and guilty for having wondered fleetingly whether the kidnapping had been faked—that is, if the boy had been taken in a custody battle. Now, it seemed impossible to believe that the mother could be faking such heartbreak. And a look at the father's eyes, red-rimmed from tears (or from blinking back tears, depending on the kind of man he was), made it seem certain that he, too, wanted his son back and didn't know where he was.

And yet, and yet . . . Will would not rule out the possibility of a staged abduction. He gave himself the same lecture he gave his reporters: He would try not to let his emotions take over.

I wonder why they're not married anymore, Will thought. Did it matter?

"Agent Graham, are you able to tell anything significant from the notes with the newspaper lettering?"

"You mean other than where they were mailed from? Not yet. Various scientific tests are being done. I'm not sure I could give you information on that, even if I had it. Which I don't."

There were a few more routine questions. Then Graham adjourned the session and said that further briefings would be scheduled as needed.

Will lingered near the back of the pack until the room was nearly empty. He caught Graham just before he left the room.

"Jerry? It's Will Shafer. Remember me?"

"Will? Will!" Graham smiled broadly and shook hands, showing none of the reserve he'd displayed in the press conference. "Gosh, it's good to see you, Will."

"Same here, Jerry."

They told each other the high points of the last decade or so of their lives. Both were still married to the same women, both had a son and a daughter.

Graham said his wife was an art teacher. "And what's Karen doing, Will?"

"Deep into social work. She has her master's now. She writes articles for journals, does some counseling."

"Gosh, that's great. Say, I read about that old murder case up in Bessemer. The town is still talking about it, I'll bet."

"You bet right."

"But what brings you here, Will?"

Will sighed. "You remember Fran Spicer? Covered city hall, sometimes the Federal Building."

"Name's familiar."

Will told Graham the basics.

"That's a damn shame," Graham said. "I knew there was a bad wreck the other night. I never connected. . . . Anyhow, I'm glad the *Gazette* has you covering this thing. Off the record, I get sick and tired of dealing with smart-ass young reporters."

"Off the record, so do I."

Graham laughed. "Come on, Will. Coffee's on me."

The police station was connected to the Long Creek city government building, which had a small cafeteria in the basement. Will and the FBI man took a corner table. While Graham went to get coffee, Will looked around. Scattered among the clerks and political gofers on break were several sullen-faced cops.

When Graham returned, Will said, "This isn't exactly a friendly town."

"Sugar? No, it sure isn't. It's got all the ingredients for bad government and bad policing. Decaying tax base, aging population, entrenched political machine, old-fashioned, pig-headed, out-of-work union people. And it's all tied together, somehow. You saw the police chief."

"How is he to deal with?"

"He's staying out of my way, mostly. That's the best I can say. Oh, I suppose he does his best."

Will felt refreshed by the coffee, and seeing someone from the old days took his mind off Fran Spicer. Then he thought again how much he would rather be home, and that made him miss Karen and the children, and that reminded him of the kidnapped boy and his parents.

"What do you think about all this, Jerry?"

Graham put down his coffee. "This is one old friend talking to another. I wouldn't say this to anyone else." Graham stared into his cup for a long time. At last, he looked at Will and said quietly, "I pray to God I'm wrong, but I think the boy's as good as dead."

"Jesus."

Graham nodded, and for a moment two fathers shared an understanding of something unspeakably horrible and sad. Then Graham's eyes changed, and Will knew he was the FBI man again.

"I don't know how much of this you can use, Will. Maybe file it away for . . . whenever. The fact that the boy has been gone for this long lessens the chances for a safe return. That's often how it works. The kidnappers panic and, well . . .

"Then there's this ransom thing. That first demand, fifty thousand. Such small potatoes, really, if you're going to go to the trouble of kidnapping someone. So now, days later, there's another demand. This time for two hundred fifty thousand. It's like the kidnappers have suddenly said to themselves, Oops, we've been acting like small-time punks here; let's grow up and act like big-time criminals."

"And that's a bad sign?"

"I think it is. If these guys planned all this out well in advance, as I think they did, and then ask such a petty amount to start with—that tells me they had to work up their courage to do it in the first place. They really are small-time punks, as the first demand indicates.

"Then it sinks in what they've done, and they realize they've risked a whole lot for very little. So they want more, a lot more money. Which they ask for a few days after the first demand. But they still haven't told us how to get the kid back, or where to drop the ransom.''

"And what's that tell you, Jerry?"

"I'm not sure. Either that they don't really know what they're doing, which wouldn't surprise me, or that they're completely cold-blooded and want to keep us off our guard. That last makes sense, because in a way anyone who kidnaps someone—for money, I mean—has to be pretty cold-blooded.''

Graham paused to stare into his empty cup. Will waited.

"See, once they tell us how to deliver the money, the kid is no good to them. Worse than that, he's a liability. And if these guys are true amateurs—that's what I fear more than anything—they might panic and kill him. If they haven't already.''

"The parents, Jerry. From where I sat, they looked like they didn't know anything.''

"I think that's right. At least for her. You saw how she was. Him . . . ? Well, I don't think so, but I can't be sure.''

"And the chauffeur?"

"Straight-arrow, we think. No record, no unsavory connections. Seems okay. Oh, this is off the record completely, but the kidnappers gave him a threat.''

"And what was that?"

"That they'd rape the boy if we didn't cooperate.''

"God Almighty.''

"Yeah. So that's where we are.''

"Can you find anything from whatever tests you do on the ransom notes, Jerry?''

"My official answer is yes. If somebody's dumb enough to leave a fingerprint in the glue he uses to paste up the letters. Or if the fibers in the paper match those found on someone's desktop blotter someday.'' Graham snorted. "It's all bullshit, Will. The paper the letters are pasted on is lined notebook, the kind you can buy in any store. Ordinary five-and-dime glue. The newspaper lettering . . . well, come on. I'll show you.''

"They gave me my own little office, Will. If I breathe deep, I can smell the soap and disinfectant, I think.''

Graham gestured to a chair, and Will sat. The agent unlocked a desk drawer and pulled out a sheet of thick cardboard about two feet square, held it up for Will to see.

The notes were displayed under a transparent sheet. The newspaper letters, all capitals, made up a jumble of typefaces. The first one read:

WE HAVE JAMEY. WE WANT 50G OR HE DIES. GET RANSOM READY. WE WILL TELL YOU WHAT TO DO.

"They spelled the boy's name wrong," Will said. "It is really J-A-M-I-E, isn't it?"

"Yes, they got it wrong."

"Unless they ran out of the letter *i*, which isn't likely."

"No."

"Maybe they're just stupid," Will said, half-joking.

The second note said:

THE RULES HAVE CHANGED. PRICE RAISED TO 250G'S. COOPERATE OR BOY WILL BE KILLED. MORE INSTRUCTIONS TO FOLO.

"What do you think, Will?"

"What do *I* think?"

"You're a word person. Give me your gut feeling."

First, Will had to clear something up. "Jerry, I'm here as a newspaperman. How much of this is supposed to be on the record?"

"Will, I'd like you not to mention the misspelling when you write your story. I'm also asking you not to write what I said a minute ago, about our not being hopeful that we'll get anything from tests on the notes. Can you do that?"

Will was uncomfortable, and he knew his face showed it.

"Will, I'll share stuff with you that I won't with anyone else. You know that. Help me in return, is all I ask."

Will ran it through his mind. He thought of all the times he'd lectured reporters about not getting trapped in deals to keep things off the record. Then he thought about how the publisher had imposed on him by sending him to Long Creek in the first place. Then he thought about how a lot of situations just weren't covered in the rules.

But first he had a question. "Why me, Jerry? You guys have access to all the science and experts in the world."

"Experts? Sure, Will. And if I want a good, perceptive reading of these ransom notes, which happen to be pasted-up newspaper letters, what should I do? Call a semantics expert from the state university a hundred miles away? And where do I get an expert on newspaper lettering? I'm looking at one. I'm looking at a professional word person. What do you say?"

"Sure, Jerry. I'm a man first and a newspaperman second. And I've got kids of my own."

Graham put his hand on Will's shoulder. "You're straight as ever, Will. You'd have made a good FBI agent."

"I'm not sure that's a compliment."

"You son of a bitch." Graham laughed. Then he held the cardboard up again. "Tell me what you see, Will."

Will studied the letters. Was there something? Yes.

"What do you see, Will?"

"You asked for my gut feelings, so here goes. Look at the first note. The boy's name is spelled wrong. The '50G' without an *s* after the *G*. And 'Get ransom ready.' The level of expression is rather crude." Although not much worse than that of some of my reporters, Will thought ruefully.

"And the second note, Will?"

"It's more literate. The words *cooperate* and *instructions*, for instance. You don't have to be a genius to use them, but they do indicate a higher level of sophistication than shown in the first note, I think. And where he has the ransom demand: He uses the apostrophe and the *s* with the *G*, which is more correct usage. Oh, and using *f-o-l-o* for *follow*. That's a deliberate abbreviation, almost certainly."

"I agree. What else?"

"Well . . . it's ordinary, I mean pretty common newspaper type, I think. Bookman Roman, Bookman Italic, some other fonts I recognize. But . . . yes, it's the kind of lettering you see all the time in newspapers. Nothing out of the ordinary."

"Good, Will. Anything else?"

Will studied the notes line by line. "No, I don't think so. These notes were done by different people, weren't they?"

"I think so."

"And what's that mean, Jerry?"

The agent shrugged. "For sure, that the second was written by someone a little smarter. That one was written by a man, another by a woman? Or maybe it's just a division of labor. I imagine it takes a while to paste up a message. Maybe the one who did the first note said, 'Hey, you do the next one. It's a pain in the ass.' "

"But Jerry, you already knew there were a couple of kidnappers. So the fact that the notes were done by different people is no surprise, is it?"

Graham frowned. "No. It's just that whatever scraps of knowledge we get might help us to . . . well, to get a conviction someday. Even . . ."

"Even if you can't save the boy."

"Right. So maybe one kidnapper is a lot smarter than the other. Maybe that's why they're squabbling, if they are. Maybe that helps explain the higher ransom demand. I don't know."

"So, Jerry, when you catch the guys, all that will help you turn one against the other to build your case. Right?"

"Maybe. But if these guys are divided, if they're at each other's throats and their nerves are frayed, it doesn't help the kid's chances. If he still has any."

"If they are amateurs at heart, it reduces the boy's chances, doesn't it?"

Graham nodded yes. "Setting up the ransom delivery is the biggest source of worry for them right now. That, and the boy himself. Who, after all, can identify them. That's assuming they haven't already, um, decided how to solve that problem."

"Damn."

"You're right about amateurs being more dangerous, Will, because they're not sure of what they're doing. Trouble is, except for political terrorists, all kidnappers are amateurs."

"Are you here for the duration, Jerry?"

"I think so. I can't be certain. Part of what I do is hand-holding for the parents. And that's tougher in this case, because they live apart.''

"Is there any chance at all that they, you know. . . ?''

Graham measured him coldly for a moment before his eyes softened. "I think their emotions are genuine, Will. That's all I can say. I'll tell you what I can tell you, and when I can. You know I'm good on that.''

"You always were, Jerry. I haven't forgotten.''

Will shook hands with the agent and left. On his way back to the hotel, he remembered something Graham had done a lot of years before. It was in Bessemer in the 1970s, and some student radicals (or so the *Gazette* had called them) at the Bessemer state university branch had staged several protests over the various investigations into the 1971 Attica prison riot that killed more than forty inmates and guards.

The radicals had seen conspiracies and whitewashes everywhere, and they had sided with the prisoners time and again. They had infuriated most of the people in Bessemer, and the police had broken up several demonstrations by enthusiastically using dogs, clubs, and tear gas.

Jerry Graham—at that time, a young FBI agent, and as buttoned-down and conservative as he looked—had been at one of the protests. Will had been sent to cover the disturbance, and he watched from twenty feet away as a wild-eyed young man with dirty hair and even filthier clothes rushed up to Graham. "Fascist motherfucker!" the young man screamed in Graham's face.

Looking sad rather than angry, the agent had calmly wiped the young man's spittle from his face, then had prevailed upon a Bessemer police officer not to arrest the screamer. "Everyone's entitled to be an asshole once," the agent had told the cop.

Will had been close enough to hear, yet he was sure that Graham hadn't seen him and wasn't feigning compassion for the benefit of the press. Indeed, Will had never told Graham that he had seen what happened. And Will had never forgotten what Graham had said in his office sometime later: "I think those students are a bunch of naïve jerks, but this is still a free country. That's off the record.''

Only later did Will appreciate how principled Graham had

been, and how much professional damage he had risked. Graham had given him a lot of "no comments" back then, but he had never lied to him. Never.

So here they both were again, Will thought: the aging FBI man and the aging journalist. Jerry, you always were a cut above most lawmen, FBI or otherwise. Maybe this is where I pay you back.

Nine

■ ■ ■

The hermit did not always know when the sadness would fall on him. When it did, it was like a weight on his shoulders. Sometimes it was so heavy, it drove him to his knees. Then he would cry like a child, filled with self-disgust, until he couldn't cry anymore. Wolf knew enough to leave him alone then. The dog would retreat to the corners of the cabin, or hide in a thicket until his master's sadness was over.

If only the crying made him feel better. It didn't; it was something he could not help, but it would never make things right.

Sometimes he could shake off the weight before it settled over him; he could do this by swinging an ax, or trotting through the woods, or—whatever. But more often than not, when the weight settled on him, he just gave himself up to the sadness. And the whiskey.

It was getting dark, and he had just made the long cut off the highway, over farmers' fields, through thick patches of woods, and down a wooded hill, until he came out on the winding dirt road. The road was a little wider than a logging trail, but it got little more traffic than that.

He hated shopping trips, so he always figured his needs so that he had to make a trip only once every several weeks. Now, his backpack was heavy with cans of meat and fruit, a bag of flour, coffee, potatoes, batteries. And whiskey; he always bought whiskey.

When he was at a place in the road where the hills were high on one side and a gulley sloped sharply away on the other, the weight of sadness fell on him. Maybe it was because he was tired, or perhaps it was the gloom. Whatever. The sadness came on him, and his eyes filled with tears.

He stopped, adjusted the straps on his pack, felt the deepening cold in his nostrils. Tonight he would drink whiskey, as much as it took to go to sleep. He would put away his supplies in the morning.

If the cabin he and Jo had built had not burned, Jo would still be alive. Wouldn't she? They hadn't done that much in heavy drugs. Yes, Jo would still be alive.

"No. No, no, no, no." He was startled by his own voice; yes, it was on him, the sadness. He hoped the rest of it wouldn't come—the screams, the voices calling to him for help, the voices he heard in his dreams.

Faster, faster. He left the road, went down a leaf-choked gulley where it was even darker. He sobbed again, loathed himself for it, was glad a rushing stream masked his sounds.

Jo was gone, forever, with their unborn child. He cried for them, cried for himself. Only the hills and trees would know.

He pushed forward. It was getting too dark to see, but he knew the way by heart.

He heard a sound. God, no, don't let it be the voices again. Jo was dead, their child dead, their life together dead.

The boy Jo was carrying would be a young man now. (Somehow, the hermit knew that the child had been a boy.) Would his son have liked living in the woods? Would Jo have changed?

There was a low, cold wind. It shifted slightly, bringing the sound of the rushing brook closer to him. It was then that he heard the sound.

"Mommy . . . Daddy . . ."

The hermit put his hands over his ears, shut his eyes as hard as he could to dam up the tears. He didn't remember ever hearing the ghost voices this clearly before. When he felt the wind shift, he took his hands away from his ears and opened his eyes. The wind, that was it. The wind had made the noises. He was not crazy.

His dog barked. The hermit could tell from the sound that Wolf was a couple hundred yards back, at a different bend in the stream.

"Wolf!"

The dog was silent; the hermit listened for the sound of the dog running after him. Nothing.

Wolf must have flushed a rabbit, the hermit thought.

"Wolf!" the hermit shouted louder, to be heard over the stream. "Damn you, Wolf." The dog could hear him, he knew. There was almost nothing the dog didn't hear.

The wind shifted slightly again, making the sound of the stream a little louder. He heard another noise, or thought he did. It was almost a low moan. Then the wind changed yet again, and the sound was gone. He was relieved; he had heard enough ghost voices.

"Wolf." He heard the dog tromping through the snowy brush. "Good, Wolf. Okay."

The dog was next to him now, and panting. Trying to tell him something?

"All right, Wolf. Come on."

The hermit took the flashlight from his deep pocket, shined it into the darkness to be sure he was headed where he thought.

The dog yelped, whined.

"No. No time to play, Wolf."

The hermit smelled fresh dirt. Shining the light down at the dog, he saw that the animal's front paws were dark and wet.

"Damn you, Wolf. You would have to dig." The hermit was tired and didn't want to have to clean mud out of the cabin from Wolf's paws. All he wanted to do in the cabin was shut out the cold and the ghosts and drink some whiskey. He pointed the light where he wanted to go and slapped his side with his gloved hand, the signal to the dog that he was out of patience.

Reluctantly, Wolf obeyed.

Ten

...

Will had some time before he had to file his story, and the rest of the day lay beyond him like a gray landscape. He was homesick. He was still worried about Fran.

The hospital was only a block away. Maybe there was some improvement . . . .

The hospital had been built during the Great Depression. The cornerstone said 1935, but just as telling was the WPA–style architecture. Not to mention the several decades of grime stuck on the masonry like burned skin, a reminder of the time when the mills and smelters had brought prosperity with their soot.

Just as Will entered the building, he heard a woman's voice: "Mr. Shafer?"

Will turned and saw the nurse he'd met earlier in the intensive-care unit. "It is Mr. Shafer, isn't it?"

"Yes. Hello again."

"I'm Heather Casey, Mr. Shafer. Your friend is sleeping very soundly. There's no change."

"Ah. Well, then, I guess there's no point in my going to see him."

"Not really." Nurse Casey frowned, hinted to Will with a shift of her shoulder that he should follow her outside.

They stood on the front walk. "Have you been friends for a very long time, Mr. Shafer?"

"You could say that. Yes. Fran has had his ups and downs. Especially downs lately, but he used to be a fine newsman, and he taught me a lot. More years ago than I care to recall all of a sudden."

"I know what that feels like. About the years racing away, I mean. But I must tell you—I'm not optimistic."

"But you said there was no change."

"No, as far as his vital signs are concerned. But considering his overall condition, the longer he goes without rallying . . ."

"I see."

Will was startled when the nurse put a hand on his shoulder. Startled because the gesture was a warmer one than he had expected from his first meeting with the nurse. Startled because her hand felt good on his shoulder, and he saw that she was a far younger-looking, more handsome woman than he had perceived at their first meeting.

"This is tough, I know," she said.

"Well, it's no sadder than a lot of the things you see, I guess."

"I'm sure you see some sad things in your line of work, too, Mr. Shafer."

"Hmmm. And if Fran does make it, he's going to be charged with drunken driving, isn't he?"

"Oh, he already has been, Mr. Shafer. Nothing will happen, of course, until Mr. Spicer is . . . able to respond."

"There isn't any doubt, then, I guess? About Fran's being drunk, I mean?"

"I'm afraid not. I know the police at the scene took pictures of the interior of his car. That's standard practice in such cases. There were several empty beer cans in the car. And I drew the blood sample myself right here at the hospital. He tested one point five. Well into the drunk-driving area, I'm afraid."

"And a young woman was injured. And she was lucky she wasn't killed. Lord. Fran was doing so well for a while. He was a recovering alcoholic. I mean, he wasn't a common drunk. Isn't a common drunk."

"I'm sure not." Heather Casey smiled kindly. "My father was an alcoholic, Mr. Shafer, so I have some personal knowledge in this area. So was my . . . Well, I guess that's why I don't drink. I have to go."

"Thank you. I do appreciate your kindness. Should I stop by later, do you think?"

"If you wish. If you're here much later, I may be gone." Heather Casey turned to leave but paused. "If you see a policeman outside the IU unit, it's because he's keeping a watch on Mr. Spicer. They're not being mean. It's just that technically . . ."

"I know. Thanks."

Will decided to go back to his room. He had nothing better to do now than file his story. Besides, he would be writing it on a portable computer and sending it to the *Bessemer Gazette* via telephone. Young reporters did that all the time, but Will, while not a total computerphobe, had started his career in the typewriter and pencil era. He thought he had best allow himself extra time.

Back in the hotel, Will called Tom Ryan at the *Gazette* and told him he thought a thousand words would be adequate for his story. Ryan sounded nervous and obsequious.

"Any change in Fran's condition, Will?"

"Nope."

"Reason I ask, publisher's been in and out of the newsroom all day. Asking about Fran, mostly. Once or twice, he asked if you'd filed your story yet."

Will shook his head in annoyance: Ryan tended to get nervous with big stories. Now Ryan was clearly worried that Will would screw up badly and it would reflect on him somehow. "Ry, don't worry. If I can't hack it, it'll be my ass, okay?"

"Ha! Will, you can do this. We have faith."

Will sent a test message, heard back a minute later that his computer was sending garble-free copy back to the *Gazette*. That was a relief, because he thought he heard thunder outside. Electrical storms could play havoc with computers.

Then, with his homesickness momentarily banished by the butterflies, Will began to write.

> The hunt for Jamie Brokaw and his kidnappers took a new turn today as investigators received an ominous new ransom demand. And the boy's parents issued emotional pleas for the child's release before going back to their separate homes to pray and wait.

Will paused after that first paragraph, read it several times. As an editor, he was constantly preaching clean, terse lead paragraphs with a minimum of cluttering clauses, abbreviations, and proper nouns. Now he dare not violate his own principles, or he would lose face among the people he was supposed to be supervising.

This isn't bad at all, he decided finally.

Will wrote swiftly and smoothly. He had made a list beforehand of the points he wanted to cover, and roughly in what order, and his prose had always been clear, if not always beautiful. The only trouble was deciding how far he could go in reporting some of the things Graham had told him. Well, he knew damn well that journalism courses didn't cover every situation.

In about an hour, Will was done, and he pressed the TRANS-MIT command. After a minute or so, he got the message that his story had arrived intact and that he would hear in a little while whether there were any questions. As he waited, Will made a note to himself to be more understanding from now on when reporters on the road got irritable.

The phone rang.

"Will, your story is fine. Just fine," Ryan said. "Us old guys can show the young squirts how it's done, huh?"

"You betcha, Ry." And that was as far as Will would go with Ryan on the forced camaraderie; even that took some effort.

"Can I ask you a few things?"

"Shoot."

Ryan's questions (most likely some had been relayed from

other editors) were good, sensible, to the point. Will fielded
them all, after which Ryan said, "I mean it, Will. It'll be
good for the staff to see that their boss can do a story like
this."

"Thanks." And because Will wondered whether he'd been
too curt before, he said, "I appreciate your help."

"Now the publisher wants to talk to you, Will."

And Will was instantly on his guard.

"Will? Will? Can you hear—?"

Will recognized Lyle Glanford's voice, knew that the publisher had become confused, as always, by the phone system.
Over the line, Will heard feet scurrying as Ryan tried to
prevent the publisher from cutting himself off.

"Now I . . . Will? I've got it, I think. Can you hear me,
Will?"

"Loud and clear, sir."

"Nothing new on Fran, Will?"

"No, Lyle." No sense telling him more right now, Will
thought.

"You'll let me know soonest, I'm sure. Will, I had a story
idea. I already bounced it off Ry, and he thinks it'll fly. What
about a roundup of other famous kidnapping cases of the
past?"

"We could do that if we have space, Lyle. I'm sure the
wire services are moving something like that, if they haven't
already."

"We thought you could do a better job from where you
are, Will. I know you can. And we're going to make as much
space in the paper as we need. Did Ry tell you yet about the
editorial?"

"Editorial? No, Lyle."

Will was baffled, but only for a moment. Then the tentative, trying-to-please voice of Tom Ryan came on the line
again: "Page one day after tomorrow, Will. The *Gazette*'s
coming out in favor of reinstating the death penalty in this
state for kidnappers."

"That's why I want this backgrounder, Will. I want it
under the byline of our executive editor. You are there, after
all. And it'll lend a little weight to the package, don't you
think?"

"That could be, Lyle." What else could he say?

"Will, this whole thing has made me sick," the publisher went on. "I don't know if you remember, but I was on the State Parks Commission for a stretch when Jamie Brokaw's father was a member. Salt of the earth, salt of the earth . . ."

In an instant, everything was much clearer to Will: the publisher's early and intense interest in the kidnapping, his eagerness to send Will. Hell, seeing to Fran Spicer's welfare was only part of it. Maybe the smaller part, at that. The publisher had it in his head that the presence of the *Bessemer Gazette*'s top editor (never mind that he was functioning as reporter and errand boy) would—what? Make the FBI try harder? Put a hundred police officers on the case, instead of fifty? What?

"Salt of the earth, Will."

"I'm sure, sir. If you want a background story with my byline, then I'll get you one. I really can't do it for tomorrow, though."

"Day after tomorrow, Will. Your background story, plus the lead-all on whatever breaking news there is, plus an editorial on page one."

Overkill, Will thought. He heard himself say, "We'd better pray there's no other news we have to get into the paper."

"What?"

"I said, we can all pray that our newspaper, that getting something into our newspaper will play a part in the safe return of the boy."

"Amen, Will." The publisher was saying good-bye, Will knew.

"Will? I'm still here, Will. Just one thing."

"Yes, Ry?"

"I wonder at the beginning of your story, Will. I mean, I was brought up short for a moment by the reference to the parents in their separate homes. . . ."

"Why? The parents are divorced, in fact. It lends a little poignancy, I thought."

"Yeah, but the publisher kind of tripped over that part. . . ."

Will shook his head in disgust. No wonder his reporters complained about the editing they got at the *Gazette*. Ryan was probably reacting not to something the publisher had said but to something he thought he *might* say.

"Ry," Will said evenly at last, "you just go ahead and do whatever you have to."

Will hung up, went to the window, and stared out. A gray sky hanging over a gray city, almost low enough to smother it.

He lay down, closed his eyes, tried to let the tension flow out of him. He'd better; otherwise, he'd have a dandy headache.

He tried to remember what a therapist had told him again and again about self-esteem and control and thinking and acting in ways that were "appropriate"—appropriate not in a social sense but in a psychological one.

He knew that some people thought of him as a "lifer" at the *Gazette*. Sometimes he thought of himself that way, although he doubted if his job was that secure lately. The publisher was too mercurial, and Will had committed the unpardonable sin over the years of finding out too much about the personal problems of the publisher and his family. It wasn't that Will had tried to find out such things; it was just that inevitably he had. And he sensed sometimes that Lyle Glanford held it against him.

Sometimes Will chided himself for not having had a sense much earlier of his own entitlement. He had gone to college on a scholarship provided by the *Gazette* for being a good delivery boy and, later, a good copyboy. He might not have gone to college at all (even if his father hadn't committed suicide in the midst of his money problems) if it hadn't been for the *Gazette*. So Will had gotten a job as a cub reporter, then as an editor—feeling all the while that he was paying back what he owed.

In fact, he was a pretty good journalist. He knew that now—intellectually, he knew it, even if in his heart he still sometimes felt as if he was in debt to the *Gazette*—but he was on the wrong side of forty, and his wife was well established in the counseling she sometimes did in Bessemer, and his kids loved it, and they had a lovely comfortable house with a porch deck and a big backyard, and his life really wasn't so bad. . . .

Enough of those thoughts; they were the last thing he needed now. Should he call home? No; later would be better, when his mood would be mellower.

First, he had to do some research.

It is one of the paradoxes of newspaperdom that a paper in a poor, small town can not only survive but make a lot of money. The reason is simple enough: A lot of people still need a newspaper for *something*, whether to check the TV schedule, or the supermarket ads, or if any of the neighbors have died.

Will knew that the *Long Creek Eagle* made money, although Will's own paper had nibbled into its circulation with its Country Edition. Will knew, too, that he would get a cordial reception at the *Eagle*. Competitor or not, he was a fellow newspaperman.

His pant legs felt damp as he went up the steps of the *Eagle* (Have to see about some laundry, depending on how long I'm going to be around, he thought), and the wind-driven sleet and rain seemed to chase him inside.

In the lobby of the *Eagle* stood a globe perhaps six feet wide. It reminded him briefly of the globe in the lobby of the *New York Daily News*, except that the *Eagle*'s was smaller and dust-covered and the lighting around it much dimmer.

A small man in his sixties sat behind a wooden counter. He seemed to have his hands full with the switchboard and a tuna sandwich, so Will ignored him. Instead, Will followed the arrow that said NEWSROOM and that pointed to a winding staircase.

At the top of the stairs was a door, and just inside a teenage girl sat behind a desk. She was wearing a Madonna sweatshirt, eating french fries, and carrying on a giggling conversation by telephone. She put down the phone and swallowed long enough for Will to introduce himself and ask to see someone in charge. The girl nodded, pressed a couple of buttons, mumbled something into the phone, pressed another button, and went back to the french fries and giggling chatter.

Before long, a young man with a firm handshake and an eager manner came out and introduced himself. If he was surprised that the *Bessemer Gazette* had sent its executive editor to Long Creek, he had the tact not to show it.

Will and the younger man traded small talk about what a terrible thing the kidnapping was and how busy everyone was on the *Long Creek Eagle* because of it.

The young man led Will to a small, narrow room lined with metal file drawers, showed him how to work the microfilm machine, and explained how the rolls of film were filed.

"I think you'll find this useful," the *Eagle* editor said, putting a small metal box of three-by-five index cards on a table. "Ruth, our old librarian, was what you'd call a human-misery buff. She kept her own file of the biggest disasters and most celebrated crimes of the twentieth century. The cards here give the names of the principals, whether we have separate bio files and art on them, and the numbers of the microfilm spools that apply."

"Beautiful. This has to be better than the public library."

"The Long Creek Public Library's a joke, unfortunately."

"I know. I stopped on my way over here. They don't even have complete *New York Times* microfilm."

"We have that, as well as microfilm of the *Eagle*. 'Course, for national stuff, you're better off with the *Times*. One reason we have a better microfilm collection than the public library is that we have more money coming in. It's one of the few things our publisher's family isn't doing on the cheap these days. Listen, if you need anything else, press that buzzer right there. That'll bring a copy kid."

Will didn't bother to look up the most famous of all American kidnappings, that of the Lindbergh baby in 1932. He had read a couple of books on it.

He half-remembered another case, from when he himself was a small boy. Yes, that must be it on the index card. A six-year-old boy had been abducted from a school in Kansas City, Missouri, in 1953. His father, a wealthy car dealer, had agreed at once to pay a six-hundred-thousand-dollar ransom. A lot of money back then, Will thought. A lot of money today, for God's sake.

Will found the microfilm he wanted and threaded it into the machine without too much trouble. It took him only a few minutes to realize that scanning the microfilm was going to be as draining as it was interesting. He had to squint to read, unless he positioned the film just right on the screen, and to get it just right he had to go so slowly that it tried his patience.

The Kansas City boy had been killed soon after being taken, it was later found out, and his body buried in a hole filled with lime.

Will remembered his own parents talking about that case: how terrible it was that the kidnappers had demanded the money after they had already killed the child. That they had meant to kill him all along. His life didn't matter to them, except as an annoyance.

Will recalled how horrified he had been to imagine the boy thrown into a lime pit. No matter how many times he had told himself that it didn't matter—the boy was already dead, his soul gone to heaven—the image had brought him near tears.

"God Almighty," Will muttered. "You couldn't make this stuff up." Even though he didn't believe in capital punishment, he was glad that two kidnappers had been caught and executed.

The case had been a cause célèbre for a long time. But even four decades later, Will was disturbed reading about it. He advanced the microfilm.

Will picked up his pace. He selected only the most celebrated cases, got the microfilm, scanned it as quickly as he could while still taking accurate notes. He felt the strain in his eyes. Yet while he was eager to be done with the task, he couldn't help pausing now and then. It was fascinating to see again what had been popular on television, what the clothing styles had been, how much chuck roast and eggs had cost a decade or two or three ago.

And something else, something he hadn't expected and most definitely wasn't ready for: As he rolled the microfilm, he couldn't help thinking how old he had been back then. I was little Will Shafer, he thought. A shy boy who thought he was doing the best he could, and who was ashamed of his parents sometimes, the way they fought and never had enough money. . . .

Will shook those thoughts out of his head and wound the roll to the end in a blur.

Giving his eyeballs a break from the microfilm, he flipped through the cards again. Oh, there was a case he remembered from the late 1960s. A young woman, daughter of a wealthy executive, kidnapped and buried in a coffin-size ventilated box. Found alive by the FBI a few days later. Will remembered the case. God, he was only in his twenties at the time. He hadn't met Karen yet, and he was still going to church. Hell, he had even prayed for that girl. Maybe it had worked: She had been saved, and the kidnappers had been caught and sent to prison.

In the few minutes he spent taking notes on that case, he was visited by another wave of sadness he hadn't anticipated. When he saw the headlines from the late sixties—race riots in the big cities, the counterculture, hippies, and, most of all, Vietnam—he thought of his own youth, and the big stories he had dreamed of covering and never had. And now never would.

Of course you didn't, you dumb bastard. You were at the *Bessemer Gazette*. You could have moved on, if you'd had the guts. . . .

"Enough," Will said to his demons. "Leave me alone, for God's sake."

He thumbed the cards again, stopped at a case from the late 1980s. The heir to a newspaper business in the Midwest had been seized and buried underground in a box (son of a bitch, the bastards must have gotten the idea from the case of the young woman), but the crude ventilation system had failed, and the man had died.

"Dirty bastards," Will hissed. He was sorry the kidnappers had only been sent to prison.

And here was a case from South Carolina. A businessman had been abducted, and a big ransom demand had been made. Will thought that the case might be worth a look, so he got out the microfilm.

The kidnapper had specified that the money be left attached to a piling under a bridge that spanned a river. Lawmen had kept the bridge under surveillance, of course, and, when a man rowed quietly up to the bridge in a boat and started nosing around the pilings, they had arrested him without trouble. After all, it is hard to escape quickly in a rowboat.

The South Carolina kidnapper seemed laughably stupid. In fact, the whole episode would have been hilarious—except that the victim had never been found.

This time, Will could tell from the microfilm, the kidnapper was on South Carolina's death row.

Will checked a few more cases, got out a few more rolls of film, took a few more notes, and abruptly decided to stop. He was getting bored. Bored and depressed. Reading the microfilm had reminded him that there was no limit to the cruelty and greed of people—some people, anyhow.

There was no limit to stupidity, either, it seemed. And when amateurs made mistakes, they were apt to panic. And kill. And then Will remembered what the FBI agent had told him: Virtually all kidnappers were amateurs.

Eleven

...

"**F**ran died."

"Oh, Will. When?"

"Not quite an hour ago. Hospital called me. They said, uh, that his general physical condition was such . . ." He had to stop.

"Will, I'm so sorry."

"I know. Thanks. I'll be here another couple of days, I guess. Sorry."

"Just do what you have to do and get home safely."

"I'll try."

Will told his wife all that had happened. "And it's cold here," he said. "Colder than Bessemer, even. I try not to think too much about that little boy."

"I know. You pray to God, you . . . whatever. Sometimes shit happens. *Evil* happens. How are his parents handling it?"

"Oh, I think they're numb. Separately. They can't even lean on each other."

"Is he dead, do you think?"

"The FBI thinks maybe. Oh, that's another thing." Will

told her about Jerry Graham's surfacing in Long Creek, and Karen told Will to send Graham her best.

They talked some more, and Will realized that Karen had steered him away from the depressing business at hand with chatter about routine, even trivial, events at home. "And Brendan has decided he wants a dog," Karen said.

"Sure, and Cass will help him take care of it, right? Ha!"

"They've been arguing over what kind to get."

"Figures. We'll have to get the yard fenced."

After they said good night, Will thought about what he would say to Tom Ryan, who had sent Fran Spicer on the last reporting assignment of his life. Ry, don't worry. No, Ry, it's not your fault. (But it was, Will thought. Damn it, it was.)

No. Fran, God rest his soul, was the one who had had the drinking problem. *His* problem, Will thought. And sometimes mine. Will thought back to the time just before Fran had gone into the *Gazette*'s rehab program, to the incident that had led to his entering the program, in fact.

Three, four years ago? Will had gotten the call at his desk. A county judge Will had known for years called to say that Fran Spicer was at Rotunda's, a tavern restaurant near the courthouse, and was incoherently drunk. Will had gone to Rotunda's immediately. It was one thing for reporters to drink—Will didn't give a damn about that, had even done a little in his youth—but it was intolerable for a *Gazette* reporter to be stinking drunk at Rotunda's, a hangout for judges, lawyers, and court clerks.

By the time Will got there, Fran had passed out. Will could still see the spilled schnapps on the table and the beer that Fran had been working on. The cabdriver had balked at first about taking Fran home, so Will had given him a twenty. The driver had helped to load Fran into the cab. Poor Fran, Will thought. Dead drunk and reeking of—

Oh. That's funny. Will let his mind back up, went over the thought that had stopped him. Something was not quite right. Now what the hell was it?

Will stood at the counter for half a minute before getting the sergeant's attention.

"Yeah?" the sergeant said at last. It sounded like a challenge instead of a greeting.

"Good afternoon. My name's Will Shafer and I'm . . ."

"I know who you are. What do you want?"

Will looked into the sergeant's eyes, tried to match the steel, but it was no contest. Nice cops in this town, Will thought.

Will took a deep breath. Talk slow and steady, he told himself. "There was an accident a couple of nights ago, on the two-lane from the expressway. A friend of mine was fatally injured."

"I know the wreck you mean. So?"

"I'd like to see the report on it."

"By what authority?"

This cop is more than small-town officious, Will thought. He's a big-league prick. But Will didn't feel like asserting his rights: Drive an hour in any direction, and one was still in Hill County. Law and order, Hill County–style, could mean being hassled like never before.

Besides, Will thought the sergeant was on solid ground. It was part of Will's job to know what was public record and what wasn't, and, if he recalled correctly, accident reports were not automatically available for anyone to look at.

"By what authority?" the sergeant repeated.

"I was only making a request, Sergeant." Will's knees trembled, from anger as well as from fear. He mustered all his control. "Sergeant, I'm not trying to make your job tougher. The guy who died worked for me, and he was on company business. That means, or it might mean, that the young woman who was injured is entitled to some money from my company. That's why I'm interested."

If I keep practicing, I might get good at lies and half-truths, Will thought.

The sergeant relaxed a little. "You talk to her yet?"

"I plan to do just that. Believe me, all I want to do is help her. I can talk to our insurance carrier and . . ."

The sergeant had done an about-face and walked to a desk in the corner. He came back a moment later with a sheet of pink paper. "Tell you what," he said, "I'll read the high points to you, if you like. But I can't let you see it."

"Fine." Will knew this was as much as he would get.

"Now then," the sergeant read. "Driver number two appeared to have been drinking. Several empty beer cans were found in right front seat. Driver's clothing smelled of alcohol."

Will listened intently; he wasn't interested so much in what the report said as in what it *didn't* say. Fran Spicer, God rest his soul, had been a creature of habit. Oh, in a pinch he might have drunk anything if he went off the wagon. But if he had stopped to buy alcohol, he probably would have bought schnapps and beer, if he could. And he would have started with the schnapps. What the hell did it all mean?

"Got what you need?" the sergeant asked, a shade less threateningly than before.

"Yes. Thanks for your trouble. Maybe I can help the lady get her money faster. But if I'm going to do that, I need her name."

"Suzanne Glover. First name with a *z* and an *e* at the end."

"Thanks a lot."

Will had noticed what looked like a grotesque paperweight in one corner of the counter. It was like a giant wood shaving resting on a metal block, except that the shaving was of blue steel and many times larger than any wood shaving Will had ever seen.

Will picked up the object, which weighed several pounds, and studied it from several angles. He was really stalling for time, working up to asking one last question.

"That thing, that thing was made at the mill," the sergeant said. "The mill's shut down now. Maybe you better . . ."

Will was about to ask his last question when Chief Robert Howe appeared next to the sergeant, whose face went white. The sergeant retreated.

Without a word, the chief took the paperweight from Will's hand, so roughly that Will's palm was scratched slightly.

"Chief, I was just admiring the office furniture," Will said.

"My brother made this, Mr. Smart Ass from Bessemer," Howe said. "You got a problem with that?"

"Nope. I meant no disrespect. I was just asking the sergeant about the accident report from that fatal the other night.

I thought maybe I could help the woman get her insurance money faster. You see, the man involved worked for me—''

''So?''

''So I wonder if you could tell me the name of the officer who investigated the accident and wrote up the report.''

''The officer who investigated the accident is not available, for reasons that are none of your business. And no one from my department will give you any more information on the accident without checking personally with me.''

Wonderful, Will thought.

The chief slammed the paperweight onto the counter, as though he wished Will's hand was under it. Then he turned and disappeared.

Outside, Will tried to breathe slowly; the chief's behavior—just short of a physical threat—had alarmed and angered him, and given him a huge rush of adrenaline. I'm probably on the chief's bad side forever, Will thought. And what had the sergeant said? ''I know who you are.''

There were times when a reporter had to have a tough hide, or pretend that he did. He thought again of Fran Spicer. What had happened to Fran was sad, so sad. No, not just sad. What happened to you, Frannie? What happened?

I'll find out, Frannie. I may have to grow some calluses, but I'll find out.

Will found the house near the end of a short street not far from the railroad tracks. Even before he mounted the creaking porch steps and knocked on the paint-peeling door, he felt sorry for the people inside.

The door opened a crack and a woman (heavy, tired-looking, fortyish going on seventy) looked out. ''I don't know what it is, but we ain't buying,'' she said.

''No, no,'' Will said. ''I'm looking into an auto accident.''

''It was my daughter who got hit. She already told the cops everything.''

''Right, right. I'd just like to talk to her to be sure she gets everything that's coming to her.'' Will wasn't comfortable with the half-truth, but he had decided to take that tack.

''You an investigator or something?''

''Yes, actually. I am doing an investigation.'' Will waited

until he was inside to elaborate. "My investigation isn't, uh, official. The other driver, Mr. Spicer, worked for me—"

"So you ain't a cop."

"No. I didn't mean to give you that impression," Will lied. "I just wanted to be sure, I mean, if Mr. Spicer was at fault . . ."

"What do you mean *if*, god damn it! That fucking drunk son of a bitch almost killed my daughter."

"Enough, Mother."

Will turned to the young woman in the doorway between the living room and kitchen.

"Enough, shit! He totaled the car, and he almost killed you."

"Enough, Mother. Okay? It's over." Then, to Will: "What do you want with me?"

Will sat, uninvited, in an ancient easy chair and flinched when the springs sounded as if they were coming through the pillow. "As I said, Mr. Spicer worked for me. He was on assignment, actually. I can't promise anything right now, but my company . . ."

"You said he *worked* for you," the young woman said. "Did he get fired over this?"

"Mr. Spicer died a short time ago," Will said. "I'm sorry. I thought you knew."

Their expressions softened a little. Mother and daughter sat on the sofa.

"It's a damn shame he's dead and all," the mother said. "But it's his own fault. He almost killed Suzanne. Ask the police."

"I did," Will said. And they practically ran me out of the station.

"I'm Suzanne Glover," the younger woman said.

"My name is Will Shafer. I'm the executive editor of the *Bessemer Gazette*. How do you do."

The mother said nothing, so Will ignored her.

"I don't want to start trouble," Suzanne Glover said, "but if there's gonna be a hassle getting paid, I'll get myself a lawyer right now. We're not rich, as you can see."

"Who gives a shit?" the mother hissed. "Rich or not, who gives a shit? That son of a bitch ran into you. Show the bruise on your shoulder, Suzanne. Never mind being modest. And the cut on the back of your head.''

"Mother."

"I am sorry, really," Will said. "I know Mr. Spicer had a problem. That's why I'm here, to offer . . ." To offer what? Will thought. A check for a hundred bucks out of the *Gazette*'s petty cash, providing the publisher would agree. Well, the *Gazette*'s insurance will pay.

"The son of a bitch was drunk," the mother said. "The police said so."

"Did you see anything?" Will asked Suzanne. "I mean, right afterward?"

"Like what?" Suzanne said.

"Just ask the police!"

"Mother, be quiet. After he hit me, it was like every bone in my body was sawdust. When the world stopped spinning, I was in a ditch. God, it must have taken me five minutes to crawl out of the car. At least it seemed that long. It was dark, except for a set of headlights. Or maybe I was dazed like and, you know, imagining stuff. Then I heard a siren, from over the hill. Then the lights of the cop car."

"So you didn't call the police?" Will said.

"How the hell was she gonna call the police, for Christ's sake!"

"Mother! No, I didn't. I went and sat in the cop car afterward."

"Ah. Do you remember the name of the officer?"

"No. Just a guy. He was nice and all. Made me keep still."

"I don't suppose you have a copy of the accident report?"

"No. Should I have?"

Will avoided that question. "You never saw Mr. Spicer?"

"Not until they took him in the ambulance. When I raised my head, I could see the officer take a six-pack, what was left of it, out of the car. I saw him dump part of a can of beer on the road. Your friend's car, it was all caved in. I knew he had to have been hurt real bad. I didn't know he . . . I'm sorry."

Will nodded; his mind was racing. "Miss Glover, do you recall seeing anything else? Anything at all? I mean, did the police officer take anything else out of the car?"

"Like what?"

"Oh, another bottle maybe. Do you know what a bottle of peppermint schnapps would look like?"

"I'm not sure. But I don't remember anything else."

"You're sure?"

"She just said so," the mother said.

Suzanne Glover flashed the older woman a look that said, Shut up. Then she said firmly, "I am sure."

"All right," Will said. "Thank you. I'm sorry for all that's happened. I know Fran would be, too." Just before he went out the door, Will said, "You might want to get your own lawyer. But I can promise you personally that you'll get what's coming to you."

Twelve

■ ■ ■

The flashlight had gone out a long time ago, and Jamie was in the dark.

His feet were wet and cold. He had managed to squirm them into the blankets, but in doing that he had kicked the water bottle. The bottle had gone all the way down to where his feet were, and the top had come off. Jamie had felt the water on his feet. Now they ached from the cold.

They had left some food. Jamie had eaten a candy bar first. Then he found a sandwich. It didn't taste very good; it smelled bad and the bread was hard. He got angry and threw the sandwich way down past his feet.

Now he was getting hungry again. He wished his mother and father would hurry up and find him. It stunk where he was.

For a long time (it seemed like a long time), Jamie had been hearing a whistling noise. He knew that was from the wind blowing by the chimney. Now the whistling got louder, and there was another sound: *ting-ting-ting-ting*.

Rain.

The *ting-ting-ting* got louder. So did the whistling. Then there was a real loud whistle and a *cling-cling* noise, and then the wind got real loud. Then he felt water on his chest. Water was running down the chimney.

A yellow light flickered over his chest, shone for a moment on his metal world, then was gone. Then he heard a loud crash.

Thunder.

There was a smaller crash, and the thunder rolled away like barrels in heaven.

"Mom-MY!"

They would come pretty soon. He wished as hard as he could that they would come soon.

Thirteen

■ ■ ■

"Today," Agent Jerry Graham told the reporters and TV cameras, "we received another ransom note from the people holding Jamie Brokaw. The envelope bore a postmark from Deer Run. For those of you who don't know, Deer Run is right along the Pennsylvania border, some forty miles southeast of Deep Well, where the second ransom note was postmarked. This latest note gave instructions for the delivery of the ransom.

"That is all I can tell you, except to say that the ransom will be delivered as instructed, and that we renew our plea to the kidnappers to return the boy safely."

"Sir," a reporter shouted, "could we please see the ransom note? And the earlier ones?"

Jerry Graham shut off the microphone and stood up, ignoring the questions shouted at him. Will saw Graham look toward him and shift his head slightly—a signal.

"Sit down, Will. I don't think anyone saw you come in." Almost comically, Graham looked up and down the corridor before flinging the door shut.

"You seem a little on edge, Jerry."

"Do you blame me?" Graham sat down at his desk and unlocked the top drawer.

Graham was holding up a cardboard rectangle with the same kind of pasted lettering Will had seen on the previous ransom notes. "For your eyes only, Will. And off the record, please."

Will read:

> PUT 250G'S IN TIGHT WATERPROOF BUNDLE. NO BIGGER THAN 20'S, NO NEW BILLS IN SEQUENCE. TAKE BUNDLE IN MARKED POLICE CAR NORTH ON LOGGER HILL ROAD OFF RTE 126 IN DEER COUNTY. CAR MUST STOP EXACTLY QUARTER MILE NORTH OF 126. THROW BUNDLE OUT RIGHT SIDE INTO BRUSH AT LEAST 20 FEET FROM ROAD. DO THIS BETWEEN 4 AND 5 PM DAY YOU GET THIS. NO TRIX. WE CAN MOVE BOY AT WILL WITHOUT YOUR FINDING. HIS LIFE YOUR HANDS.

"Today?" Will said.

"Today. Now, Mr. Word Person, tell me again what you see."

"Lord. He really thought this out, didn't he? Assuming there's one mastermind."

"Yep. Very detailed. He wants delivery made just as it's getting dark."

"Do you think he'll be watching?"

"My hunch? Yes. That area is deep woods. If he gets set up in a spot, and he has binoculars, he's pretty safe. Especially, say, if he's wearing camouflage clothing. Besides, they still have the boy, so he probably figures we won't get too cute. And he's right. But tell me what you see here, Will."

"Damn, Jerry. What do *I* know?"

"As much as me, probably. We're nowhere on this, Will. I'd roll the dice to make something happen, except I don't know where the dice are. What do you see here?"

"It's more like the second note than the first. He's no fool. By comparison, the writer of the first note sounds unintelligent. You're probably way ahead of me, but he must know this whole region pretty well. A hunter, maybe? An outdoorsman?''

"Or at least someone who knows the land around here. What else, Will?''

"He's, well, he's fairly literate. There, the possessive *your* in front of the gerund *finding*. The misspelling of *tricks* is a deliberate shortcut, nothing more. See, he gets tired of clipping and pasting. 'His life your hands.' He leaves out *is in* because he's getting impatient with the cut-and-paste task.''

"Tell me more.''

"Hmmm. . . . The same crazy-quilt of typefaces. Ordinary, commonly used newspaper fonts. Oh. Where he says 'quarter mile,' he managed to find the entire word *quarter* somewhere in a headline, so he pasted it intact. Saved himself some snipping.''

"The impatience you spoke about, Will.''

"Instead of cutting letters, he cut corners.''

"Nicely put, Will. We'll do tests on the paper and paste, but I'll bet my mortgage it's like the other paper. Ordinary five-and-dime stock.'' Graham bit his lip, as though deciding something important. "Will, you're one of the few newsmen I trust totally. That's why I'm inviting you right now to come with me, if you'd like. On the stakeout, I mean. When the ransom is delivered.''

Will filed his story early, called the *Gazette* to verify that it had been transmitted intact, fielded a few routine questions. The thrust of it, of course, was that there had been a third ransom note, with instructions, and that the authorities intended to comply.

Will almost lied when Tom Ryan asked him whether he knew any details of the ransom delivery. Will said he had written everything that officials were willing to say with certainty. That was true enough, technically, and Will felt honor-bound not to go further.

He left the motel before anyone at the paper could phone him back with sharper questions. He found a decent diner and ordered the pasta special. It turned out to be simple spaghetti and meat sauce, but it wasn't bad, and it would give him the body warmth he'd need later on. Then he found an army surplus store, where he bought a thick sweatshirt with a hood, a pair of flannel-lined hunting pants, rubber and leather hunting boots and socks to go with them, and a water-repellent canvas hunting jacket.

Will put it all on his credit card, but he would damn well put it on his expense account.

He went back to the motel to change into his new outdoor gear, and by three o'clock he was in a car with Jerry Graham, who was dressed the same way.

"I'm getting too old for this stuff, Will. That's what I think sometimes."

"Me, too, Jerry." In fact—and there was no hiding it from himself—Will felt invigorated. He might pray to God (and he had) that the kidnapped boy come home alive, but it was still exciting to be at the center of events as they unfolded. It was what had first drawn him to the newspaper life, years ago.

"I'm sorry about your friend, Will."

"Thanks. I got the funeral arrangements made. Fran's body is on its way back to Bessemer. Maybe he's home already, in fact."

"He'd gone off the wagon in a big way just before the wreck, I guess?"

"It looks that way. I mean, his clothes smelled of beer and everything, and he tested high on blood alcohol. . . ."

"Any reason to have doubts? Other than wanting to give him the benefit of the doubt because he was a friend?"

"All right. I won't deny my emotions might be getting in the way. If I'd been in the office, I never would have sent him over here. The kidnapping is a big, big story, and I would have worried about the pressure being too much for him."

"He didn't have what it takes?"

"Once, he did. Quite a long time ago. Quite a few drinks ago."

Will knew the geography well enough to tell when they had crossed into Deer County. The day was raw, damp, windy. Now and then, Graham worked the windshield wipers. Some of the gusts were strong enough to push the car to one side or another.

"We've all known sad cases, Will. I know some talented agents who rubbed someone's ass the wrong way, ran afoul of some federal chickenshit. So they crashed and burned. When that happens, people get out or they get bitter."

Will waited, sensing that Graham would say more.

"This guy Fran, Will. You knew him way back when?"

"For a while, he was a mentor. When I was new, he taught me a lot. So the years went by—more than I want to think about, actually—and things went a certain way for him, another way for me."

"And suddenly you're the guy in charge, watching over him. Role reversal."

"Yes. And I suppose"—Will was about to share more than he'd intended to—"I suppose I'm operating on some not-quite-resolved baggage from years ago. My father committed suicide, and there was a sense of shame attached to it, back then. Which I can't do anything about. Now, Fran will always be the drunk who crashed into a car and injured a young woman as his final act."

"The gutter reaching up to drag him home?"

"Something like that. So I've been sort of snooping around to see if there could have been any mistakes. Or anything else. Off the record, Jerry, this is an angry little town in some ways, and I'm not sure how much I'd put past the cops."

"Meaning what, Will?"

"Meaning I don't know what. I did wonder if the young woman had a friend in the police department who was going to help her collect a big insurance settlement off a stranger."

"Pretty farfetched."

"I know. And the young woman doesn't seem like that kind of person."

"You went to see her about this?"

"About the wreck, I did. Just to try to satisfy myself. And there were a couple of other things."

Will told Graham about Fran Spicer's old drinking habits (whenever possible, schnapps first, then beer) and his lingering suspicions about the blood test.

Graham listened—skeptically, Will thought. Finally he said, "Be careful, Will. You're right about one thing. Long

Creek is an angry little town. Isolated, suspicious of strangers. Don't get on the wrong side of the cops, if you can help it.''

After a while, they turned off Route 126 and started uphill on a narrow two-lane road that was asphalt in some stretches, dirt in others.

"We're going roughly parallel to Logger Hill Road, Will. It's over that way." Graham gestured to his right with a thumb. "About three-quarters of a mile, actually. You in shape?"

"For my age, not bad. I jog a little."

"Good."

Jerry Graham found a hard spot by the road and pulled over. Will stood next to the car, flexing his legs to get the warmth started. The turf under his boots had lost some sponginess; the ground would soon freeze, and might not thaw again until April.

Graham opened the trunk, took out two pairs of binoculars. "One for day vision and one for night, Will. Do me a favor and carry one pair."

Then Graham took a rifle out of the trunk and slung it over his shoulder. "An old three-oh-eight Winchester semiautomatic, Will. Stop anything on the continent. The telescopic sight that's on it right now"—Graham took a foot-long tube out of the truck and put it into a deep pocket—"can be replaced with this night-vision sight in a few seconds."

"If you see someone picking up the money. . . ?"

"I'll just try to see where he goes, that's all. Get a general description, if I can. But it's a good bet the kidnappers, or one of them anyhow, is in the area, and we want to be ready."

Graham took out a small compass and held it as far as possible from the rifle barrel so that the needle wouldn't be affected by the metal. Then he pulled up the back of his coat and took a black radio off his belt. "This is Eagle Visitor," he said into the radio. "I'm moving in now."

The agent took a path up a hill, through thick underbrush, then into a stand of old evergreens. Will had been able to see the top of the hill from the road, and it hadn't seemed like such a steep climb. But it was plenty steep enough, Will decided after a few minutes.

Then Will figured it out: Instead of taking the most direct

route to the top, Graham was deliberately varying his path. "You're trying to stay out of sight, Jerry."

"More like not wanting to go in a straight line, in case someone's drawing a bead on us. Whoever he is."

Wherever he is, Will thought.

Soon, they emerged from the evergreen stand and were climbing up a steep slope carpeted with decayed leaves and dead limbs. Will could see the sky overhead—gray, cold, wet—and then they were back under evergreens, but shorter ones this time.

Except for the wind, which rocked the evergreen boughs and rattled the bare branches of the leaf-bearing trees, the woods were quiet. So fear shot through Will like a current when he heard the rustle in the brush just up the hill from them. Graham heard it, too, because, as fast as Will could flatten himself against the slope, the agent had unslung the rifle and was aiming it uphill.

"Shhhh," Graham said softly.

Will could smell the rotten leaves as he pressed his face to the slope.

The noise from above came again, louder and closer. Will raised his head very slightly, enough to see Graham squinting into the rifle sight. Suddenly, Graham lifted his face off the rifle stock and smiled broadly. "Go home, Bambi."

Will looked up in time to see the white tail just before the deer bounded out of sight. Of course, he thought. It had to be an animal, for God's sake. But Will's legs were shaking.

Graham stood up, slung the rifle over his shoulder again, and they went the rest of the way to the top. The agent checked his compass, then pointed to his left. "If I'm right, Will, we just have to walk a couple hundred feet this way. Then we can hunker down."

Will followed Graham along the ridge line. To his right and below, Will heard a gurgling creek. They picked their way through decades-old pine trees. Then they came to a small clearing.

"As promised, Will. This little open space. A deputy from Deer County gave me pretty good directions. Their sheriff has three guys planted around here. Plus six guys from Hill County and Long Creek, if you count me."

Looking down from the clearing, they could see the tops of trees, and beyond them a short expanse of brown field. And beyond the field, clearly visible, a stretch of dirt road.

"That's Logger Hill Road over there, Will. In a while, a police car is going to come by and toss a bundle off to the other side of the road. Just about dead center in our line of sight."

The view reminded Will of the vista from a hole on the Bessemer Country Club golf course. The road was a good quarter of a mile away. Anyone on the road, or near it, would probably not see anyone on the ridge line above, yet Graham and Will had an unobstructed view.

"I didn't see anyone else, Jerry."

"The idea was for people to get in place well ahead of time."

"So there's a lot of eyes looking where we're looking?"

"Yep. Seems all the cops and deputies around here hunt and fish. Easy for them to do a stakeout like this and stay out of sight, Will. I'm just a city boy."

"Me, too."

After scrounging a bit, they found places to sit that weren't too wet or uncomfortable.

"Thanks for keeping your word on the stories, Will. Not breaking confidence. Not that I thought you would."

"You're welcome." Several seconds went by before Will realized something. "You've seen copies of the *Bessemer Gazette*, then."

"A place on the main drag, about three blocks from police headquarters. They sell out-of-town papers. Not to mention numbers and cheap cigars."

"That's good to know. About the out-of-town papers, I mean. I know my paper has had distribution problems over here in Long Creek."

"You still don't know how long you'll be around here, Will?"

"No. I've been here longer than I expected. I need to do some laundry, in fact."

"I'll point out a laundromat when we get back. Maybe we can have dinner and a couple of drinks later."

"I'd like that." Sitting in the wet almost-quiet of the

woods, Will knew he would have to decide for himself when to go home. There was no one at the *Gazette*, except for the publisher, who would decide for him.

Lord, he thought. My problems are nothing. I worry about when I can go home, and Jamie Brokaw's parents are wondering whether their child is alive.

A car came into view on the road, and Graham tensed as he peered into his binoculars. "Just an old clunker, Will."

Now they could hear the car's grinding, sputtering engine. It took the sound a second or so to reach them, so that the car seemed to be ahead of its own noise.

The car passed out of view.

"Depressing around here, isn't it, Will?"

"Yes. I can see why people want to leave. Are the cops really as bad as they seem?"

"Oh, yes and no. With some of them, their heart's in the right place. Just not a lot upstairs. Some others seem pretty shrewd, but I don't know how honest they are."

"Do you have anything to base your suspicions on?"

"Other than the rumors that reach the bureau? Just my gut. It has a ping in it sometimes, Will. I believe in instinct. It's got nothing to do with stars or sheep entrails. It's the sum of all I know about law enforcement and people, from my life as well as my work, trying to tell me something."

Will decided to wait until later to tell Graham about his clash with the police chief.

They waited some more. It grew dark in the woods behind them, even though they could still see clearly to the road.

"Any time now, Will."

Just then, another car came into view. Graham peered into the glasses. "That's him, Will."

Graham's radio crackled. "This is Messenger One. Slowing down."

"Messenger One is the deliveryman, Will."

The radio crackled again, one voice after another.

"Deer Watcher One here; we see you. . . ."

"Deer Watcher Two, I have you in sight. . . ."

"Long Creek Two, we see you. . . ."

Finally, Graham spoke into the radio: "Eagle Visitor here. I have you in sight."

Graham handed Will the binoculars. "I can look just as easily through the gun sight, Will."

Will peered through the glasses. Suddenly, the car was amazingly, startlingly close. The driver got out carrying a bundle, then kicked the door shut. The sound seemed to take forever to reach Will's ears. The man looked up the road, then down it. Then he walked to the edge and tossed the bundle into the brush, where it rolled a couple of times before nestling to a stop in the tall, wet grass.

Through the glasses, Will watched the man get into the car; again, the noise of the door closing seemed a light-year away.

The car drove away.

"We'll wait for a while," Graham said. And into the radio: "Eagle Visitor here. I have the bundle in sight."

"Deer Watcher Two. So do I."

"Long Creek One. I see it."

Will breathed as slowly and evenly as he could to keep the glasses steady. He could see it clearly; if he ignored the distance distortion of the binoculars, the bundle seemed only half a football field away. A chill ran down his backbone.

"Jerry, the kidnapper could be watching right now. Just as we are."

"Possible."

"There's real money in the bundle?"

"A quarter mil. Small bills, just like the note said."

"Marked?"

"I can't hear you, Will."

"Are they mar—?" Will caught on, and shut up.

After a long moment, Graham said, "We have lots better technology for things like that than we did when I first joined the bureau, Will. Can't tell you any more."

Slowly at first, then rapidly, the gloom of the woods crossed over them, darkening the field between them and the road, then making it harder to see the road itself.

"Here, Will." Graham handed him the other pair of glasses. "Funny thing about these, Will. They actually work better when it's darker."

Graham took out the other scope, put it on the rifle in place of the day sight, then settled back to watch.

Minute by minute, Will's view through the night binoculars grew sharper. Will was looking at a world of sickly green, a world in which a few things stood out sharply and darkly. One of those things was the bundle.

Soon it was completely dark in the woods. Will was warm enough in his hunter's clothes, but he could feel the descending chill on his face.

Time passed. Will put down the glasses now and then to relieve his eyes, but Graham squinted constantly through the rifle scope.

Will was about to ask how much longer they would wait when Graham said into the radio, "This is Eagle Visitor. I think I'm going to call it a day. Are we all clear on the surveillance?"

"Deer Watcher Two here. Roger."

"Long Creek One. Heading home. I see my relief coming up the hill."

Graham stood up. "That bundle will be watched constantly, Will. We have teams of watchers set up around the clock. Part of me wants to stay here and look through the telescope."

"And the other part?"

"That part says I've been working sixteen hours a day and need my rest in case I have to make life-or-death decisions. My guess is that one of the kidnappers will find a way to get that bundle and not get caught. That's off the record."

"Understood. They have the cards, then. The kidnappers."

"They have the boy, Will. If I had a chance to grab one of the kidnappers without the other—well, right now I don't think I'd do it. A day or two from now, especially if things change, or maybe if they don't change, I might think differently. For now, maybe we can get a glimpse of whoever picks up the bundle. A photograph, too, if we're lucky."

Will stretched his legs for the walk back, took one last look through the glasses at the bundle.

"Let's go," Graham said, slinging the rifle over his shoulder and turning on a flashlight. Graham checked his compass and charted a more direct route back to the car.

Graham said little on the drive back to Long Creek, and Will wondered whether it would be a good idea to forget about having dinner with him. But once back to town, Graham made a point of driving Will past the laundromat, past the newsstand that sold out-of-town papers, past a restaurant that advertised steaks.

"Not bad food there, Will. Shall we meet there in, what, an hour and a half?"

"Great. Time enough to get a shower and do my laundry."

Graham swung by the Long Creek Inn to let Will off. "Jerry, thanks for taking me along. I'll see you in a while."

Back in Deer County, the woods were completely dark, for the moon was masked by the clouds that shed a rain turning to sleet. The woods were quiet, save for the rain. The birds and animals had all sought cover. Those that slept at night were just trying to stay dry and warm. As for raccoons and other nocturnal creatures, few took notice of the form that appeared by the bundle. It was just about the time that Will and Graham were finishing a steak dinner and getting set to move over to the restaurant bar to compare the stories of their lives.

The deputy who should have seen the form, that of a well-built man of medium height, had been stomping his feet up and down to keep warm while he smoked a cigarette. By the time he trained his scope where the bundle should have been, the bundle wasn't there.

The deputy immediately began rehearsing his story in his mind. He would say that he caught only a glimpse of the man, not enough for a good description.

The man had easily hoisted the bundle to his shoulder and headed into the woods. He didn't turn on a flashlight until he was deep in the trees. He knew the way.

Fourteen

. . .

It was cold in the car, and Will could only hope he'd guessed right. He figured the nurse would leave the hospital by the main entrance when her shift was done, but he couldn't be sure. Nor could he be sure she'd leave on time.

Shivering in the dark, Will cursed himself. Why hadn't he just thought to look her up in the phone book and called her at home? Because you don't even know if she's listed, or how she might be listed, he told himself. So wait.

Finally, Will saw her under the light of the arch at the door. His heart rose, then sank just as quickly: She was walking out with another nurse. Damn! Will had to see her alone.

Then the two nurses smiled and waved good-bye to each other. One made a sharp turn away from the hospital, into the darkness. The one Will wanted walked straight toward his car.

Will got out and stood in the street. "Heather Casey?"

"Oh!"

"I'm sorry to startle you. It's Will Shafer again. Can we talk a minute?"

"Oh, it *is* Mr. Shafer."

"Call me Will. I just need a minute of your time. Can I give you a lift?"

"Oh, no thank you. I live just a short way from here, and I usually walk. Why don't you leave your car here and stroll with me. There's a little place we can stop for coffee."

Will was pleasant but evasive as they walked a block and a half. Heather Casey pointed to a narrow door next to a dim and grimy window. "It's not as bad as it looks," she said.

The diner was long and narrow, more shadows than light, and it smelled of decades of fried eggs and hamburgers. Heather Casey nodded and smiled at a skinny man of sixty or more who stood behind the counter next to a grill. The man wore an apron that had been white a hundred launderings ago. He frowned at Will, then picked up his spatula and slid some meat patties around the hot metal.

"If you're hungry, the food in here is not bad, believe it or not," Casey said.

She led Will to a booth at the back, past a couple of tired old men who sat hunched over their soup.

"Long Creek's not much to look at, is it?" she said after they were settled in the booth.

She picks up what a person's thinking, Will thought. "I guess it has some of the same problems Bessemer has," he said.

"Oh, more. More, I'm afraid. At least Bessemer's on the lake. Here, we're not only economically depressed but landlocked. Time-locked, too."

The man who'd been at the grill was standing by their booth. Now Will saw that he had a bad eye; it was almost opaque, and it seemed to be looking away from Will while the good eye stared right through him.

"How are you tonight, Lewis?" Heather Casey said.

"I'm just fine, Heather. What can I getcha?"

"Just coffee for me," Will said. He was a little hungry but not sure he wanted to eat in this place.

"Lewis makes great four-alarm chili," Casey said.

"Okay, I'll try it," Will said. "And the coffee."

The man went away, and the nurse looked at Will as if to say, Well?

"I don't know how to put this exactly," Will began. "I've been bothered by some things about the accident that killed my friend Fran."

"Really? What?"

"I don't know. No, that's not true. I do know, sort of."

"What is it?"

Just then, the man returned with their coffee and Will's chili. Will paused until he was gone.

"Well, to begin with, was there any doubt at all that he was drunk?"

The nurse's face changed suddenly. "Why, what an odd question."

"Is it?" Will slowly stirred his chili.

"Yes." Heather Casey studied her coffee intently. "Why do you ask, Mr. Shafer?"

"Well, the main thing is, I'm trying to be sure that the young woman he injured gets everything she's entitled to. My company—"

Heather Casey appeared troubled. The look on her face, Will's memory of how she had greeted him so kindly at the hospital when he'd gone to see Fran Spicer, and something about the way her hand had felt on his shoulder caused him to decide something in an instant.

"Cancel what I just told you," Will said. "I'm no good at lying. I did, in fact, go to see the young woman who was injured in the crash, and I do want to see that she's taken care of. But . . ."

"Try your chili, Mr. Shafer."

Will did as he'd been told. The chili was spicy and delicious. He waited.

"There is, there is something. Oh, dear. He was all wet, you see."

"Wet?"

"His clothes were all wet. There was some blood, of course, but his clothes were mostly wet from beer. He reeked of it."

"Would that be strange?"

"It wouldn't be, necessarily. Not necessarily."

Time to gamble a little, Will thought. "I can tell from your voice that something's bothering you. You've been a nurse for a while, right? Seen a lot of things. But something's bothering you.''

"It was like the beer had gotten spilled all over him a short time before.''

Will noticed that she hadn't said, "It was like he'd just spilled beer on himself.'' What did that mean, if anything? He waited.

"He was wet with it. His clothes were.''

"And that struck you as odd?''

At first, Casey sipped her coffee and said nothing. Then she touched her right shoulder with her left hand and her left shoulder with her right hand. "Have you ever spilled beer on yourself?'' she asked.

"Not recently, no.''

"Anyway, both shoulders were wet. Both of the shoulders on his coat were soaking wet.''

Will thought about that for a moment, then he caught on. "You mean, even if he had been drinking at the moment of the wreck, the beer probably would have splashed all over his chest, say, or onto his lap. But it would have been less likely to soak *both* shoulders. Is that it?''

"I'm not saying it couldn't happen that way, Mr. Shafer—''

"Will.''

"Will. It's just that there was so much. And it was so fresh.''

"Fresh?''

"Yes. I remember . . . You see a lot of things as a nurse; you can't let it get to you. But I was touched by how pathetic this man looked. With the shoulders of his coat, kind of a shabby coat, all wet. And his hair . . .''

Something lighted in Heather Casey's eyes and hardened there.

"What is it?'' Will pressed. "I can tell there's something.''

"His hair was wet with the beer, too. On both sides of his head.''

Again, Will heard something tentative in her voice. He knew what his next question would be, but he wanted her to go on.

"My father was an alcoholic. I have to discipline myself mentally not to be too judgmental when I deal with patients who have been drinking."

Will could tell from her face (a lovely and intelligent face, framed by hair that was a lustrous chestnut in the light of the diner) that she wanted to say more. He waited.

"My husband, too. He was an alcoholic. And abusive, like my father. My husband, he was the real reason that I have to force myself not to be too judgmental about alcohol. As a nurse, I mean."

"I'm sorry."

She seemed to blink back the sadness as she shook her head and forced a smile. "I'm the one who should be sorry. I don't know why I told you that. You must be good at newspaper work. Getting people to talk about themselves."

Will shrugged. "I try to keep confidences, and I try not to hurt people if I can help it."

"I know that. I can tell that about you."

"And I can tell something about you. That you're a good nurse. You're too kind not to be."

"Oh, my. We should have coffee and chili more often."

"We could do that." But Will was really wondering what it would be like to meet Heather Casey for a drink, then dinner, then to walk her home. And say good night at the door?

She interrupted his reverie. "Something strikes you as odd about the wreck involving your friend. Something's not right?"

Will shrugged, then tossed the question he'd been waiting to ask. "How do you suppose he could have been soaked with beer on both sides of his head? His hair wet with it on both sides. Is that possible?"

She just looked at him for a long moment. Will finished his chili.

"Is it possible? I've seen terrible things happen to the human body in wrecks. One night when I was a young nurse, three teenage boys were brought in. Two were already dead, it turned out, and the third lived for only part of the night. A sad and familiar story. They'd been drinking, and their car hit a tree, bounced off it, and went into a field, rolling over and over.

"Those boys were wet, with their own blood, for one thing, and yes, their clothes were pretty soaked with beer. All over."

"Well, it's possible then," Will said.

"But those boys had been going very, very fast. There was a lot of beer in the car—a couple of cases of it, I seem to recall—and the beer was in bottles. So that the impact, the rolling over and over, caused the bottles to explode and shower the bodies. With glass as well as beer; their bodies had pieces of glass in them, I remember. It was horrible."

That jolted Will's attention. "Fran Spicer wasn't going that fast, was he?"

"I'm not a policeman, Mr. Shafer. Will."

"But it's a little hard to believe, isn't it? That he would be soaked that way, on both shoulders and all over his hair. Unless someone poured beer on him, wanting to make him look like a common drunk."

"Instead of what?" she said. "An uncommon drunk?"

God, I'm tactless, he thought. But it was no time for him to ease up. "My friend Fran, when he gave in to temptation, liked to combine beer and peppermint schnapps. That's sticky stuff—"

"I know what it is, Mr. Shafer. Believe me."

"Was there any of that on Fran? On his clothes? Any sticky sweetness?"

"No. Why don't you ask the police about the accident?"

"I did. The police here are less than forthcoming." He told her about his clash with the police chief. "So I went to see the young woman. She wasn't a great deal of help, but of course how could she have been? Fran's car hit her, and she was very dazed afterward."

"Probably in shock. In which case, she may never know exactly what she saw and heard."

Something occurred to him. "Did you see the cop who investigated the wreck?"

"No. Wait, maybe that was him. I'm not sure. There was a policeman standing off in the corner, near the emergency room. But I didn't get a good look at him. Or pay much attention. It's not unusual to have police in the hospital. Very common, in fact."

"And would there be a hospital record of which police officers were there at a particular time?"

"Not necessarily. In fact, emphatically no. Our hospital's not in the best neighborhood, as you probably noticed, and it's not unusual for police to be there in connection with shootings, stabbings, bar fights, domestic violence——"

Will heard the catch in her voice, saw the momentary hurt in her eyes. He pretended not to.

"Anyhow," Casey said, "you get the picture."

"Yes." He thought of something else. "And who drew the blood from Fran Spicer? For the drunk test?"

"I did."

"You did? And how does that work?"

"We have these standard kits for testing blood in cases in which drunk driving is suspected. As soon as blood is drawn, the vial is taken to our lab for immediate testing. When the results are in, I initial the vial and sign an affidavit saying that I drew the blood, and that it tested such and such. It's for the police to use in court."

"And you did that?"

"Yes, and the lab technician, Carmine . . ." It was only a short pause, but Will caught it. "Um, Carmine did the test. It seemed all routine."

"You say it *seemed* all routine."

Again, Heather Casey's face changed, only this time Will could tell that a door had closed. "I've said all I can say, Mr. Shafer. I have to be going."

"Something was on your mind just then, wasn't it?"

She refused to let her eyes meet his as she fumbled in her purse.

"Please," Will said. "The coffee was on me. If you ever want to talk, I'm staying at the Long Creek Inn."

"I have to go," Heather Casey said. She dropped a dollar bill on the table. Will picked it up. Without thinking, he took one of her hands and gently pressed the bill into it. He held her hand a moment longer than he needed to.

"At least let me walk you home," he said.

"You don't have to. It's not that far."

"Please."

Out on the cold, dirty sidewalk, he put his arm over her shoulders. He could tell that she liked it there.

"I didn't mean to get into all that," she said. "About . . . you know."

"That's all right. You . . ." Shut up, he told himself.

"This is where I live."

"Shall I wait until you're inside?"

"No need," she said, chuckling. "I'm quite comfortable and safe here. Have been for some time."

"Right. Of course." He never had been good at gallantry.

"Good night, then. You're a good listener."

Before he realized what was happening, she leaned toward him and put her hands on his shoulders. He kissed her on the cheek and would have hugged her had she not spun away.

She started up the steps to the apartment building, then stopped. "I don't know why I told you that. I don't even know where he is anymore. My husband." And she went inside.

On the way back to his hotel, Will tried to sort out his feelings. He was drawn to her by—what? She was vulnerable, that was it. She was vulnerable, and she had trusted him. Made him feel strong, even needed. His wife had no such weakness; if anything, Will needed her, too much sometimes. Face it, he told himself. It's a good thing you're married to a strong woman.

He knew that was so. But before he fell asleep, his thoughts were about Heather Casey.

Fifteen

■ ■ ■

He showered and dressed in a hurry and went over to police headquarters. There might or might not be a briefing that morning on the kidnapping, he was told. Will thought that meant there was nothing new to report.

Several reporters were lounging around the briefing room, some drinking coffee, some smoking, all doing their best to look jaded and bored. Will picked up some of the chatter.

"Why don't they tell us they think the little bastard's dead already, so we can say it on the air and go home?"

"I'll drink to that."

"You'll drink to anything."

"Not after last night. I'm sworn off. Until tonight anyhow."

So full of themselves, he thought. Like they've been seeing movies about hard-ass journalists so they know how to act. He left before he was tempted to tell them all to shut up.

Will persuaded the desk sergeant to dial Jerry Graham's extension. The sergeant let Will through the gate none too cheerfully.

"Will." Graham nodded, pointed to a chair.

Will sat down.

"Care for coffee, Will?"

"If you are. What's up, Jerry?"

Graham stared at him, and Will saw that his eyeballs were gray. "You look awful, Jerry."

"When I have a tough call to make, I like to sleep on it. This is my toughest call, and I couldn't sleep."

"What's that, Jerry?"

Graham got up and locked the door to his tiny office. Then he opened his desk drawer and held up a sheet of cardboard with a sheet of paper full of pasted-up newspaper lettering. Will saw that it was another message from the kidnappers.

> STAKEOUT WAS MISTAKE. WANT US TO CUT OFF
> CHILD'S EAR? WE WILL UNLESS WE GET EXTRA
> 100G'S. DELIVER SAME PLACE 11 TOMORROW NITE.
> U CAN'T HIDE SO MANY COPS. DON'T TRY. WE CAN
> MOVE BOY AT WILL. OBEY AND HE GOES FREE SOON.
> OTHERWISE I KILL HIM.

"God Almighty," Will said.

"Three people besides the kidnappers have seen this, Will. The boy's father, myself, and the Long Creek police chief. Now four people, counting you."

"Cut off his ear . . . Dirty bastards!"

"An old Sicilian custom, Will. But I don't think we have too many Sicilians around here. Tell me what you see."

Will read again, letter by letter. "I don't know, Jerry. This is like the second note. Not grade-school English, like the first one was."

"I agree. And notice the word *child* there. . . ."

"I was just going to say. He got impatient, like before. He found the word *child* in a headline, so he pasted it up intact and added the apostrophe s. Cutting corners."

"What else, Will?"

"He switches. Ah, see. I said *he*. The note starts out first-person plural, but it switches at the end to singular. 'Otherwise I kill him.' "

"And?"

"Well, I guess the dominant person in this whole thing is really asserting himself. It is a man, not a woman. I feel sure."

"I agree. See anything else, Will?"

For the briefest moment, Will thought he did. The feeling passed. "What next, Jerry? You said you had a tough call."

"Which is, Do we give in or say no?"

"I don't envy you."

Graham shook his head. "The guy who has the really tough call is the boy's father. He's good for the money—ten times that, if he needs it—and he can get a hundred thousand cash like that." Graham snapped his fingers. "But I don't know what to advise him."

"You mean, will the additional money get the boy back?"

"That's one thing. Plus, the longer they keep the boy, assuming he's still alive, the more of a liability he is."

Will understood. "You're wondering whether to try to bring things to a head."

"Something like that. Will, this is all between us, in this room. When this is over, I'll share everything with you, but for now . . ."

"Not to worry. Where was this latest message sent from?"

"A little postal station way off in a corner of Hill County, almost into Steuben. About the same distance from Long Creek as the post office where the last message was postmarked, only a bit west and south."

"You think he—they?—are just trying to show how they can move around without being spotted?"

"I suppose. Toying with us. But of course, we don't have any way of knowing that the boy is with them. They could have left him somewhere. Alive or dead."

The phone rang. Will stood up to leave, but Graham motioned for him to stay. Will only half-listened; he tried not to listen, in fact. Graham uttered one- or two-word answers to whomever he was talking to.

Will thought some more about Fran Spicer. What real difference did it make whether Fran had been drunk or not? Will thought, What am I? The guardian of the insurance company's coffers? So maybe some young redneck really was drunk that night and Fran's blood sample got switched with his. So what?

So it's rotten, that's what.

Tuning out the one-way phone conversation, Will thought about the two or three times he'd met Spicer's son. Mark, that was his name. An awkward boy, sullen and self-conscious. No doubt torn every which way by his father's on-again, off-again drinking and his parents' divorce. I'll bet he can't wait to grow up, Will thought. He thinks things will be easier then. . . .

Will knew something about warped father-son relationships. More than he cared to remember. Much more.

Will had no particular feelings one way or another about Fran Spicer's son. Compassion, maybe. There was that. Compassion for Fran, too. Suppose, just suppose Fran hadn't been drunk the night he died. His son shouldn't have to grow up and live his life with that. And Fran—what should his tombstone say? "Here lies a drunk who tried to climb out of the bottle but couldn't"?

No, it wasn't right. Will couldn't let it alone. If Fran had been set up somehow, he had to find out. If he couldn't uncover what had happened, he'd at least try to find enough to point the way for someone who could. Jerry Graham? Maybe he could do something, once this kidnapping thing was over with.

Meanwhile, Heather Casey might be helpful. Sure, Will thought. You're thinking of her strictly as a news source. Keep lying to yourself. What was it about her? Some sweetness that your wife doesn't have, your wife who's had to put up with your job as much as you have, who puts up with your depression and anxiety. . . ?

The F.B.I. agent put the phone down. "There's a man with courage," he said. "I told him he was in my prayers."

"Who?"

"Jamie's father. He's made a decision, Will. The biggest of his life maybe, and I think it's the right one. Come on. I'm going to brief the animals right now. Present company excluded, of course."

As Will followed the agent, he thought of a way to chase the truth about Fran Spicer. Of course, he thought. How simple. But am I cut out for it?

"We have just today received another note, apparently from the kidnappers," Graham told the strangely hushed gathering.

"Like the others, it consisted of newspaper lettering. . . ."

In his practiced monotone, Graham summarized the contents of the note while camera shutters clicked. And then he said, "Jamie Brokaw's father has authorized me to say that we will not—repeat *not*—comply with this latest demand unless and until we have an indication that the boy is still alive."

The room was quiet for several seconds.

"Agent Graham," a reporter said, "do you personally believe Jamie Brokaw is still alive?"

"I have no way of knowing."

"Sir, would Mr. Brokaw be able to raise the money, and if not. . . ?"

"He could get the money easily. This is not about money. You there."

"Sir, how does the boy's mother feel about complying or not complying?" a young woman asked.

"Mrs. Brokaw is under a doctor's care and under deep sedation at this time. Yes."

"Sir, isn't it a pretty big gamble with the boy's life, stonewalling like this?"

Will studied Graham's face, saw that the skin was stretched tight over cold anger. "I am not the one who gambled with Jamie Brokaw's life. The kidnappers have done that. And I warn them that if any harm comes to the boy, I will not rest until I personally see them punished."

"Do you favor the death penalty for kidnapping, sir?"

"My feelings on that are my own and are irrelevant."

"And sir, what would you accept as an indication that the boy is still alive?"

"That's up to them. They could record the boy's voice. . . ."

"But then you'd have no way of knowing when the recording was made."

"You didn't let me finish. Let them take a picture of the boy holding a copy of today's paper in front of him. They can figure out what to do."

Will saw that Graham, exhausted and drained, was near the end of his string.

"Agent Graham?" The questioner was the same reporter who had asked whether the "stonewalling" was gambling with the boy's life. "Sir, what will you do if they cut off one of the boy's ears and mail it to you?"

Embarrassed for his profession, Will waited for Graham's temper to explode. Instead, the agent smiled thinly for a moment and said, "Your question is not only stupid, it shows an indecent lack of compassion. The rest of you can write that down and quote me and make it just as emphatic as you'd like. An indecent lack of compassion . . ."

"What do you think, Will? Is that going to get me fired?"

"I hope not, Jerry."

"Hmmm. It might have in the days of J. Edgar. Oh, well. I've always wanted to go to Butte, Montana. The fishing's good, I hear."

"What if nothing happens, Jerry? I mean, no sign the boy is alive and no . . . ear in the mail. Nothing. What then?"

"Then we're no worse off than we are right now. Do you want to have lunch later?"

"I'd better say no. I have to write a thousand words. Maybe fifteen hundred." Thinking of Fran Spicer, he added, "And I've got some things to sort out."

"Suit yourself. I'm going to get some soup and coffee."

On their way out, they passed the reporter who had so angered Graham. He was tall, youngish, his face set in determination. Will envied him his toughness even as he found it despicable.

"Mr. Graham," the reporter said. "You were right about my question. I'd like to apologize."

Will was tired. Hours ago, he'd written almost two thousand words on the kidnapping. Then the computer had garbled

much of the first five hundred or so, and he'd had to pains-
takingly go over it with the editors back in Bessemer. It had
been so tiring, he'd felt physically exhausted by the time he
was finished. And his spirits were sagging. He was depressed
about Fran Spicer's death and sickened by the horrible turn
the kidnapping case had taken.

Now he waited in the hospital coffee shop. It was easy to
feel inconspicuous. The visitors who wandered in to sit fid-
geting at tables had their own worries. The hospital staffers
ducked in only to get coffee or candy bars from machines.

Maybe this is stupid, Will thought. Maybe he won't show
up at all. All right: Give him another twenty minutes or so.
Then go grab him, whether there're other people around or
not.

Will was finishing his second diet soda when the man he
was looking for came in. Will got up to intercept him, but he
didn't have to hurry. The man, dressed in rather soiled whites,
glanced at his watch and took a seat in the dim light of a
corner table.

Will sat down across from him. "How's it going, Carmine?
I saw your name tag. I called earlier to be sure you'd be
working."

The lab technician leaned back, studying him. "I don't
think I know you."

"My name is Will Shafer. I'm here because a friend of
mine was in a bad wreck. They brought him here, where he
died. Does that ring a bell?"

Carmine shrugged. "Not really? Who are you? Or *what*
are you? An investigator?"

"Not officially. But I am looking into the circumstances
of my friend's death. His name was Fran Spicer. He was
supposed to have been drunk when he was fatally injured in
a wreck a couple of nights ago."

Will looked in the smooth olive face. He was looking for
fear but didn't find it.

"You did the test," Will went on. "The blood test to check
his alcohol level."

"So?"

"So I have my doubts about the accident and the blood
test. Maybe you can help me."

"How would I do that, man? And why? That's hospital business. Police business."

Will studied the face. This should be where I see the lie in his eyes, or the weakness, Will thought. Instead, he saw just a cool stare. Was it cool because Carmine really did have the truth on his side? Or was he just tough?

"I've been wondering if there was something wrong with the test, Carmine. Is there any reason I should think that?"

"Think what you want, man. I know my job. I come in here and do my job."

Carmine stood to leave, and Will blocked him. Now, Carmine's face went hard. "I have to go, man. I have a job to do. Think you're tough enough to stand in my way?"

Will studied Carmine's frame for a moment. He was shorter than Will but more athletic. And he was no coward.

"I'm not going to stand in your way, Carmine, I just wonder what happened, that's all. Did you switch blood samples? Is that it?"

"You're talking crazy, man. Keep it up and you'll find yourself in the psychiatric ward."

"Was it for money? Did a lawyer pay you? Who?"

"Out of my way, man." Carmine brushed by him, and for the first time Will was sure he saw Carmine's lips quiver, saw the fear shine in the eyes.

"That's it, isn't it, Carmine? I guessed right."

The lab tech pretended to ignore him. Will walked alongside him, into the corridor, hissing in Carmine's ear. "Why? For money?"

Carmine stopped, stared at Will, who thought he saw something else now in Carmine's eyes.

"Your pupils are real big, Carmine. It must be tough, working in a hospital and having a habit, too. Like loving chocolate and working in a candy store. Yes?"

"Go suck out of a bedpan, man."

"Good, good answer. I'm right, though. Someone paid you, didn't they? Or they have something on you, maybe. Or both."

Carmine stopped, stared at Will, his eyes cold as a snake's. "You got something on me, go to the police, man. I live in this town, and I do my job right. Like I said, you keep talking that way, and you'll be in the nuthouse.''

Will didn't know what to say next.

Carmine saw the self-doubt on Will's face, and smiled almost tolerantly. ''Your friend was a drunk, and now he's a dead drunk, man. That's how it is when you drink and drive. I'm sorry for your grief. Really. But I was just doing my job.''

''Bullshit. You switched the blood, his blood, with someone else's. Didn't you? Or did you just put something in it? Which?'' Will was shooting in the dark, but he had nothing to lose.

''You're crazy, man. Keep talking, and I'll call security myself right now.''

''You shafted my friend. Who paid you? A lawyer? Someone else? Why?''

''I'm running out of patience, man. Keep it up, and I call security. I'm not kidding. You'd best be going.''

''I'm going, for right now.'' Will was losing it; he couldn't keep his voice tough, because he had nothing to use against Carmine, and Carmine knew it.

''If you're smart, you'll be going for good, man. If I see you again, I won't just call security. I'll call the Long Creek cops, and they'll throw your ass in the can for harassing me. You'll grow old there.''

''You're the one who's going to grow old in a cell, Carmine. Someday. It's tough in state prison.''

Will thought he saw something flicker in Carmine's face. He knew he'd be ashamed of what he was going to say next, but he was playing for keeps. ''Prison can be really tough, depending on the kind of man you are. That scares you, doesn't it, Carmine? Prison. What guys do to other guys in prison. Maybe you know about those things already.''

Carmine stood still, and Will saw his shoulders slump for a moment. Then Carmine straightened; he and Will had both heard the voices coming from around a bend in the corridor.

''I belong here, man. You don't. You're keeping me from doing my job. Get out of here, or I'll have you arrested.''

Will turned and moved toward the stairs.

"Your friend was a drunk driver, man. That's why he's dead, and that's why he scored high on his test."

Will banged open the metal door to the stairs. He was out of things to say.

Will walked to his car with deliberate slowness. A wind made the air seem razor-cold, but in an almost perverse way Will savored the pain on his cheeks. The encounter with Carmine had pumped too much adrenaline into his blood.

He drove slowly. He stopped at the newsstand Jerry Graham had pointed out to him and bought copies of the *New York Times*, the *Bessemer Gazette*, and the *Long Creek Eagle*. He would wait until he got back to his room to see what, if anything, the editors in Bessemer had done to the story he'd filed the day before. Then he'd read the *Times* and the *Eagle* to see how his story measured up to theirs.

God, Will thought. Here I am, way on the wrong side of forty, and I'm still wondering how I stack up. When does it stop? Maybe when I get away from Bessemer.

But Will was in no mood to let those thoughts crawl through his head this night, so he pulled over when he saw the pink neon signs of a shabby bar on a corner. Inside, he recognized a few faces at a table: reporters he'd seen at the press conferences. He had no desire to join them.

He asked the fat bartender for a six-pack of Budweiser to go. As he waited for his change, Will's eyes settled on the bottles—whiskey, gin, rum, and schnapps, yes schnapps—set in rows in front of the mirror. No doubt about it: The bottles were tempting, at least in the mood Will was in now. And yes, he could appreciate how good it would taste: a shot of sweet-burning schnapps, chased by cold, slaking beer. Is this how it starts, Fran? With feelings like this?

For a moment, Will thought of having a shot at the bar. But after what had happened to Fran, after his talk with Carmine about doctored blood tests, that would be insane. Sure, he thought. Get myself picked up by the cops, and then Carmine does my blood test at the hospital. Nice, Will. . . .

He got his change and left. And he put the six-pack in his trunk. With the beer there, no cop could frame him. Could he?

* * *

Halfway through his second beer, he called home. Brendan answered; he and Cass were getting ready for bed. Brendan asked whether he could have a dog for Christmas. Will was evasive.

Karen came on the line. "It is getting to be that time, isn't it?" she said. "Christmas shopping, I mean."

"Lord, yes."

"When are you coming home?"

"Soon, I hope. Very soon."

"That's terrible, about the threat to cut off the boy's ear. I saw the report on the six o'clock news."

"Did the kids hear it?"

"No, God. That would have upset them."

"Upsets me. And Jerry Graham."

Then Will told his wife about his lingering suspicions about what had happened to Fran Spicer, and about his meeting with Carmine the lab technician. Some pride in his newfound toughness crept into his voice.

"That kind of thing isn't you," Karen said. "It's not you."

Stung silence. Then he said, "I felt I had to do it."

"I don't know about that. I do know you. And what you did to that . . ."

"Carmine. The lab tech."

". . . with that Carmine is not you. Your strengths are research and logic. You're not—that term you use for some reporters—you're not street-smart. You're not, Will. Any more than you're handy with tools."

That last pierced him like a dart. A couple of years before, Will had decided to cut some firewood. He'd rented a chain saw, despite (or maybe because of) Karen's anxiety over his lack of skill with tools.

The saw had hit a nail and bucked in his hands. It was sheer luck that he hadn't badly injured himself or his son, who was standing nearby.

"Bull's-eye," he said, not trying to hide his anger.

"I'm sorry. I didn't mean that. Yes, I did, but I shouldn't have put it that way. I was only . . ."

"Why explain? You couldn't have been any clearer."

"Will, I'm your wife, and I worry about you messing with

the police and this Carmine. If he is crooked in some way, you can't assume he's some harmless punk. Even if he is, he knows people who aren't.''

Will swallowed the last of his beer and waited for her to go on.

''And if you wounded this man on a personal level, Will, how do you know he won't come after you with a knife or something?''

That made him feel even worse. She was right, of course. Right about his strengths and weaknesses. He was not tough and shrewd. Even in doing what he did best—making decisions in the workaday newspaper world—he was more comfortable with stories that originated with government actions and court rulings than he was with investigative or speculative articles.

''I'll be careful,'' he said.

He got through the rest of the conversation without losing his temper. After hanging up, he cracked open another beer—is this how it starts, Frannie?—and thought over what Karen had said. Yes, he might have wounded Carmine on a personal level, might have made him hate him. For that, Will felt a tinge of guilt—and anxiety. He had been reckless in the encounter with Carmine Luna, perhaps to the point of stupidity.

He thought again of how right Karen had been, and then he remembered how he had felt with Heather Casey, how close he had come to . . .

Well, what? He knew which reporters cheated on their spouses when they traveled. He'd felt morally superior to them. ''Hypocritical bastard,'' he whispered to himself.

He forced himself to scan the newspapers. The *New York Times* account of the kidnapping was on an inside page, under a one-column headline. The *Times* article was accurate, thorough, clear, circumspect.

Will thought his own story measured up pretty well by comparison. Will skimmed the rest of the *Times*, catching up on the world.

He picked up the *Long Creek Eagle*. Even with the kidnapping, it found room for other local news: a church-renovation fund drive, complaints about smells from a landfill, a couple of drunk-driving arrests (yes, Fran's sample could have been switched), a grocery-store burglary.

Will remembered what a famous journalist had said years ago: "*All* news is local."

I guess so, Will thought. Is there anything else happening in Long Creek? The lead obituary was on a retired steelworker who had been a gunner on a Liberator bomber in the China-Burma-India theater in World War II. And there was the Long Creek mayor, cutting a ribbon somewhere.

Besides the kidnapping, the biggest local news was from the fire department. A child had been killed because he played with matches while his mother left him alone to go to the coin laundry, and two men had perished in flames after apparently using gasoline to clean up some grease.

Was there any end to human stupidity? No, Will decided.

He got into bed. He tried not to think about Heather Casey. And just before gliding into oblivion, he had the same feeling he'd had before—that he was overlooking something obvious, even trivial, and yet terribly important.

Sixteen

■ ■ ■

The hermit awoke in the dark of night, in the dark of his soul. He knew at once that he had been having a whiskey dream, that he would be hours getting back to sleep—if he did.

Sometimes the whiskey did that to him. Other times, it let him sleep. Whenever he drank a lot of whiskey, he thought it worth the gamble.

No. It hadn't been just the whiskey dream that had roused him. Wolf had stirred. The hermit could see his form in the dark. The dog was sitting up, his ears high.

"Damn you, Wolf."

He raised his head and saw the silhouette of the dog against the blue-black of the window. Now Wolf was standing on his hind legs, his front paws on the sill, his ears pricked and alert.

"Damn you, Wolf." He let his aching head fall back on the pillow. "You can't sleep, either."

The dog whined softly, then chortled.

The hermit swallowed hard against the nausea, wishing now that he had eaten more while drinking.

Wolf whined again, louder. The hermit raised his head again, saw by the silhouette that the great shepherd was looking directly at him.

"Lie still, damn you. Wolf, lie down."

Wolf snarled, then barked loudly. The hermit sat up. Only a few times had Wolf snarled and barked in the middle of the night. Once, there had been a black bear near the cabin, another time a deer. Once, the hermit had heard footsteps (human?) in the dark.

"What, Wolf?" the hermit said, getting out of bed and walking to the window. "What, boy?" he said, putting a hand on the dog's shoulders and feeling the fur standing on end.

The hermit stared into the night, held his breath as he listened. There was nothing but the soughing of the trees. Still, he tiptoed to the corner and picked up the rifle, an old lever-action .30–30 carbine. He could open the door with one hand while holding the carbine in the other, and firing it if he had to. There was something out there; he was sure of it.

In the dark, the hermit laid the rifle on the bed, then pulled on his pants and stepped into his boots. He put on his thermal vest. "Shh, Wolf. Good boy."

With a flashlight in his left hand and the rifle in the right, he tiptoed to the door and put his ear to it. Nothing.

Wolf sat down next to him, whined, scratched the door. Without turning on the flashlight, the hermit opened the door, felt a gust of cold wind.

"Wolf, come."

Outside now, he closed the door quietly and listened. There were only the tree noises. No, there was something else: a scraping sound. The darkness and the wind played tricks; the sound could have been a stone's throw away, or way over the next ridge.

Suddenly, Wolf bolted and ran. The hermit turned the flashlight on, caught Wolf in the beam thirty yards away. The dog paused, looked back at him, his eyes red and huge. Then the dog turned and ran.

The hermit followed.

Stepping high so as not to trip in the dark, he trotted behind the dog. He tried to keep the flashlight steady, but the beam danced helter-skelter as it poked into the blackness. About every fourth step, the light picked up Wolf trotting ahead as though drawn to something.

"Wolf!" The hermit hissed as he stopped to catch his breath. The light caught Wolf's red eyes staring back at him. "What the hell is it with you? Stupid dog."

The hermit trotted on, catching Wolf in the beam. The dog was farther ahead, eager. Going back the way they had come earlier. Almost to where he had been digging earlier. Was that what this was all about?

"Wolf, wait! Damn you."

An impatient bark from ahead.

"All right, god damn it."

Then he heard the sound, like an echo from far away. Christ, don't let me be hearing this. I ain't been drinking so much that I deserve this.

He heard the sound again—a moan, a scream, an echo— and dropped to his knees, letting his carbine and flashlight fall. He put his hands over his ears. He held his breath and uncovered his ears.

Again the sounds. Hard to make out, tumbled by the wind, but boy sounds. Real. He was too awake from the cold for it not to be real. Wolf barked. The echo-moan came again; Wolf barked again, went on barking.

Yes, there it was. From deep in his memory came the cries of the son he had never had, the one he had let die in Jo's belly.

"Mom-MY . . . Dad-DY . . ."

He knelt on the chill bed of pine needles.

"Help me. . . ."

Once, the hermit had managed to get the rifle muzzle almost to his face. It was after a really bad whiskey dream, and he had almost convinced himself that if he could get the muzzle into his mouth and pull the trigger before he had time to think about it, he could see Jo again. And the baby? At least he'd be with them, wherever that was.

But he hadn't been able to do it. He'd been afraid of the pain if he didn't die right away, afraid to die slowly in the woods. He'd even been afraid how the gun oil and old cordite of the muzzle would feel on his tongue.

"Jo, I'm sorry. I couldn't. I couldn't." What did the trees and the night care?

Maybe this time he could really do it. Shoot Wolf first? No, let him have his chance. If any dog could make it in the woods, he could.

He stood up and almost fell back down. The whiskey had taken a sledgehammer to his head, and, while the night had sobered him, it had not deadened the pain inside his skull. A drunk like this was enough by itself to make him want to die. Why not fire a bullet into his head. His brain was mush, anyhow. It couldn't even tell what was real anymore.

There came the sound again, a child's moaning. It sounded near and yet far away.

If he did it tonight with the rifle, would the sound of the child follow him?

Whiskey. There was some left in the cabin. He would swallow it all and go back to sleep—forever, if he was lucky.

The wind shifted; it was in his face now, and he breathed deeply to clear his head. And now the wind brought a scraping sound. Yes, there it was. It was real. Just then, he heard the unmistakable *ping* of metal on metal.

Again, he heard the moan of a child, followed by Wolf's bark. Wolf went on barking, and the moan rose to a shout, a scream. "Dad-DY! Puh-LEEZE! Get me out. . . ."

There, over there. He flashed the light in the direction of the sounds and stumbled toward them. The hermit tried to control his own breathing, the better to hear the night sounds. There was the *ping* of metal on metal, and the scraping sound: a shovel digging into dirt. And then the sound of a man's voice, angry, cursing.

The beam of light danced crazily with his steps, catching ground, branches, treetops, Wolf's eyes. And beyond Wolf, something else: There in the light stood a man holding a shovel. Next to him was a small mound of fresh-dug dirt, and next to that a larger mound with something sticking up out of it.

Wolf snarled, moved toward the man, who raised his shovel as if to swing it.

The hermit worked the lever of the carbine to put a round in the chamber. "Wolf!"

Transfixed, the man in the light beam looked toward the hermit.

"Help! Daddy, get me out! Get me *out*!" The child's voice sounded as if it was coming from a well. In there, the hermit thought, looking at the bigger mound. In there.

"Wolf!"

The dog stopped several yards from the man, who switched the shovel over to one hand as he stooped, still looking toward the light. With his free hand, the man picked something off the ground: a newspaper. He put the paper under his arm and fumbled some more on the ground before he found what he was groping for: something box-shaped, like a camera.

The dog advanced toward the man, snarled again. The man extended the sharp edge of the shovel toward the dog's face.

"Wolf!"

The hermit put the rifle to his shoulder, pointed it toward the sky, and squeezed the trigger. The sound crashed over and over down the hills and ravines. Somewhere, an owl stirred.

"Help *me*! Get me *out*!"

The man backed out of the light beam and turned to run. The hermit worked the lever of the carbine again. Hearing a new round being chambered, the man dropped his shovel and ran off into the darkness.

"Wolf, come!"

But there was no need for the command: The dog was already digging furiously at the larger mound of dirt.

"God Almighty," the hermit said. "God Almighty." He walked slowly to the mound. Dirt and leaves from Wolf's digging spattered off his boots.

"Mom-MY! Get me out. . . ."

The hermit leaned over what looked like a stovepipe and shined his light into the opening. "Jason?"

"Dad-DY! I'm in here."

"Jason? Jason! God Almighty!"

"Get me out!"

His father had sent a man to find him! Jamie knew his father could do it, knew his father wouldn't let him die. He knew!

Jamie could hear the scratching and digging. He shouted as loudly as he could—in joy now. He heard a dog again. He could tell it was a big dog. Jamie liked dogs.

He heard the shovel sounds, faster than before. Faster, faster, faster! He heard a man grunt. He knew that the man was shoveling as hard as he could.

Jamie shouted as loudly as he could. His own voice rang back in his ears, but he didn't care.

The dog barked again—what a big dog it must be!—and Jamie made a sound that was part laugh and part cry.

The sounds of the shovel were close now. The man was grunting hard.

Now the shovel banged on the metal. Again and again. Jamie heard the man swear. Then Jamie heard a *thump*, *thump*, and then a screeching noise like old nails being pried loose.

There was a *clang*; Jamie saw a flash of light and smelled cold, clean air. Then there was another *clang*, like something snapping shut again. Jamie heard the man say, "Shit!" Then the prying noise started again. The prying noise kept going, going, going.

Clang.

The cold, clean air blew all over Jamie's face. A light in his eyes was so bright, it made him squint. When he opened them, he saw the upside-down head of a dog, the biggest dog he had ever seen.

"Wolf, back."

Jamie felt big, strong hands on his shoulders, felt himself being pulled out of the metal place.

It was night.

"Jason," the man whispered close to his ear. "Jason."

"My name is Jamie."

Seventeen

. . .

Will slowed his car when he saw the gouges in the earth. He pulled over and stopped.

Will got out, stood by his car, shivered in the wind. Fran had come down a curving hill—not the kind of hill you wanted to take at sixty miles an hour, but not one that seemed particularly dangerous, either. Had the accident report mentioned anything about snow, ice, whatever? No. Nor had Suzanne Glover.

"Were you really drunk, Frannie? What happened?"

Having struck out at several saloons—no bartender recalled serving schnapps and beer to a man in a dark gray suit on Thanksgiving Eve, or, if they did, they wouldn't say—Will stopped at the liquor store he'd passed earlier.

Yes, he thought, it would make sense if Fran's last great temptation had been right here: The liquor store was not that far from the expressway; it was on the two-lane heading into Long Creek. Jesus, Frannie might've been tempted after seeing a bar back there, then resisted until spotting this place.

114

Will parked in the dirt lot. Coming out of the store were two young men—teenagers, Will thought—in dirty work clothes. One carried a brown paper bag. They got into a battered pickup and drove away.

I hope the store owner's halfway friendly, Will thought. But suppose he isn't.

He started toward the door of the store, then spotted the phone booth. He had an idea.

"Good afternoon," Will said.

The man behind the counter in the liquor store looked up, nodded, and said, "Help you?"

"I hope so. I'm checking on something, actually."

Will saw the man's eyes harden.

"I wonder if you remember a man who might have stopped in here the night before Thanksgiving. Middle-aged, wearing a suit?"

"Suppose I did?"

Not friendly, Will thought. "I'm interested because this man is, was a friend of mine. He's dead now, from injuries in a wreck down the road." Will paused, locked onto the man's eyes. "If my hunch is right, he might have stopped here not long before."

"Hold it right there, mister! I don't sell to drunks, so if you're trying—"

The man cut his voice the instant the door opened and a customer walked in. Will stepped back, pretending to check the scotch brands, as the man rang up a sale to a whiskey buyer wearing overalls and a red face.

Will had heard fear as well as anger in the man's voice. He was glad he'd called the *Gazette* from the booth outside and had the paper's morgue check something.

The customer left, and the owner turned to Will. "Like I was saying, I don't sell to drunks."

"And you don't sell to minors. The liquor commission made a mistake when it suspended your license. Twice."

"How do you—?"

"It's public record. Look, it's okay. Just listen." Will tried to keep the tremble out of his voice. "I believe you, all right? I can understand why you're upset. It's okay, really." The man's eyes softened. "I'm not looking to get you in trouble. I have personal reasons for checking. I think my friend might have stopped here. Your place is the closest liquor store to where the accident happened."

"So what? How do you know he didn't stop at a bar? Couple of them up the road a way."

"I know. No one remembers my friend. Besides, when my friend drank and had the choice, he liked to start with peppermint schnapps. If he stopped to drink schnapps in a bar, he would have drunk until he passed out. My friend was an alcoholic. And you can't buy a bottle of schnapps in a bar to take out. Legally, you can't. You follow me, don't you? So I think my friend might have stopped at a liquor store to buy schnapps and beer. Do you remember?"

"Who buys what in here is no one's business. Now get the hell out of here."

Will had never been much of a poker player: He couldn't bluff. Now he had to bluff. "I'm a newspaper editor, and if you don't help me I promise there'll be a team of reporters looking into how you managed to keep your license. Trust me on that."

The man's eyes hardened again.

"Look," Will went on, "I'm not trying to hurt you. Now, if a man came in here to buy schnapps and beer the night before Thanksgiving, you'd remember. Wouldn't you?"

"He was here just before closing."

"Ah. And what time was that?"

"Couple minutes before seven."

"You're sure?"

"Told you, didn't I? Night before Thanksgiving, I was closing early. Not many people get a bottle of schnapps and a six-pack, unless they're planning to tie one on. Which he was."

"Oh? And how do you know that?"

The man snorted contemptuously. "I been selling booze a long time. I asked him if he needed any cups. He said no and acted like it never crossed his mind."

"But you think it did?"

"Told you, I been selling booze a long time. Face like

that, it's easy to tell. My guess is, he was gonna give himself a jolt as soon as he could find some privacy.''

"And you still—'' Will bit off his words. He wanted to call the man every name he could think of for selling liquor to someone he thought was an alcoholic. But what was the point in that? He needed information. "So my friend would have left here just about seven?''

"He was my last customer. I about shit when I heard about the wreck. You gotta understand . . . .''

"Yeah, I understand.'' Will turned to go, then stopped. His instinct told him to leave this man with some pride. "Look, I'll trade you promises. I'll keep quiet about this, and maybe I can keep your name out of the paper someday. And you forget I was ever here.''

"Deal.''

To seal it, Will bought a pint of scotch, which he probably wouldn't drink, put down a twenty, and left the change.

He drove back toward Long Creek. The accident report said the wreck had happened at 7:30. Will drove at the speed limit, then slowed down a little. Maybe Fran had slowed for a time because of the darkness? The weather? The unfamiliarity?

Sure enough, before many minutes passed, Will came to the top of the hill down which Fran Spicer had driven to his doom. It was clearly marked with a diamond-shaped yellow sign and an arrow indicating the direction of the curve. Will slowed a little more, took the hill curve without trouble, came to a stop on the shoulder at the bottom. It had taken Will less than ten minutes to travel from the liquor store to the accident site. And he hadn't been speeding at all, not like Frannie had been, at least at the end.

What happened, Frannie? What happened in the other twenty minutes? Was the police report that far off?

On the way back to Long Creek, he saw a small, low building with the windows covered with plywood; it was one of a dozen or more boarded-up buildings he'd seen around Long Creek. The sight depressed him; what was happening here could happen in Bessemer (hell, it *was* happening in spots), although his home city at least had a state university branch and a couple of fledgling high-tech companies going for it.

He thought of Suzanne Glover's shabby house. He hoped the insurance company would treat her all right. He'd check when he got back to Bessemer. Then something else occurred to him; he had a reason to see her again.

"Hello, remember me? Will Shafer."

"Yes, hi," Suzanne Glover said. "I'm sorry my mother was so rude to you."

"Oh, no. That's okay." Shivering on the porch, Will was pleased at his good luck: the mother must not be home.

"It isn't, really," Suzanne Glover went on. "She's just protective, is all."

"I understand."

"Would you like to come in?"

"Oh no, thanks. What I wanted to ask you, you're sure the accident happened near seven-thirty? Not closer to seven, maybe? Or perhaps later?"

"Does it matter?"

"Well, possibly."

Before Will was forced to improvise, Suzanne Glover went on: "Anyhow, I am sure. I was watching the seven o'clock news with my mother before going out to the store for a couple of things. You know how the news ends like at seven twenty-six or so? I left right after that."

"I see. Thank you again."

"It shouldn't matter, should it? The time?"

"No."

But it does, Will thought. He turned to go, then thought of something else. "And you're sure you don't know the police officer who helped you that night?"

"No. I told you before."

"I know. I just thought, small town and all . . ."

"I might have seen him around, and I might not. He was just a cop."

One last thing occurred to him. "Did you say something before about a second set of headlights the night of the wreck?"

"I, I don't know. Don't remember. I was dazed. I was almost killed, for God's sake."

Even before she shut the door, Will knew from Suzanne Glover's face that he probably wouldn't be welcome again.

Back in his room, Will called Tom Ryan on the *Gazette* city desk and told him he expected to file a fairly routine story on the kidnapping, saying in effect that there was nothing new to report. Then he got to what was really on his mind.

"Ry, what time did Frannie leave the office to head for Long Creek? Do you remember approximately?"

"Late afternoon sometime. Things were winding down here. It was getting toward dark."

"And did he seem eager to go?"

"I guess."

Will had a hunch. "Switch me back to the coffee shop, Ry. . . . Yes, the coffee shop."

Will's hunch turned out to be a good one. After talking for no more than a minute to the counterman in the *Gazette*'s coffee shop, Will had himself switched upstairs, to the medical department. He was lucky again: Doc Quick, the *Gazette*'s company physician and about the only good internist in Bessemer, was in.

When Heather Casey finished her shift, Will was waiting for her in the lobby. She had agreed to talk to him again.

"Have you been waiting long?" she said.

"Hi. Just a few minutes." Will felt as awkward as a teenager—and almost as eager. "So, how are you today, um. . . ?"

"Just call me Heather. Fine, thank you."

They went to the same dingy-looking diner they'd visited the first time. This time, the man behind the grill was noticeably more pleasant. The nurse let Will buy her coffee, and he ordered a hamburger and a soft drink.

"You said you wanted to talk about your friend, Mr. Shafer."

"I said you could call me Will. Remember?" For God's sake, he thought, I kissed you.

"I'm sorry. Will. How can I help you?"

"I paid a visit to Carmine. Not a friendly visit."

"And where was that?"

"Right at the hospital. I waited for him in the little room with the food and drink machines. And I asked him about the blood test on Fran Spicer."

"What did he tell you, Will?" The nurse's voice had gone flat and cold.

"Not much. It's what he didn't tell me, actually."

"And why do you persist in this?"

Will was doubly dismayed the way the conversation was going. She seemed so guarded, he wondered how much information he could expect. Worse, she was cool to him personally. "I'm persisting because it isn't right," Will said. "Before he fell apart, Fran had real good newsman's instincts. 'Trust your instincts,' he told me a long time ago. My instincts say something is wrong here. I mean, what happened to Fran."

"And you're a newsman, aren't you?"

"Oh, I'm that, all right. Not the world's best, but far from the worst. But see, this is more than a story. Something terrible happened to a friend of mine, someone who worked for me. Someone I feel responsible for. He's dead. And I don't like the label that's being pasted on his corpse."

"A label?"

"Here lies a drunk. He couldn't kick the bottle, and he died a drunk. Carmine said something like that. 'Your friend was a drunk,' or some such."

"Carmine said that?" Heather Casey shook her head in dismay. "What else did he say?"

"Oh, a few things that were pretty hostile. Especially after I told him of my suspicions. Told him I thought the blood sample had been phonied up. Or switched outright."

"Did you say you suspected him?"

"Yes. That was the unmistakable message." Will chewed on his hamburger while Heather Casey slowly stirred her coffee.

"Did you give him a reason for suspecting him?"

"I sort of implied he'd done it for someone else. For money, perhaps. Or . . ."

"For drugs?"

"Well, yes. I guess I leaned on him. I don't have to guess. I did lean on him. I made some remark about his being tempted by working so close to drugs and all."

"And you think the police would have put him up to it?"

"That's one inference. I've already had one big fight with the police chief, and the cops generally don't seem that friendly."

"And you don't know whom to trust."

"No. I know the FBI man who's in town because of the kidnapping. We go way back, in fact. But I'm reluctant to bother him about Fran Spicer when he's got a life-or-death case on his hands. Anyhow, back to Carmine. Have you known him a long time?"

"Oh, a few years. He does decent work, cares about what he does, although he can be moody. He's absent a little more than he should be. And I've wondered about his personal life."

"About whether he has a habit?"

"That and . . ."

"Whether he might be gay."

"Yes. I hate stereotypes, I really do. But he does have a manner about him."

"When I was leaning on him, I mentioned something about what happens in prison. I think that got under his skin."

"Newspaper people don't mess around when they want something, do they?" She had never sounded less friendly.

"I'm not like that—normally. And after I leaned on Carmine, I had second thoughts about it." Will deliberately avoided mentioning that it was his wife who had given him the second thoughts. "Heather, listen. I wouldn't have gone to Carmine and talked to him like that . . ."

"You didn't mention my name?"

"No. I wouldn't have gone to him like that, except I have reason to believe there's something awfully wrong with Fran Spicer's death."

"Just because of that schnapps thing? That's no reason . . ."

"Fran Spicer did buy a bottle of schnapps. And a six-pack. I found the liquor store that sold the stuff to him."

"Well, then. He probably threw the schnapps bottle into a ditch when he was done with it."

"I don't think so. I don't think he had time to drink that much before the accident. The liquor store was closing at seven, and Fran came in just before closing. The guy in the store remembers that."

She sipped her coffee and waited for him to go on.

"Now, this is crucial. The accident happened just about seven-thirty on the nose. I talked to the young woman who was hurt, and she's positive. Could Fran have gotten that drunk between seven and seven-thirty? And if he could have, which I doubt, what happened to the schnapps bottle?"

She frowned skeptically. "I can tell you that one person's body doesn't behave like another's. Your friend wasn't in the best of health. People have different tolerances. You know yourself what happens if you drink on an empty stomach, for instance."

Now Will could not help but smile in self-satisfaction. "I don't think Fran drank on an empty stomach—if he drank at all. I checked the coffee shop at my newspaper. When Fran rushed out of the office Wednesday afternoon, heading for Long Creek, he stopped and bought a couple of sandwiches for the road."

"Perhaps he hadn't eaten them."

"My guess is that he had. It's close to three hours from Bessemer to Long Creek, and Fran was almost done with the trip when he had the accident."

"You've really tried to piece this together, haven't you?"

"Yes. I talked to a doctor today. My newspaper's doctor. A pretty decent internist. He thought it highly unlikely that Fran could have been sober at seven and legally drunk at seven-thirty, assuming that there was anything at all in his stomach. I bet you don't disagree with that."

"But you don't know if he was sober when he stopped at the liquor store just before seven, do you?"

"He must have been. If he'd stopped anywhere else before that to drink . . ."

"He never would have left. Yes, that sounds familiar from my own childhood." A cloud came over her face. "Not just my childhood. Well, then."

"It doesn't add up, what happened to Fran."

"It's intriguing, I'll say that. And I understand your concern for your friend."

"Frannie didn't have a lot going for him the last few years. Now he's dead. He has a son."

"I see. How could I possibly help you? Would you want my help?"

"I'd welcome your help. And your company." Will waited, but she seemed not to hear that last. "Tell me where Carmine lives. I need to talk to him some more."

"Perhaps it would help if I went with you."

"That's very kind. I'd like that."

"As I said, I've usually gotten along okay with Carmine."

"And he tends to be absent a lot?"

"He called in sick today, in fact. Let's pay him a call."

"Wonderful."

Eighteen

■ ■ ■

"Jason," the hermit whispered. "Can I call you Jason for a little while?"

He sat in a chair sipping his whiskey, listening to the light snoring of the child. The hermit was being careful not to swallow too much whiskey. The man he'd seen at the burial place might come back, and the hermit wanted to be ready. He was: His lever-action .30–30 lay across his lap.

The hermit reached down and patted Wolf on the head. The dog liked Jason; it wasn't jealous at all. Good.

The hermit kept his rifle clean. Every so often, he killed a deer, even though he hated to do it. Over the years (he had been in the woods a long time), he had learned to cook the deer and store it so it lasted.

No matter how hard he thought about it, the hermit could not understand how the boy had come to be put in the ground like that. Had someone meant to keep him there for a long time? Like some kind of pet?

Did the boy belong to the man the hermit had seen in the woods? No, that made no sense.

Sometimes it was hard to separate what was memory and what was nightmare, what was real and what was wish.

The hermit took a long, hard gulp of whiskey, then reached up to touch his face. He could still remember the pain from the fire all those years ago. Yes, that was real. Jo and the unborn baby had died; that was real, too. The fire had been real. He ran his fingers over the stretched, shiny skin of his cheeks, then over the ridges of scar on his forehead and where his eyebrows had been.

The boy was stirring.

"Jason," the hermit whispered to the sleeping child. "I'll call you Jason."

Jamie's feet were warm and dry. That was the first thing he felt as he came up from a deep sleep. He wiggled his toes, then moved his feet. They didn't bang into metal anymore; his back didn't ache anymore.

He opened his eyes and looked into flames on top of flat gray stones. A fireplace, he thought. But not the fireplace in his father's house.

Oh! His father must be coming to get him. He tried to make words, but before he could even open his mouth his eyes were closed again.

When Jamie's mind bubbled up from sleep the next time, it didn't go back down. He moved his arms and legs. Good. It felt soft and warm around his arms and legs, not cold and hard like in the metal place. The blankets around him felt good on his skin.

Oh! He didn't have any clothes on. Jamie felt a rush of shame to think that someone had taken off his clothes and looked at him. But the shame was hot on his skin now, and he felt like crying. He looked all around the cabin again. Where were his clothes?

"Dad-dy. Dad-DY!"

Jamie started to cry, and, as he did, he felt a big cough in his throat. He coughed, which only made him cough harder. The cough seemed to come from way down in his chest, and it hurt. Now, even with the shame, Jamie suddenly felt cold. He started to shiver. Where was his father?

* * *

The hermit laid the rifle on his bed, got up and poured a little whiskey into a cup. He added some sugar, then some warm water from the kettle on the wood stove.

The hermit stirred the whiskey drink. Was it too strong for the boy? No. It would put him back to sleep, which would probably be good for him.

Jamie coughed. His chest hurt, and his throat was sore. Where was his father? Where *was* he? Jamie thought of all the times he'd had colds, and he'd coughed at night and felt bad, and then his father had been there, sitting on the bed, and one of his father's strong hands had patted his back and held him up and patted his back . . . . There, there. There, there. His mother had whispered that to him, softly in the night, before she'd gotten mad and taken him away. There, there . . . . And his father, with his strong hand gentle on Jamie's back, had given him something in a teaspoon that was strong and sweet in his throat, something magic that made him go back to sleep almost as soon as his head touched the pillow again.

Jamie wanted his father (and his mother!) more than ever. He sobbed hard, and his chest and throat felt worse than ever.

Something cold and wet touched Jamie's ear. Jamie lifted his head and looked into the eyes of the biggest dog he had ever seen. The flames from the fireplace shone in the dog's eyes. Jamie remembered there had been a dog when the man got him out of the metal place. The dog opened its mouth to pant; Jamie smelled the strong, wild breath, saw the teeth. Was he dreaming this? The teeth were yellow and unbelievably long, like the teeth of a . . .

"Wolf," a man's voice said. "Get back, Wolf."

The dog went away. Then Jamie felt a man's hand reach under his head and lift it, saw the cup in front of his face. He recognized the smell in the cup. His father sometimes drank in front of the fireplace at night, just before he put Jamie to bed.

"Drink, Jason. You'll feel better. Drink."

Why did the man keep calling him Jason? The man tipped Jamie's head up, then brought the cup close to his face. Jamie filled his mouth with the strong, sweet taste. He swallowed, and his throat started to feel better. The man's hand brought the cup up again (the fingers smelled like wood and dirt and dog and smoke), and Jamie drank some more. It felt warm and good in his stomach.

The man's hand was not behind his head anymore. Jamie lay down, felt his eyes getting fuzzy. The warmth in his stomach was spreading to his toes. He wasn't shivering anymore. His chest was warm inside; the cough had gone away.

Something big bumped Jamie and rolled up against him. Jamie could smell the dog's fur. The dog was cuddling up next to him! Jamie liked the dog.

He heard a voice; it sounded far away: "Lie still, Wolf. Lie still, boy. Go to sleep, Jason."

Why did the man keep calling him Jason? Where was his father?

Jamie slept again.

The only drug the hermit still did was whiskey. The hard stuff from his long ago had painted mind pictures that lasted for days. But this was real. The boy sleeping by the fire was real. And out there was someone mean enough to bury him alive. Just to be mean? But inside the foul-smelling tube (the hermit was pretty sure it was an old hot-water tank), there had been a flashlight, a bottle, and some food scraps. Had someone left him there just for a while as punishment?

That made no sense at all. But as he thought that, the hermit touched the scars on his forehead. He thought of the long-ago fire that had killed Jo. Someone had been mean enough to set that fire; someone had been mean enough to put a little boy in the ground. There wasn't any explanation; none was needed.

Someone out there was mean enough. Hell, I saw him, the hermit thought. I saw the man who put the boy in the ground. Had he been coming back to dig him up? Or to shovel dirt down the pipe and bury him forever? Whatever he had meant to do, the man might come back. It would take some doing to find the hermit's cabin, unless he found it by accident. Suppose there was more than one man next time. . . .

All right. The hermit knew the woods better than anyone. Wolf could hear almost anything that moved outside. And the hermit had plenty of ammunition.

Jamie was coming up out of sleep again. The blankets stuck to him as he moved. He had been shivering and sweating at the same time. Now he didn't feel cold anymore. He coughed, but it didn't hurt. His throat was not as sore.

Dog. The dog was not there now. Jamie was now awake, but he still didn't know where he was.

Jamie listened as hard as he could. He was alone. The man wasn't there anymore. But a log in the fireplace was still burning; Jamie felt the heat on his hair and shoulders.

He sat up; the blankets fell away, reminding him of his nakedness. He did not want the man to see him naked. Oh! He already had. Where was his father? Where was he?

The hermit was almost done stringing the line. In a rough circle, he had wrapped the twine from tree to tree, about waist-high and fifty feet or so from the cabin. Pairs of tin cans dangled every several feet.

"Pretty neat huh, Wolf?"

Lying contentedly under a tree, the dog looked at him with a puzzled "if you say so" look.

Snap went a branch on the hillside. Wolf's ears stood up, and the hermit grabbed his rifle. For a second, the hermit saw a tan and white blur, then nothing. Deer.

"Okay, Wolf."

The sky looked as if it might be gathering rain—or snow. The air was an in-between cold. Some morning soon, he would wake up and there'd be half a foot of snow on the ground and the rain barrel would have ice on top.

Thinking of the weather, the hermit got angry: Who would leave a little boy buried in the ground this time of year? Anytime, for that matter, but, with weather like this, it was only luck that the boy hadn't frozen.

The hermit tugged on the twine, and the cans jangled. If someone sneaked up at night, the hermit would hear it. Even if he didn't, Wolf would.

* * *

Jamie sat up, looked all around, and was afraid. This was the first good look he had had at where he was. He had never seen, or even imagined, such a place. He was in a cabin with walls of rough dark wood. Though the cabin was small, it seemed to be stuffed full of things. Jamie's eyes swept all around; he saw bed, fireplace, small wooden table and chair, wood stove near a sink on steel legs. There was one window, near the foot of the bunk; a door next to the window; and a second door next to the sink.

There were shelves on all the walls, and they were full of cans and boxes of food, blankets, folded clothes, flashlights, bottles of whiskey, cans of dog food—more different things than Jamie could count, more than he had ever seen in such a small place.

The place smelled like a barn. Or almost. The cabin had the smells of a grown-up's sweat and dirty socks; of wood smoke and cooking; of mud and leaves and firewood (there were logs behind the stove and next to the fireplace); of kerosene from the lanterns hanging from hooks; of dog.

Jamie didn't want to stay in this place. He wanted to put his clothes on, with no one watching him, and go home with his father.

Jamie started to cry. Thinking of his father made him feel even worse, and he let out a sob that turned into a scream.

A door banged open. There was the great big dog. And there was the man, whose face Jamie had not seen clearly before. Jamie looked at the man's face and screamed again.

Nineteen

...

In the dim vestibule, Heather Casey pressed the button marked LUNA, CARMINE. She leaned close to the microphone as she pressed the buzzer again. Will hadn't suggested it, but he was glad she was going to talk to Carmine first. He was sure Carmine would never see him otherwise.

A third time she pressed the buzzer. Nothing.

Shit, Will thought.

Heather Casey looked at him with raised eyebrows that said, Now what?

"As long as you went to the trouble to come here with me, let's try the super," Will said. He pressed the button for the building superintendent.

After a few seconds, the inner door opened. The man in the doorway was short, slim, over sixty, and his flannel shirt smelled of cigar smoke. "Yeah?" he said.

"Sorry to bother—"

"We're here to see Carmine Luna," Heather Casey interrupted forcefully. "I work with him at the hospital, and he didn't show up today."

The super opened the door to let them in. "I think I heard him go out a couple hours ago," the super said.

"Did you hear him come back?" Will said.

"I ain't even sure it was him goin' out. But let's go have a look."

They followed the super up a foul-smelling dark staircase whose apple green walls were peeling. Will remembered the guilt he'd felt when his wife had chided him for going after Carmine. Now, seeing the drabness that was Carmine's apartment building, Will felt sorry for the man. Then he remembered how Fran had looked in the hospital bed, and the feeling went away.

"I hope he's in," Will said.

The super led them partway down a short brown and yellow corridor on the second floor, stopped in front of a door, and knocked loudly. After several seconds of silence, he knocked again. Nothing. "Ain't here," the super said.

"Could you please check," Casey said. "I wouldn't want him to lose his job. Or fall behind on his rent."

The thought of lost money shone briefly in the super's eyes, and he took a giant key ring from his belt.

The super opened the door, flicked on a light inside, and stepped in. In the moment before they followed him, Casey looked at Will and whispered, "The hospital doesn't pay people like Carmine very much."

Dust balls rolled like tumbleweeds where the brown wood floor met the gray plaster walls. A table and chair stood on a throw rug in the middle of the room.

Will's first impression was that the room was like countless others lived in by young bachelors.

"Anyone home?" the super said. "Guess not."

The place smelled of dust, old food, and stale breath. Along the wall farthest from the door were a sink, small stove, and refrigerator. As Will reached the middle of the room, he caught a sour odor from the dirty pots and dishes piled in the sink and strewn along the counter.

Will's mind went back two decades, to his own days as a single man. He had let his dishes and laundry pile up, but what he was seeing (and smelling) now was different. It was not just clutter; it was filth. On just about every square inch of shelf, there were encrusted dishes, empty beer cans, grease-stained cardboard containers from take-out meals eaten many days ago.

"Well?" the super said impatiently.

"This place is a sty," Will said.

"Hey," the super said. "I don't provide maid service. Okay? How he lives is his business."

"Right," Will said. But there was something about Carmine's living space that spelled sickness, decay, corruption.

Without asking permission, Casey walked to the door on the left wall, which obviously led to the bedroom and bathroom. She pushed it open and turned on a light. "Carmine?" she said, knocking on the nearest closed door. "It's Heather Casey."

"Look," the super said. "You can tell he ain't here. All right?"

"Carmine?" Casey turned the doorknob and pushed. "It's stuck."

Will held his breath. For no logical reason, he half-expected the bathroom door to bump against a body if Casey pushed on it again. She did, and the door gave.

Heather Casey turned on the bathroom light. Will was standing over her shoulder, still holding his breath. Will exhaled in relief when he saw the wrinkled towel still partly jammed under the door.

"Time to go, folks."

"He doesn't keep a very neat place, does he?" Heather Casey said, ignoring the super.

Dust and hair lurked in the corners of the bathroom, along with dirty towels and underwear. Will was thankful that the toilet lid was down; that way, only a hint of an awful smell reached his nostrils.

Will edged past the superintendent and stood next to Heather Casey in the tiny hallway illuminated weakly by the light from the bathroom. They faced another closed door. This time, Will tried the knob. Locked.

"Suppose he's takin' a nap?" the super said with annoyance.

Ignoring him again, Casey knocked loudly. "Carmine? Carmine!"

Will looked at the super. "I think you should check in there."

"Suppose he's sleepin' off a drunk or somethin'? He's entitled."

"Something's not right," Casey said sternly. "Please open the door."

The super produced his key ring, fumbled for a moment, and unlocked the door. Heather Casey opened it but deferred to the super, who reached around her to find the wall switch.

Again, Will held his breath and was relieved when the light showed an unmade bed, a dresser of dirty unpainted wood, and clothes strewn everywhere. The window was open a few inches, but the air in the room was foul. It smelled of dust, dirty laundry, and . . .

Heather Casey noticed it first: The bed was slightly cock-eyed, and the covers had been pulled down on the side facing the wall, as though something or someone had rolled off the bed into the narrow space and caused the bed to slide.

The nurse stepped into the room far enough to see between the bed and wall. Will saw her recoil in shock, but only for a second, before her professional control took over. "We'll have to call the police," she said coolly.

Will tiptoed to her side and looked between the wall and bed. Carmine was there, lying on his back, his head toward the foot of the bed. He was wearing pants but was barefoot and shirtless. A belt was wrapped tightly around his left arm. His right arm lay across his chest, the hand near the bulging left biceps, where the hypodermic needle was embedded. Carmine's eyes were half open and death-glazed, the lips drawn back from clenched teeth, almost as though he had steeled himself for the final leap.

The room smelled of dust, dirty laundry—and death.

They waited for the police in the building super's office. Will had never gotten used to death, and the sight of Carmine lying on the floor with his eyes empty was burned into his mind as clearly as a snapshot.

He avoided Heather Casey's eyes, afraid that he would see in them an accusation—that if Will hadn't confronted him, Carmine would still be alive. But that was crazy. Wasn't it?

The police arrived: two uniformed patrolmen and a detective. Will, Casey, and the super told the detective how they had found the body. They were all sure they hadn't touched anything except light switches and doorknobs.

"Doesn't much matter," the detective said. "Never saw a plainer overdose."

He said it in such an indifferent, almost contemptuous way that Will was pleased when Heather Casey said quietly, "Carmine worked at the hospital, where I work, and he was a human being. Like all of us."

Will studied the detective: a big man, with some fat but also thick slabs of muscle, reddish face, dark curly hair. Why was there something vaguely familiar about him? Will didn't think he'd run into him at police headquarters.

In bored, perfunctory tones, the detective questioned the three of them. Most of the questions were directed to the building superintendent, and they had to do with whether he had seen any other recent visitors to Carmine Luna's apartment (no) and whether he had heard any strange noises from there (no).

Will continued to study the detective's face, still trying to figure why it was vaguely familiar. Finally, the detective looked at Heather Casey. For the first time, he smiled. "I didn't mean to sound like such a hard ass. I remember you now. It's been a while. How have you been?"

"Fine, thank you. It has been a while. Since before you were a detective." The nurse's tone was a bit softer.

"Right. And you came here just now because Carmine didn't show up for work?"

"That's right. I just wanted to check up on him."

"And he called in sick?"

"Yes."

"And you wanted to be sure he was all right?"

"Yes."

The detective looked puzzled, maybe even skeptical. "Well, my guess is that he couldn't wait for a fix. He got it, all right."

Heather Casey shook her head sadly. "It's not like I was a friend of Carmine's. I wasn't. But it's such a sad thing. Such a . . . waste."

"It is that," the detective agreed. "But I'm not quite clear why you came by to check on him—the two of you—when he wasn't even a friend."

Will decided he had let Heather Casey carry the ball for him long enough. "I wanted to see Carmine," he said.

"What about?"

The moment of truth, Will thought. What to tell, what to hold back? To hell with it. "I'm a newspaperman from Bessemer, here to follow the Brokaw kidnapping. One of my colleagues, a reporter, was fatally injured the night before Thanksgiving. An automobile accident."

"I know the wreck you mean. And now I know who you are. You worked with that guy, huh?"

"Yes."

"What's that got to do with the late"—here, the detective had to check his notes—"Carmine Luna?"

Casey came to Will's aid again. "Carmine was a lab tech. He did the blood test on Mr. Shafer's friend after the accident. I drew the blood."

"Which had plenty of booze in it, if I remember right," the detective said to Will. "Your friend was drunk."

"I have reason to think otherwise," Will said.

"Meaning what?" A challenge.

"Meaning I think Carmine monkeyed around with the blood test one way or the other."

"And what makes you think that?"

Will told him as succinctly as he could about Fran Spicer's drinking habits and the time of his stop at the liquor store and the time of the accident, and how it all didn't add up.

When Will was finished, the detective looked at him with cold, hard eyes and spoke quietly. "Some people would say you're interfering with police business."

"That's not my intention." Like hell, Will thought. "But I don't want my friend remembered as a man who died a drunk."

The detective studied Will, who studied him back. Will still wondered why the face was familiar.

"And just why would Carmine, or anyone else, screw up a blood test?"

"I don't know that."

"You don't know that," the detective mocked. Then he turned to Heather Casey. "You know anything about this?"

"Mr. Shafer has shared his feelings with me, yes," she said evenly. "And I must say, I do have some misgivings myself."

God bless Heather Casey, Will thought.

The detective shrugged, looked at Will, and said, "For whose benefit would this Carmine guy do something like that?"

"I don't know."

"You don't know. You're the one making the accusation."

"I'm not accusing . . ." But I am, Will thought; I am accusing somebody. "I don't know for whose benefit."

Just then, there were heavy steps in the corridor outside. The blanket-covered body of Carmine Luna was being carried out on a stretcher. A patrolman leaned into the room and said to the detective, "Nothing special upstairs. A couple bucks on the dresser, is all. And no drugs. He probably bought a bag and popped it all at once."

"So," the detective said to Will, "unless the deceased has a big bank account, which I strongly doubt . . ."

"I don't have the answers," Will said. "Only questions."

"That's fair enough. As I recall, the other person involved in the accident was a woman from town."

"Yes. I've talked to her. She seemed like a nice young woman."

"Well, then. The accident was officially your friend's fault, regardless of whether he was drunk or sober. So the young woman has nothing to gain by trying to get the blood test fixed, does she?"

"No. I guess not."

"You guess not. And she seemed to you like a nice young woman. And living around here, she probably doesn't have enough money to bribe somebody even if she wanted to. Fact is, about the only guy around here who's rich is the father of the kidnapped kid."

Will said nothing. What could he say?

"Anyhow," the detective said, "I'll pass along your suspicions."

"And then what?" Having gone this far, Will didn't bother to hide his annoyance.

"Then probably nothing happens," the detective said.

"Because, frankly, I think your theory is a crock of shit. Excuse my French, miss."

"Okay," Will said. "Then you tell me what happened."

"I don't have to tell you anything. And my main suggestion to you is that you get on the two-lane and head on up to the main drag and go on back to Bessemer."

After a long, cold silence, Heather Casey spoke. "I'm sure Mr. Shafer is upset about his friend and doesn't mean any disrespect."

Her elbow brushed Will's, and he took the hint. "Right," he said, swallowing hard.

"And Will, I'm sure Detective Howe will keep his promise and relay your suspicions to higher authority."

"Howe?" Will said.

"John Howe," the detective said. "That's right. Same last name as the chief. That's because he's my brother."

Of course, Will thought. That's why the face is familiar. God, am I an outsider.

"If you're finished with us, perhaps we could go," Heather Casey said.

"You can both go," Detective Howe said. "I'll tell the chief what you said. Tonight, maybe. We're playing poker at his house."

Will stopped in front of Heather Casey's apartment building and shut off the engine.

"Would you come in for a few minutes?" she said. "I'd like you to."

He had been afraid she would say that, and hoping she would. "Sure," he said.

"That sofa's comfortable. I'm going to have some wine. Would you join me?"

"Please."

The living room of Heather Casey's apartment was small, Spartan, immaculate. A long, narrow table of cherry wood stood in front of the sofa, and beyond it a fireplace.

"It isn't real," Heather Casey said, sitting down next to him and pouring two glasses of white wine. "The fireplace, I mean. It's just for looks."

"It's pretty." God, he thought, I haven't lost my touch when it comes to making small talk. I can always find something stupid to say.

"Would you like some crackers and cheese? I think I have some cashews."

"No, nothing else. This is fine. You read a lot, I see." The shelves on either side of the fireplace were crammed with books.

"A lot of self-help stuff. A mystery now and then. Nothing too scary. Living alone, I'm not eager to frighten myself before I try to sleep."

"You've been alone for a while?"

"A while, yes. Here's to life."

"To life."

They touched glasses and drank. Then Heather Casey set down her glass, put her face in her hands, and cried.

Will hesitated a moment, then put his arm around her. Her body slumped against him, and she leaned her head on his chest.

He had meant only to comfort her, but her warmth and closeness was arousing him. Will breathed deeply, filling his nose with the scent of her skin.

Heather stopped crying. Her breathing slowed. Will kept his arm around her shoulders. He bent a little lower, gently kissed the top of her head.

Finally, she sat up and looked at him. Her eyes were shiny through the tears. "Thank you," she said.

He didn't know what to say. But he knew what he felt. He hadn't been with another woman since he'd been married, had scarcely been tempted, and now here he was.

She smiled knowingly. "You're married," she said.

"Yes."

"Of course. Of course." Her face showed a hint of sadness. "I needed you to come inside tonight. After finding Carmine like that."

"God, yes. Carmine." Will took a long drink. He would have his own demons to wrestle with tonight, and not just about Carmine Luna.

"It wasn't only Carmine," she went on quietly. "The

reason that detective, the chief's brother, recognized me and vice versa is that he came to my home once. It was a while back. When he was a uniformed officer, and I was still married.''

Will understood what had happened. He sensed, too, that Heather Casey needed to tell him. ''It was what they used to call a 'domestic disturbance,' '' she said. ''In my case, it meant a black eye and a bloody nose.''

''I'm sorry.'' Will poured more wine.

''Thank you. Al was sorry, too. He was always sorry. And he always got drunk again, and . . .''

''And it never got better.''

''It did, actually. That last time, I got an order of protection. It was a big, big step, especially since I've been in Long Creek all my life, and you know how that is. Everyone knew. But it wasn't going to happen to me again. Not that.''

''You say it got better after that?''

''It got better after Al left. Got drunk and left Long Creek, left my life.'' She sipped her wine, and bitterness flashed in her eyes for a moment. ''Left a bunch of debts, too, as a matter of fact. But I still had my job and my life. There're worse things than being alone, believe me.''

''Have you been alone since?''

''Oh, mostly. I may not always be, but for this phase of my life it works.'' She paused. ''What's your wife's name, Will?''

''Karen.''

''Kids?''

''One of each. Good kids.''

''And your wife, does she have a career?''

''Social work.'' Will told her a little about Karen's work with teenagers, her counseling, the articles she wrote. ''All in all, she's one of the most competent people I know. No, more than that. She's . . .''

He stopped himself. To tell her about his wife seemed hypocritical, and he was afraid that saying more would squander this moment.

''You're lucky. Both of you are. Thank you for coming inside with me. And for listening.''

She had slid closer to him on the sofa, and he put his hand on hers. She smiled, and he put his arm around her again. God, let me do the right thing, he thought. Whatever it is.

Without disturbing her, he drank the rest of his wine. Her head was on his shoulder now, and he turned toward her. He caught the scent of her perfume, her hair. And when he kissed her on the lips, he tasted the wine again. Her eyes were closed, and she smiled softly. He squeezed her shoulder softly and let her slump completely against him.

"I really needed someone here tonight."

He caught the past tense, and was not sad. Prayer answered, Will thought. "Heather, will you be all right?"

"Yes. I know you have to go."

She saw him to the door and put her hand on his arm. "Your wife is lucky," she said.

"And your husband was a fool."

She smiled, then shrugged. "Good night, Will."

His head full of more emotions than he could sort out, Will drove back to the Long Creek Inn. On the way, he stopped at the newsstand and bought the *New York Times*, the *Bessemer Gazette*, and the *Long Creek Eagle*.

In his room, he opened the bottle of scotch he'd bought at the liquor store out on the two-lane, poured a jolt into a glass, and added a little water. He sat in a chair, tried to force himself to relax.

No luck. He drank some scotch, knowing his head would pay for it in the morning.

Will would talk to Jerry Graham, try to persuade him to investigate Fran Spicer's death. Was that something the FBI would do? Will didn't know.

There had to be something fishy about it. Heather Casey had thought so, too (he forced himself not to dwell on the time in her apartment), and had said as much.

As far as the Long Creek police were concerned, Will knew he was vulnerable. One just didn't get on the bad side of cops on *their* turf.

Unwinding a little, he scanned the newspapers. As always, he devoted more attention to the *New York Times*—and had the feeling again that he was overlooking something trivial and yet very important. What was so special—?

God Almighty.

Will dialed his home. As he'd thought, Karen was just getting the children squared away. He said good night to them, then asked Karen to look up the number for Harvey Bober.

"Harvey Bober?" She was incredulous.

"Yes. I'll explain soon."

"Hmmmph. Just a minute."

After she gave him the number for Harvey Bober, the *Gazette*'s circulation director, he cut short the conversation with apologies and pledges of undying love, which did nothing to lessen his nagging guilt over his attraction to Heather Casey.

"Damn," Will whispered to himself as he dialed Bober's number back in Bessemer. "Can this be?"

Will reached the circulation director, asked him a few questions, and got the answers he had expected.

He hung up, tossed down the rest of the scotch in the glass, and didn't know whether to feel stupid or triumphant. It had been there all along, and he had just now caught on.

"Hey," he said to the room, "better late than . . ."

Damn, Will thought. Latin Condensed. Yes, Latin Condensed. He could hardly wait to get another look at those pasted-up ransom notes.

Twenty

...

Jamie felt a lot better. The man with the hurt face had washed Jamie's clothes, hung them near the stove to dry, then left the cabin so Jamie could get dressed with no one looking. The clothes smelled of smoke, but they felt clean on his skin. Not like in the tin place.

For a while, Jamie had been afraid to ask the man his name. When he finally did, the man laughed and said, "What do you want to call me, Jason?"

"My name is Jamie."

The man's eyes had looked sad (it was hard to tell about the rest of his face), and at last he said, "All right. Jamie it is."

"Why do you keep calling me Jason?"

The man's eyes looked really sad. "That's a long story. An old story."

The man told Jamie that Jason was going to be his son, but that Jason's mother was burned up in a fire before Jason even got to be born.

"Is that what happened to your face?"

"Yep."

"Does it hurt?"

"My face? Not anymore."

Jamie didn't understand why the man didn't just marry someone else and have a new son. Just like he didn't understand why his mother and father couldn't still live together. There were a lot of things about grown-ups that he didn't understand.

Then Jamie remembered that the man hadn't answered his question. "What's your name?"

"Oh, boy. How about I just tell you my dog's name. Wolf."

"Okay. But what's *your* name?"

"Hmmm. Well, I'm a hermit. Okay? I don't use my name much."

"What's a hermit?"

The man laughed and said, "A hermit is a crazy guy who lives alone in the woods with a ferocious dog 'cuz he likes dogs better than people."

Jamie didn't quite understand. "Are you really crazy?"

"No. Sometimes maybe."

Jamie still didn't understand. "Is that really a wolf?"

"No. This is an honest-to-God German shepherd."

The dog came up to Jamie and butted him with his head.

"Wolf likes you," the hermit said.

"I like him, too." Jamie patted the dog on the head. He had never seen such a big dog. Jamie could spread his hand on top of the dog's head and still not touch the ears.

"Did you get him when he was a puppy?"

"Sort of. When he was only a little ways grown, I took him away from a farmer who wasn't treating him right."

"Really?"

"Yep. I was doing an odd job for the farmer, like I do sometimes when I have to have a little money, and I felt sorry for the puppy, and I told the farmer I wanted him. And he let me take him." Especially when I told him I'd break his head if he didn't give him to me, the hermit thought. But he wouldn't tell the boy that.

"How old is Wolf?"

"Six."

"That's older than I am. I'm five."

"Jamie, where're your mother and father?"

"Back home."

"Where's that?"

"My father lives in a house on a hill near Long Creek. My mother got mad and left. I go to see my father a lot."

"Jamie, do you know who stuck you in the ground?"

Jamie got tears in his eyes.

"Don't cry, Jamie." The hermit felt badly. He shouldn't have talked to a kid like that. "I'm sorry I made you cry. I didn't mean to."

The dog put its paws on Jamie's legs, stood on its hind feet, and licked the side of Jamie's face. It tickled so much that Jamie laughed.

"See, Wolf wants you to feel better."

"I have to go to the bathroom. Then I want to go home and be with my father."

"Your mom must miss you, too."

Jamie frowned. "She got mad and left. I feel sorry for my father sometimes."

"In there, Jamie. When you're done, I'm going to give you something to eat. Then I want you to tell me what happened to you."

"Then will you take me home?"

The hermit thought about the man he'd seen in the night. "Yes, Jamie."

"I want my daddy."

"I know. I know." The hermit didn't want the boy to cry anymore. "Just go in there, Jamie." To his astonishment, the hermit was embarrassed. "If you have to do anything but pee, take some lime—the white stuff in the can—and throw it in the hole. Okay? But don't get any in your eyes."

When Jamie came out, he heard sizzling sounds from the stove. He smelled cooking.

"I saved some warm water in the sink for you to wash your hands, Jamie. Around here, we don't waste water."

Jamie stood on tiptoes to dip his hands in the soapy water, then wiped them dry on a raggedy towel hanging on the side of the sink.

"Sit here, Jamie. Your cough is almost gone, do you know that?"

"Yes." It was, Jamie realized.

"That jolt of whiskey fixed you right up, didn't it?"

"Yes." Jamie didn't know quite what the hermit meant. "What should I call you? You still didn't tell me."

Jamie watched the hermit stand by the stove, scraping stuff around in a frying pan. His dog sat near the stove, looking right at the hermit.

"Tell you what, Jamie. I'm going to take you home pretty soon, so what we're doing right now is just, oh, sort of a visit. Okay?"

"Okay." Jamie didn't know what he meant.

"It's just a visit. So we can play a game. If you want to, you can call me, uh, call me Da—" Suddenly, the hermit was overwhelmed with sorrow and shame. He turned away, shook his head, forced himself not to cry.

Jamie didn't know what was happening. He was glad when the hermit looked at him again. The hermit's eyes were shiny.

"Tell you what," the hermit said. "I live in the woods, so you can call me Woody. How's that?"

"Is that your nickname?"

"No."

"Then why. . . . ?"

"It'll be my nickname if you call me that. Starting right now."

Jamie didn't quite understand. "I don't get to call many old people by their first names."

"If it makes you feel better, you can call me *Mr*. Woody." Just then, Wolf whined. "Wolf, you'll get your share, you greedy bastard. Oops, excuse me, Jamie."

Jamie laughed at the funny name, laughed at the swearing. "The men who took me away swore a lot."

"When was that, Jamie?"

"A long time ago."

"How long?"

"I don't know. I thought they were going to do things to me."

"Did they?"

"No. But they hit me. And two men put me in that tin place. With bread and water."

"You mean where I found you?"

"Yes."

"How long were you there?"

"I don't know. I couldn't tell when it was night."

God, the hermit thought. "Where were you before that, Jamie?"

"In a long cement room with no windows. It was a bathroom."

"A bathroom?"

"Yes. It had a toilet and a sink. I remember men talking."

"How long were you in that place, Jamie?"

"I don't know. At first, I couldn't tell when it was night, because there weren't any windows. But when I got sleepy, I guessed it must be night. Only, there were times when I wanted to sleep but when I was too scared."

"How many times did you sleep, Jamie?"

"A couple, I think. I don't know. I was scared."

"I bet."

"They gave me baloney sandwiches to eat and a toy furry bear to play with. But I was still scared."

"Jamie, where were you when the bad men first took you?"

"With Tony. He was driving me back to my mother."

"Who's Tony?"

"He drives me and my dad places. He's real nice."

"So he's like a chauffeur?"

"Yes." Jamie remembered the word. "I'm allowed to call him by his first name."

"So, Jamie, your mom and dad don't live together?"

"No. My mom got mad and left, and then she made me go with her."

"It's okay, Jamie. Okay to cry. Here."

Jamie took the rag from the hermit and wiped off his face.

"Let's eat, Jamie. We can talk while we eat."

Jamie looked at the big plate of food: chunks of meat, potatoes, carrots. It smelled good.

"Stew, Jamie. The vegetables are from cans. Do you like venison?"

"What's that?"

The hermit decided not to tell him. "It's like beef, Jamie. It's a kind of beef."

Jamie started to eat. He had had stew before, but never like this. It was good. Jamie was surprised at how hungry he was.

"Eat as much as you can, Jamie. 'Cuz you know what? In just a little while, I'm going to take you home. Or close to it."

"To my father?"

"To your mother and father. Before it gets dark. Now tell me some more, Jamie."

Proud that the boy seemed to like his cooking, the hermit let him eat. Every third or fourth spoonful, the hermit asked a question, letting Jamie answer in his own good time.

Jamie was getting used to Mr. Woody's face. Wolf sat next to Jamie, and when he felt full Jamie asked if he could give the dog what was left on his plate. Mr. Woody said he could.

When the hermit thought he understood what had happened to the boy, he said, "I'll bet your dad has a real big house, Jamie."

"Yep, he does. I have a pony there."

Rich, the hermit thought. "Jamie, I think someone kidnapped you to hold you for ransom."

Jamie gave him a blank look, and the hermit reminded himself that the boy was only five.

"Can I go home?" Jamie said.

"Sure, Jamie. It's fun to visit, though. Isn't it?"

"I want to see my father," Jamie said. "You're not my father."

"I know, Jamie. I know." The hermit turned his face away to hide his sadness.

"I think I have to go to the bathroom again." Jamie had eaten a lot.

"Okay. You know what to do."

Alone, the hermit stood up and tried to clear his mind. He felt ashamed for almost asking the boy to call him Daddy. What a rotten thing to do. The boy had seen through it, too: "You're not my father."

Oh, Jesus Christ. The hermit sat down on his bed, put his head in his hands. Guilt was heavy on his shoulders. He grabbed a bottle of whiskey and gulped once, twice, three times. He swallowed more than he meant to.

Good, the boy hadn't come out yet. The hermit lay down and closed his eyes. He would rest for a few minutes, clear his mind.

Jamie was surprised to see Mr. Woody lying down. Then he heard the snoring. Jamie wanted to go home, but he was afraid to wake up the hermit.

Something cold and wet touched his hand. Wolf had nuzzled him.

"Wolf, do you want to play with me?"

The dog's eyes were friendly, and his tail was wagging.

Jamie decided to play outside with Wolf until Mr. Woody was done with his nap. Jamie wanted a dog of his own someday.

Jamie put on his outdoor clothes as quietly as he could. Then he opened the door and stepped outside. He could smell the trees. "Come on, Wolf."

Wolf didn't seem to know what to do. The dog looked toward the figure snoring on the bed, then at Jamie. Finally, he followed the boy.

Jamie closed the door quietly and took a step in the fluffy snow. Then another step, and then he was running in the snow, kicking it up, and Wolf was right next to him. Jamie laughed. Wolf was almost as much fun as the pony back home. Jamie made little snowballs and threw them at the dog. The dog liked the game: He ran away from Jamie, then turned around and came racing back, as if he was going to run right into him. But he always turned away at the last second, and Jamie could tell from the eyes that the dog was having fun. Jamie wished he could take Wolf home. Jamie felt snow on his face, felt the wind.

The hermit stirred when he heard the tin cans jingle. The whiskey had left him sluggish, but he knew he hadn't dreamed the noise. Why didn't Wolf bark? The damn dog was supposed to be guarding—

The hermit sat up, looked around the cabin. Empty. "Jason! Where are you? Wolf . . ."

He leaped out of bed, grabbed his rifle, opened the door. He saw the tracks of boy and dog, heard the boy laughing and the dog snorting playfully on the other side of the cabin.

"Jas . . . Jamie! Come back in here! Wolf!"

A moment later, the boy appeared at the door, looking frightened.

"We, we have to get ready, Jamie. I'm sorry I, uh, fell asleep."

"I was playing with Wolf."

"I know. I know."

There was a light snow already on the ground, and the wind was picking up. The air was colder, and the graying sky hinted at still more snow. Hard weather to travel in—or maybe good weather to travel in. He knew the woods better than anyone.

The boy had said there were two men who had kidnapped him. The hermit had seen only one. Maybe the two of them would come looking. Maybe they were both out there right now. The hermit cursed himself for having been careless.

The wind gusted, and all the cans jangled at once. Big snowflakes appeared.

The hermit closed the door. "We're going for a long hike, Jamie. A hike in the snow. We're going to take you home."

Jamie pouted. "Can I play with Wolf some more?"

"Not now."

The boy looked disappointed.

"Jamie, you want to go home, don't you?"

"Yes, but I was having a good time with Wolf. And I wanted to build a snowman."

"It'll have to wait. We have to go now."

"All right. Mr. Woody?"

"What?"

"Can Wolf come and see me?"

"Maybe, Jamie. Maybe."

He got the boy snug on the sled, wrapped him in a blanket, and handed him a woolen ski mask. The hermit saw fear in the young face.

"What's wrong, Jamie?"

"The men who took me had masks like that."

"This is just a mask, Jamie. It'll keep your face warm. You can see out of it."

Jamie put the mask on. It itched. "One man held a big gun in front of Tony's face."

"A gun like this?" The hermit held up his carbine.

"Bigger even."

Shotgun, the hermit thought. "I bet they wanted to make your dad pay a lot to get you back, Jamie. I bet that's what happened."

"How come my daddy didn't just buy me back?"

The hermit was angry with himself for upsetting the boy. "Maybe he wanted to, Jamie. Maybe something went wrong."

"Do you ever get lost in the snow?"

"I don't get lost in the snow, Jamie. You know why? Because this is my home, these woods. Even deer hunters get lost out here sometimes. But I don't."

The hermit thought he saw the boy's mouth wrinkle into a smile under the wool mask. "Jamie, you won't be afraid of me if I wear a mask, will you?"

"No. I'll know it's still you."

"Right. It's still Mr. Woody." The hermit put his mask on. Next, he fastened a sling to his carbine so he could carry it across his back. Finally, he checked his pockets: compass, two extra pairs of gloves, extra socks, extra cartridges for the rifle. In the deep pockets of his coat, he had two bags, one with bread, another with chunks of cooked deer meat— enough for himself, the boy, and Wolf. On the sled, strapped under and around the boy, he had put ponchos, with blankets tucked between them for dryness. He had also packed a thermos of coffee and a big canteen of water.

"Anything comes loose from the sled, you holler. Okay, Jamie?"

"Okay."

The hermit put his back to the boy and tugged. The sled began to move.

"Are we going to Long Creek?" Jamie asked.

"Nope."

"Where are we going?"

"To Deer County."

"How come? Is it closer?"

"No."

"How come we're not going to the closer place? I want to see my daddy. And my mommy."

The hermit thought fast. "I can't explain why, Jamie, but this is the quickest and safest way, even if it's farther. Do you trust me?"

Just then, Wolf appeared by the sled. The dog's face was all happy. Jamie reached out and touched the dog's back, and Wolf swung his head to brush Jamie on the leg. Jamie giggled.

"Do you trust me, Jamie?"

"Yes."

"You sure?"

"Yes."

"Better tell Wolf you trust me."

"Wolf, I trust"—Jamie giggled at the funny game—"I trust Mr. Woody."

The dog looked at the boy, chortled deep in his throat, then trotted on ahead.

Jamie was happy. It was fun being pulled on the sled. Mr. Woody had fixed it so Jamie's back was resting on the blankets and ponchos. It was like sitting in a chair, only better.

Jamie kept looking at Mr. Woody's back as the sled glided along. The back looked big and strong. Jamie's face was warm inside the mask. He saw lots of big snowflakes, and they made him think of the night the bad men had taken him away. But this time it was fun to look at the snow. Now and then, a flake settled on Jamie's eyelashes and tickled as it melted. He was going home. Jamie closed his eyes and went to sleep.

The hermit glanced back, saw from the angle of the boy's head that he was napping. Damn, he thought. I'm doing something for someone. Who would have thought? Jo, if you're watching somewhere, look what I'm doing.

He kept a steady pace, deliberately going a little more slowly than his body wanted. He was saving his energy, just in case.

The weather was getting worse. It was borderline: cold enough, especially with the wind, and snowy enough to be dangerous—for anyone who didn't know the woods. The hermit knew the woods.

He was glad the boy hadn't pestered him too much about why he didn't just go into Long Creek if it was closer. How to tell a kid about fear and hate from a long time ago? How to make him understand? He couldn't. It didn't matter.

The first few miles, the hermit spotted a couple of deer. Running ahead of him, Wolf flushed several grouse from their hiding places beneath the evergreens. The dog barked as the birds exploded from cover, drumming the air with their wings as they darted away through the trees and snow.

Every few minutes, the hermit would stop and stand still. Seeing his master motionless, Wolf would trot back and stand next to him, ears high. The hermit was nervous: The man he'd seen in the night near the burial place had to be one of the kidnappers. And now that the boy was free, the man would probably come back, looking for the boy. To kill him?

Each time he stopped, the hermit heard only the sounds of the ground and the trees and, now and then, the birds and animals.

The snow kept coming, though the wind let up a little. Depending on where he was, high ground or low, he could see fifty to a hundred yards.

When he was hungry, the hermit took out a big piece of bread and a few pieces of meat. He chewed slowly, so he could still hear around him. He gave a piece of crust and part of a hunk of meat to Wolf.

Let the boy sleep. Blessings on you, little man—is that how the old poem went? Damn, I hope I didn't give him too much whiskey. Naw. He didn't seem to have a headache. He's just warm and happy, almost. I only wish he was safe.

The hermit ate an extra piece of bread, gave a nibble to the dog, and took the sled rope to press on again. It was then that he thought he heard something behind him. Wolf's ears went up like spikes. The dog looked in the direction of the sound. It had been like a branch snapping, but not from a deer.

The hermit breathed in and out slowly, straining to hear.

There it was again, the snap of a branch. From a man's foot. Wolf growled deep in his throat.

"Shhh." The hermit dragged the sled with the sleeping boy up onto a little rise and hunkered down under a big pine tree with Wolf next to him. "Shhh," he commanded again, and with his hand he ordered the dog to lie low.

Snap. The noise was closer now, and suddenly there he was. The man stood in a little clearing about seventy-five yards back. Through the swirling snow, the hermit saw that the man wore camouflage clothes and carried a rifle. A hunter? Most of them were smart enough to wear bright orange or red. The hermit didn't even know whether it was deer season yet; he hadn't heard any rifle shots.

Maybe the man was hunting out of season. There were plenty of hunters like that, and the camouflage clothes would make it harder for game wardens to spot him.

Or maybe this was another kind of hunter—hunting him and the little boy.

As the hermit knelt and watched, the man stood still, looking all around. Then he looked down at the sled tracks and footprints of man and dog. Following us? Was he the same man? He could be, the hermit thought. He has the same height and build as the guy I saw in the dark. I think he does.

The man was studying the tracks, which were being erased by the wind and snow. He started walking again, toward the hermit's hiding place. The hermit shifted his position slightly to relieve one knee, and, as he moved, his shoulder brushed a bough, knocking loose some snow that plopped onto the sleeping boy.

"Daddy!" The boy awoke with a start. Wolf growled, then barked. In his wake-up terror, Jamie kicked and punched at the air, and the sled moved. It slid down the little rise, slowly and harmlessly, coming to a gentle stop only a few yards away—but in plain sight of the stranger with the rifle.

The hunter walked toward them, rifle at the ready. The hermit saw that the rifle had a telescopic sight.

The hermit had his own weapon ready, with a round in the chamber. The man was less than fifty yards away now, and for a moment the hermit wondered whether the thing to do was just to shoot him and be done with it.

No. He had never shot anyone, and there was no way to tell whether this was the guy he'd seen at the burial spot or just another poacher.

"Daddy!"

"Jamie, don't move! Stay down!"

Now the hunter stopped, looked straight at the hermit, and seemed to raise his rifle. The hermit brought his carbine to his shoulder, aimed to the stranger's left, and squeezed the trigger.

The noise of the shot echoed through the woods. Wolf barked, Jamie screamed, and the stranger seemed paralyzed in his tracks. In an instant, the hermit had chambered another round and was aiming at the man's chest.

The man backed up. His head was shaking and his mouth was open in disbelief.

"Get out of here!" the hermit shouted. "Get away, or the next one's right in your chest. I swear. The boy's staying with me."

The stranger turned and ran, and the hermit changed his aim. This time, he fired behind the man, close enough for the snow to kick up near his heels.

The echo died away, and the hermit knelt next to the sled and the weeping boy. "He's gone, Jamie. No one's taking you away again. I promise."

Twenty-one

■ ■ ■

Will slept badly: too much scotch and tension, not enough rest. When he awoke, he tried at once to call Jerry Graham. No answer.

Trying to ignore fleeting thoughts of Heather Casey, he dressed and showered quickly, grabbed a breakfast of toast and coffee, and went to the police station. There, he found more commotion than usual for so early in the morning. It was two hours before the normal time for a briefing on the kidnapping.

Something had happened—Will could tell that at once from the crowd of reporters, camera people, and technicians. Please, God, Will thought, don't let the kid be dead.

Will went with the crowd, down the corridor toward the briefing room. He spotted Jerry Graham coming the other way. "Jerry, what happened?"

"Glad you got here, Will. I would have sent for you in another few minutes."

"Is the boy. . . ?"

Graham leaned toward him and whispered. "We think the boy's been spotted, Will. Alive."

And before Will could say anything, the FBI man was gone.

Chief Robert Howe sat at the long table, waiting for his audience to settle down. As the chief studied the gathering with thinly veiled contempt, Will studied him in turn: Yes, there was a strong resemblance between the chief and his brother, the surly detective (although he had been much less surly with Heather Casey, but then Heather Casey wasn't an outsider).

Jerry Graham sat next to the chief, waiting to be introduced and looking impatient.

God Almighty, Will thought. Why do we need a toastmaster here? Will felt like shouting what he had figured out the previous night. He thought it would be an eternity before he could talk to Graham alone. Latin Condensed, for God's sake.

"This morning, I'm going to turn the proceedings over directly to Special Agent Graham," the chief said.

"Good morning, ladies and gentlemen," Graham said. "Very early this morning, we received a report of a child, approximate age five to seven, seen in the dense woods near the border of Hill and Deer counties in the company of an adult male. We have reason to think that the child is Jamie Brokaw."

There was a momentary commotion, during which Jerry Graham sipped coffee from a plastic cup. When the noise subsided, he went on: Early that day, a man identifying himself as a deer hunter had called the Deer County Sheriff's Department, reporting that the previous day he had seen a man pulling a sled on which was strapped a child. The man had been accompanied by a very large dog, apparently a German shepherd, and had fired two shots when the deer hunter approached.

On the phone, the deer hunter had acknowledged that he was hunting illegally, before the start of the regular season, and he had therefore been reluctant to call the authorities.

"But his conscience got the better of him, and he finally called," Graham said.

Graham went on to summarize what little the authorities knew: that the hunter had described the man in the woods as being medium height and build, wearing a ski mask—"You will recall that the kidnappers of Jamie Brokaw wore ski masks''—and that the sighting had taken place while it was snowing.

"The fact that the boy appeared to be strapped to the sled, plus the fact that the man fired two shots, makes it probable that the boy was Jamie Brokaw and the man with him one of the kidnappers," Graham said.

One of the kidnappers, Will thought. Well, what about the other one? He could hardly concentrate on the questions and answers that flew by, so intent was he on getting Jerry Graham alone.

"Mr. Graham, would you please answer yes or no on whether the kidnappers managed to escape with the latest ransom bundle despite heavy surveillance of the drop site, and does this indicate that the authorities have lost control of the case?" The questioner was the beautiful young television reporter. One tough cookie, Will thought.

Graham kept his face impassive. "The ransom was delivered as per instructions, and I will not comment on the other parts of your question."

The reporter with the dirty raincoat was on his feet. "Agent Graham, in view of the fact that the authorities issued an ultimatum, namely that there must be proof the boy is alive and well before any more ransom is delivered, what do you think this sighting means?"

"I don't understand the question."

"Well, sir, I mean, do you think the kidnappers are moving the boy to a different hiding place? More to the point, has he been under your nose all the while?"

"I have no way of knowing that," Graham said. "There's a lot of places a child can be hidden. And moving him from one place to another would probably not be that difficult. How many vans and pickup trucks are registered just in Hill and Deer counties? Thousands. And you don't have to drive very far to find some of the densest woods in the Northeast. We've got a couple hundred square miles of forest that start just a short drive from here."

"Agent Graham, in view of what you now know, might it not have been wise to conduct a thorough search of the woods in the region?" asked the reporter with the big biceps.

Graham bit his lip, then answered. "It's not that simple to conduct a thorough search, as you put it, of dense woods. Especially when the weather is iffy. But as a matter of fact, I can tell you now that state police aircraft have been keeping their eyes open, so to speak."

Will couldn't help but be amused. Graham had practically chewed his last words. Will recalled that Graham had trained in hand-to-hand combat. Perhaps the FBI man was even now fantasizing about being in a room alone with Big Biceps and bouncing him from wall to wall. . . .

"Mr. Graham, no doubt the boy's parents have been notified. How are they reacting?"

"Like any parents would. They are, naturally, hopeful that the child sighted is indeed their son, and that no harm has yet come to him."

"What do you mean by that, sir?" It was Dirty Raincoat again.

"I shouldn't have to spell that out," Graham said coldly.

Jerry, Jerry, Will thought. Learn to suffer the fools.

"Sir, some of us have heard a rumor that the kidnappers threatened to assault the boy sexually? Can you comment?"

"I have no comment," Graham said, barely in control. "Except that whoever would spread rumors like that is beneath contempt."

That brought silence to the room. Impatient to get things over with, Will stood up. "Jer . . . Agent Graham, is a search of the woods being done now, and was the man who called the Deer County Sheriff's Office able to pinpoint the sighting?"

"Yes. As we speak, a search is under way in a selected area, in the section of woods where the hunter thinks he saw the man and the boy. The weather forecast is not promising, but we have no choice but to press the search at this point."

Another question occurred to Will, one so obvious that he was surprised no one else had asked it. He must phrase it as though he knew it to be a fact: "Agent Graham, I assume the Deer County Sheriff's Office tape-records its incoming telephone calls. Is the tape of the hunter's call being analyzed, or will it be, and what do you hope to find out?"

"Yes, the tape of that call will be analyzed. For what it's worth, we think from the tone of voice and the caller's tendency to mumble certain words that it was an older man. And I don't know what we'll find out, other than that he has loose dentures."

There was a low collective chuckle in the room. Several pairs of eyes turned respectfully to Will, who would have been flushed with pride except that he was dying to talk to Jerry Graham alone.

The lovely TV reporter raised her hand. "Mr. Graham, what about the previous messages from the kidnappers? I mean, their having been sent from different locations and all? What does that mean in view of the boy's being sighted in the deep woods?"

Which was precisely what Will was trying to guess at.

"Who can say?" the agent replied. "We already know there were at least two kidnappers, after all. If I had more answers, I might have the boy."

"Well," the gorgeous reporter pressed, "do you think the different locations used in the ransom mailings were meant as a diversion, or are the kidnappers just toying with you?"

"I don't know," Graham said. "I suggest you ask the kidnappers. When we catch them. Which we will."

"Sir, are you yourself going to the search area? And will the press be allowed to accompany the search party?"

"I am going out there as soon as we're done here. And we can't have all of you tromping all over the place. So the chief and I have decided to have a pool arrangement. Two representatives of the print media, meaning one reporter and one photographer, and one cameraman and reporter from TV. Ladies and gentlemen, this is not negotiable, so please do not push me."

A rumble of discontent went up: even though whoever was selected for the pool would be obligated to share what they filmed or saw, those left out would be furious. Sure, Will thought. That's why we all got in this business once upon a time: to be where the action is. Not to have someone else tell us about the action.

The next voice was the police chief's: "Everyone come up here and write your name on a piece of paper from this pad. Put it in this basket, and we'll shuffle them and see who gets to go."

All but oblivious to the grumbling around him, Will stood in line to sign his name. He was frustrated and furious. He had cooperated with Jerry Graham early on—lent him some of his expertise, for God's sake!—and now he, Will Shafer, was about to be shut out unless the luck of the draw favored him.

Will signed his name, put the piece of paper in the little basket, tried desperately to get the attention of his old friend the FBI agent, who was standing off to one side, seemingly intent on ignoring him. Will had never been good at being pushy, and he envied reporters who were. Now that feeling came back to him, and he felt humiliated as well as angry. *Jerry, don't do this to me!*

"All right," the police chief said. "I'll draw the names now."

Of course, Will's name was not one of those drawn, and his face stung as though he'd been slapped. He would get out of the newspaper business and get a job in public relations. This time, he really would. But first, god damn it, he was going to try his damnedest to get out to the woods with the searchers, even if he had to get arrested. . . .

"All right," Jerry Graham said, "those of you who have been picked can come with us. There's a van waiting out back. The rest of you, well, you can wait here, I guess. There's not much point in your trying to follow on your own, because the roads leading into the area will be blocked off at a certain point. . . ."

One last time, Will tried to catch the eye of his old friend Jerry Graham (the man he'd been with on a stakeout in the woods, the man he'd had dinner and drinks with, for Christ's sake!), but in vain.

Well, Jerry Graham could shit in his hat and pull it down over his ears as far as Will Shafer was concerned. Will thought he just might put everything he knew in his next story, including the stuff that had been off the record. He wasn't going to be treated this way.

Will left by a side entrance. It was getting colder, snowing again. A good day to stay in a second-rate hotel and consume what was left of the scotch, then file a story that the editors back in Bessemer would have trouble translating. He wouldn't be the first reporter to get drunk before writing a story. Ah, Frannie, I don't blame you, Will thought. I really don't. Will had never felt lower, or madder.

He paused as he opened the door to his car. Should he go back and find someone—anyone—to tell what he knew? Screw it. Maybe he'd talk to Jerry Graham later. And maybe—

Just as he was getting into his car, a powerful hand clutched his shoulder, so suddenly that Will felt a jab of fear.

"Mr. Shafer?" It was a cop. Midthirties. Hard, square face, partly hidden by amber sunglasses, the kind of glasses cops sometimes wore on the pistol range. "Relax, Mr. Shafer. Agent Graham sent me to get you before you got away. Come on with me."

"Will, I'm sorry for the little charade. A necessity, I thought. Want to come along?"

"Of course, you bastard. I was fit to be tied."

Graham laughed, then gestured to the cop who'd retrieved Will. "Meet Officer John Raines, Will. One of the few people around here who seems to know what he's doing."

Momentarily startled by the FBI man's candor, Will shook hands with the smiling officer, who had removed his shooting glasses to reveal cool gray eyes.

"You have something to tell me before we go, Will?"

"Yes. It's about the ransom notes."

"John, would you excuse us for a minute?" Graham said. "Officially, the bureau doesn't operate quite the way I am now."

"No problem. I've got something to do anyhow before we leave. Good meeting you, Mr. Shafer."

"It's Will. Same here."

As soon as they were alone and the door was locked, Graham opened the desk drawer and took out the cardboard sheets. He held them up and raised his eyebrows, as if waiting for Will to prove something.

"It's with the second and third ones, Jerry. Remember how we thought maybe one guy had done the first note but not the others?"

"Right."

"And we noticed the shortcut he took there, with the abbreviation, and most important right there." Will leaned forward to point to something in the third note. "There, Jerry, that word *quarter* that's pasted up intact. It's Latin Condensed type, Jerry."

The agent looked at Will as though his old newspaperman friend was speaking Chinese.

Will went on. "Latin Condensed is an old-fashioned typeface, Jerry. Rather formal for the look most papers want nowadays. Stuffy, even. Not that many papers use it."

Graham nodded. "And you know the ones that do?"

"Not the *Bessemer Gazette*, Jerry. Not the *Long Creek Eagle*. In fact, none of the hometown papers from this area. It's the *New York Times* Jerry. The *New York Times* uses Latin Condensed type in some of its headlines."

"The *New York Times* . . ."

"Jerry, I feel like a fool. I'm so used to seeing it, because I read the *Times* every day. So it didn't dawn on me that it was unusual. In fact"—Will bent forward and pointed to two other letters, both on the second ransom note—"those letters there are Latin Condensed also."

The agent listened with razor-sharp concentration.

"Jerry, the *New York Times* has trouble getting its papers into this region. Geography, weather, shipping problems, most of all the lack of a good satellite printing plant. You can buy the *Times* in only a few places around here. It's available here in Long Creek, though sales are sparse. The next-closest place is Bessemer."

"You're sure?"

"I verified it last night by calling the *Gazette*'s circulation chief."

"So," Graham said. "Whatever it means, those postmarks all those miles apart on the ransom notes, and the bragging about being able to move the kid at will . . ."

"Jerry, some of the newspapers used in the pasteups of the second and third notes were bought right here in Long Creek."

Graham put the ransom notes back in his drawer and locked it. "We've got to get going, Will. How would what you just told me dovetail with the boy's being sighted in the woods?"

"I don't know. There are at least two kidnappers. We know that."

"Right. Could be those distant postmarks are supposed to divert us. Or maybe the kidnappers just get their rocks off by toying with us. God, I don't know."

Will felt a little let down. He had been proud of his discovery (belated or not) and had expected Graham to . . . what? Be more enthusiastic? Offer a new theory?

"Will, Officer Raines can drop you at your hotel for a minute if you want to get your hiking boots or whatever. He'll drive you out to the search area. Okay?"

"Sure." Why am I going with this guy Raines? Will wondered.

"I'm afraid your fellow journalists would be all over my ass, Will, if it was obvious that I was bringing you along outside of the pool arrangement. So I'd appreciate it if you'd stay close to Officer Raines and be inconspicuous."

"Sure." That made sense, but Will thought Jerry seemed hesitant and embarrassed.

"Oh, and Will. As I said, I don't know exactly what to make of this thing with the Latin, Latin . . ."

"Latin Condensed type."

"But if you could, you know . . ."

Will knew. In for a dime, in for a dollar. "It's off the record, Jerry. For now, anyhow."

Raines drove him to his room, where Will called the *Gazette* and told the editors to go with a wire-service story on the kidnapping if he couldn't file in time for the first edition.

"My instincts tell me to stay with the searchers no matter what, even if it means not being able to file," Will said.

Hanging up before anyone could argue, he grabbed his boots, heavy jacket, and hat and was out the door. God, it was great to be on a story again. . . .

Raines was quiet for much of the ride out to the country. Will was comfortable with the silence. He even closed his eyes for part of the trip. He didn't doze, but he did relax a little. He wished he'd had a bigger breakfast; there was no telling when he'd be back in town.

"You know this FBI guy from before, I guess."

Will was almost startled by Raines's voice. "Yeah. Haven't seen him for a while, but we first got acquainted back in Bessemer. When we were both just starting out."

"Him in law enforcement and you in the newspaper business," Raines said.

Raines seemed to be straining to be convivial, so Will went on. "That was a long time ago. More years than I want to admit."

They rode in silence a while longer. Will was thankful for the car's powerful heater, even though he was starting to have to fight off the drowsiness. The cop still wore his amber range glasses and kept his eyes straight ahead, on a road that was starting to get slick in spots.

Snow fell out of the pewter sky. Will wondered where Jamie Brokaw was, whether he was . . .

No. He didn't want to think about it anymore.

"Pretty sharp, isn't he?" Raines said. "Graham, I mean."

"I always thought so. He's what we used to call a straight arrow. I guess I'm dating myself a little."

"I had him figured for that, too. By the book and all."

"But not totally," Will said. "Jerry's got good instincts, I think. Hunches, whatever you call them."

"Like in poker."

"I guess so, although I don't play cards."

The mention of poker reminded Will of his encounter with the chief's brother. Since Raines was loosening up a little, Will decided to fish. "The chief and his brother play poker, don't they?"

Raines snorted. "Not with me they don't."

Ah so, Will thought. We have here a police officer who doesn't like his chief and some of the people around the chief. Perhaps that fact could be useful.

Will recognized the turnoff; it was the same road Jerry Graham had taken when Will had gone with him on the stakeout. A Sheriff's Department car with its red gumball blinking blocked the road partly, allowing room for one vehicle to pass at a time. A deputy standing alongside the car waved Raines through. Will saw eight or ten cars parked nearby along the highway: probably the curious who had learned by radio or television that a boy had been spotted in the woods.

Raines drove well beyond where Graham had stopped the day of the stakeout. The road was icy, but Raines seemed to have no trouble. There was a lot more snow out here in the open country than back in Long Creek.

"You're used to these conditions, I guess," Will said.

"Sure am. I grew up north of Albany, where we got just as much snow as here. Plus, I got studded tires."

"You do any hunting around here?"

"Some. Don't get much chance. I'm a good shot, though."

They went up a long hill, and the swirl of snow seemed to thicken as they climbed.

"Weather's gonna make it tough for the copter pilots," Raines said. "But they'll fly as long as they can."

From the top of the hill, Will saw a big clearing off to one side of the road. The area was jammed with police vehicles. Will also spotted an ambulance, a truck that appeared to be a communications center, several portable toilet booths, and a canteen that was dispensing coffee and sandwiches.

Dozens of lawmen, some wearing uniforms, many carrying rifles or shotguns, stood in clusters.

"This here clearing is owned by the Deer County Rod and Gun Club," Raines said. "It was the handiest place for a base of operations."

Raines parked at the end of a row of cars, and he and Will stepped into the snow. Instantly, Will felt himself shivering, but only partly from the cold. The rest was pure adrenaline, triggered by the scene around him. The air was alive with the sound of generators, snowmobiles, and helicopter engines. Will watched one copter lift off, its rotors beating down the air in a cyclone of snow, then bank as it veered toward the dense woods.

This was worth writing about, no matter how it turned out: that a lot of brave people were risking their lives for a little boy.

He walked past a helicopter, saw two people in flight suits jotting on clipboards. The blond hair of one of the pilots curled out from under her helmet.

Will looked for Raines; he didn't want to loose track of him. There he was, being briefed with several other cops a few yards away.

Will looked back at the helicopter; the pilot had climbed into the plastic blister of a cockpit. Oh, the woman was in the copter, too. Good story, good story, Will thought. Got to find her later, talk to her, weave her into the story gracefully without making too big a deal out of it.

The copter's blades started to spin, faster, faster. The craft lifted off, the snow flung like sparks into Will's face, the air like thunder. And then, suddenly, the copter was up, away and gone, heading after the other aircraft toward the deep woods.

"Goddamn," Will whispered. "I do love this so, don't I?" For a moment, he felt silly. Then he didn't give a damn; the truth was, he felt like a little boy watching a big fire. The pure excitement of it was wonderful. Any reporter who didn't feel it was no damn good, and any who denied feeling it was a liar.

"You game for a snowmobile ride?" Raines said.

"Hell, yes," Will said. He wondered what had become of the journalists in the pool. He hoped they were far away; he wanted as much of this as possible for himself.

"Graham wanted me to be sure you didn't get hurt," Raines said. "You in decent shape?"

"Hell, yes." For an office worker my age, anyhow, Will thought. "Look, I'll try not to slow you down or get in your way. But it's not up to you to worry about me. Okay?"

"Hmph. 'Course, it's my ass that's in a sling if something happens to you."

Will was worried that Raines was going to be a pain in the ass about having him along, so he decided to push. "What are they going to do to you? They don't play poker with you now, right?"

For an instant, the eyes behind the amber glasses were anything but friendly. Then Raines forced a smile. "Get on," he said, pointing to a red snowmobile. "And hold on."

Twenty-two

∎ ∎ ∎

He saw gray through the tops of the trees: the first light of the day. The heat from the two bodies, Wolf's and the boy's, had kept him almost warm in the cocoon of ponchos and blankets. He guessed that he had slept off and on during the night: Every so often, he had been startled, and in the moments afterward had been unable to remember what he'd been thinking. Sometimes it was hard to tell what was real.

He had thought of going back to the cabin, had decided not to because he thought the hunter might ambush him. So the hermit had chosen a sleeping place on a little slope beneath the shelter of some pines. Now *he* could set an ambush, if he had to.

Wolf had been comfortable enough. God, what a tough dog. Wolf could make it in the woods without him if he had to.

The boy had whimpered now and then. Poor Jason; he'd probably dreamed about being back in the ground. It *was* hard to tell what was real.

Careful not to wake the boy, he took a long time crawling

167

out of the ponchos and blankets. Finally on his feet, he saw that the fresh snowfall was more than ankle-deep. He re-arranged the ponchos and blankets to cover the boy entirely, then walked a few yards away to relieve himself.

Lighter now above the trees. Snow still falling, swirling down through the branches. He was glad he had picked a sleeping place hidden from the wind.

He saw the faint yellow glow, and for a second he thought the moonlight was lovely on the treetops and spilling onto the snow below.

Not moonlight. The yellow glow darted and danced, grew more intense. When he first heard the sound, it was like the beating of grouse wings. Second by second, it grew louder, until it was almost overhead, chasing its own beam of light.

The sound of the helicopter roused Wolf and the boy. The hermit went over and knelt next to them. Wolf stretched, yawned loudly, and shook himself. The boy shifted, put his hand into the fold of poncho where the dog had lain.

Jamie knew it had been a dream, all of it, and that when he opened his eyes he would be with his mother and father. Then he remembered that his mother and father lived in differ-ent places, and he couldn't remember where he was, until he tried to move his feet. His feet wouldn't move, because he was in a tight place. Then he put his hand where the nice dog had been, but there was nothing there. He tried to call for his father, but he couldn't make the sound he wanted.

"Shh, Jason. It's all right. All right. It's morning in the woods. I bet you never saw—"

He heard another engine sound, from far away. But not from above.

"Daddy?"

"It's all right, Jason. It's all right." He wanted the boy to be comfortable, so he loosened the straps.

"I want to go home. I want to go home, and I want my daddy." Then Jamie thought of his mother, too, and felt sorry for her because she wasn't with his father anymore. He started to cry.

* * *

The hermit reached into a deep pocket, took out meat and bread. He chewed slowly, trying not to be bothered by the boy's crying. Up to now, he had felt sorry for the boy, had wanted only to comfort him. Now he felt hurt; the boy wasn't grateful to him at all. He just whined and said he wanted his father.

The hermit faced the feeling in himself—jealousy—and felt like a foolish child himself. It was unfair ever to expect much gratitude from a child, let alone one who had suffered like this one. For Christ's sake, the hermit scolded himself, suppose you and Jo had had that baby. . . .

A memory swelled inside him, weighed him down with sorrow. His head started to ache, and he longed for whiskey. . . .

He gave some meat to the dog, then knelt next to the weeping boy. "Jason, take this and eat it. You'll need—"

Jamie didn't like Mr. Woody calling him by the wrong name, and he didn't like the smell of the cold meat from his pocket. When the meat was held close to his mouth, Jamie slapped it away. The meat landed in the snow, where Wolf went to claim it.

"God damn it, Jason," the hermit said without thinking. "That's good meat."

Jamie thought Mr. Woody sounded mean, like the ones who had taken him. Mr. Woody had just sworn at him, too. Now, nothing mattered to Jamie except going home. He began to cry even harder, in loud, choking sobs.

"Jason, it's all right. . . ."

Jamie cried harder still. He hated Mr. Woody and the way he smelled and the way his face looked.

The hermit walked a few yards away, trying to get himself back together, trying to think straight. Hearing the boy's wailing made him want to slap his face, or hold his face in the snow until he stopped. No, no, God Almighty. It wasn't the boy's fault, wasn't his fault.

"Shut up, Jason! Shut the fuck up, for Christ's sake. I'm doing the best I can. Don't you see?"

Jamie had tired himself out with his weeping. He stood up,

then sat down in the snow to catch his second wind. In the lull, the hermit heard sómething: more engine sounds, at ground level. He strained to hear, but he could not tell whether they were coming closer.

It was lighter now above the trees; very soon, it would be hard to hide. He saw another yellow beam, coming from a different direction. He heard the copter. Then, above the sound of his own heart, he heard another one. The second one was low, almost overhead. Louder, louder, and then it was gone.

Jamie was still crying. Wolf was getting frantic, circling around. The dog was upset from the noise of the engines and the boy's crying and his master's shouting. Wolf barked loudly.

"Wolf, damn it! Shut the fuck up!"

Now all Jamie wanted to do was get away. He took a few steps, then slipped and fell facefirst into the snow.

Wolf put his paws on the boy's back, put his snout in the boy's ribs to turn him over.

The snow came through the mask, into Jamie's eyes. It was cold, cold, and he couldn't see. The dog was heavy on his back.

"Wolf! All right, fella. Let him get up, let Jason get up. . . ."

It seemed to the hermit that there were noises all around him now. There must be others with the hunter. Men in uniform, setting fires and coming after him.

"Jason, get up and come on."

The hermit felt danger nearby. He worked the lever of the carbine, putting a cartridge into the chamber. His fingers trembled as he let the hammer down into the safety position. Could the boy keep up with him? No.

"Jason, get on the sled. Get on!"

Jamie stomped his feet and wailed.

"Get on the sled, damn it! If you don't, I'll tie you on."

Jamie hated Mr. Woody now. He was just like the others.

"I want to go *home*. . . ." He choked on a sob in his throat.

"I know, I know. I'm going to take you home, Jason. I promise I will. I promise." Oh, God, do I have to lose you again?

* * *

Raines parked the snowmobile next to several others in a small clearing. An enormous deputy, frowning behind his sunglasses and holding a rifle, stood in the clearing. Will spotted a movement in the trees about fifty yards away: another lawman with a rifle. Will looked the other way; after a few seconds, he saw still another deputy with a shoulder weapon.

"What's the plan?" Will asked Raines. "To flush him out and have him trapped no matter which way he goes?"

"I don't make plans. I just follow them."

Why is it that every cop has to be a smart ass at one time or another, Will thought. God, they must hate reporters even more than they let on.

Raines moved close to the big deputy, and the two communicated in whispers and nods. Scanning the open sky over the clearing, Will saw a helicopter in the distance, circling low over the trees. He looked at Raines, saw Raines studying him in a not so friendly way. "Shafer, I'm going up this way," he said, pointing into the woods. "If you want to come a little ways anyhow, it's all right. That's what your FBI friend said."

"All right." Will didn't know exactly what Graham had told Raines, or what Raines thought Graham had told him. In a situation like this, the only thing for a newsman to do was to take whatever he could get. "How many people are out here?"

"No idea," Raines said.

"Fifty? A hundred?"

"Probably closer to fifty. You can get all that from your FBI friend."

Prick, Will thought.

"There're more coming," the big deputy said. "Some with tracking dogs."

"You ready, Shafer?" Raines said.

"Lead on."

"Stay close to me and try not to fall."

Raines picked his way through gently rolling woodland. The thick evergreens and the snow lent a hush to everything, despite the distant sounds of snowmobiles and helicopters.

Will looked all around, soaking up impressions to weave into his story. The setting was as beautiful as an Ansel Adams photograph.

Will kept up easily enough and wondered with pride whether Raines was surprised at his stamina. Best thing I ever did was take up jogging, he thought. Have to get back into it when I get home. . . .

After a while, they started on a long downhill slope. There was a stream at the bottom, and Will saw a dozen or so people standing in a small clearing along the bank. He recognized the reporters and camera people he'd seen at the briefings. Several deputies stood like herding dogs around the perimeter of the gathering.

"Right there're the pool folks, Shafer, if you want to hook up with them."

Raines was trying to get rid of him, all right, but Will didn't feel like being part of a pack, waiting in the woods and stomping his feet to keep warm. "I'd rather go with you," Will said.

"I don't know about that."

"Jerry Graham wanted me to stay out of sight of the pool reporters."

Raines seemed to think that over for a few seconds. "I don't really give a shit about that. To be blunt, I don't want to be responsible if this nut shoots you. And I don't want you to get in my way."

"I understand."

"Why don't you just hang around here?"

"Do you guys think he's probably cornered somewhere up ahead? Is that it?"

"Like I said, Shafer, I think it's a good idea if you wait back here with them other folks. Your FBI friend isn't here right now, so I'll use my own judgment."

Raines nodded toward the clearing where the other reporters were cooling their heels (literally), gave Will a final hard glance, and walked ahead alone.

Will stood in place for a minute or more, until Raines was out of view. He was annoyed by how Raines had dumped him, annoyed because he didn't know where Jerry Graham was, annoyed because he was getting hungry.

It had been a long, long time since Will had covered a big story. It made him sad to think about it, but the plain truth was that he had never done some of the things he had once dreamed about. He had never covered a presidential campaign or a revolution or a war. And he never would.

He was getting chilly standing in the woods. Had he come all this way just to stand here and let his toes get cold? He looked toward the clearing. Will was partly hidden by underbrush, and he could tell that none of his fellow journalists had spotted him. More important, none of the deputies shepherding the press had seen him. Will recognized his temporarily undefined situation for what it was: an opportunity.

Stepping as softly as he could, Will set off in the direction Raines had gone.

At last, the boy had cried himself into silent exhaustion. Rather than let himself be tied to the sled, the boy had sat down, let Mr. Woody wrap blankets around him, allowed the dog to rub against him.

"Good, Wolf. Good boy. Good. Let Jason sleep." I might have been a good father, he thought.

He took off his mask. The cold on his face made him feel more alert. He touched his forehead, felt the burn scars from long ago, remembered the fire as though it had just happened.

Was there anyone he could trust? Any place he could hide? Not for long, he thought sadly. And the boy didn't like him as much as before.

Quickly, he finished loading the sled. The boy was sleeping. You cried yourself back to sleep, Jason.

It was snowing gently now, and the wind had let up. He could better judge the engine sounds. The copters were circling closer, but the snowmobiles were still well behind him. He knew the terrain enough to be sure they'd have to come for him on foot.

Just then, he heard a new sound. Wolf heard it, too, and growled.

Dogs.

The hermit gripped the sled rope and started walking.

* * *

Will had lost sight of Raines, which was probably just as well, because if Raines saw him he'd be furious. And Raines could find a way to make Will's life tougher.

Besides, Will thought, I might need a cop I can talk to about what happened to Fran. That thought almost surprised him: For a little while, at least, he had all but forgotten about Fran Spicer's death.

He was getting tired, and he was really hungry. The terrain was more rugged, and the snow in some spots was halfway to his knees. The boots and thick socks kept his feet warm enough, but his face was getting cold. He stopped, took off his gloves, pressed his palms to his cheeks. Better.

Now and then, Will heard a helicopter. He no longer heard the snowmobiles. Had he walked that far into the deep woods? More likely, the machines had already been used to bring people up as far as possible and were now idle.

Will looked at the sky; it was a lighter gray than before. What did that mean? That the sun was trying to squint through? Or did he just think it was lighter? In any event, the snow was still falling. If he gazed up into the swirling flakes for more than a few seconds, Will felt dizzy.

For a while, he'd been able to follow Raines's tracks. Now the snow and the wind, light but enough to help erase footprints, had made that all but impossible. Before following Raines, Will had checked the sky, determined the sun's hiding place, and oriented himself. He thought he was still taking the course Raines had set out on. But he couldn't be sure. For that matter, why assume that Raines had kept going in the same direction?

Jesus, Will wondered in a moment of panic, am I lost?

No. he was still going the way he'd started (roughly, anyhow), and he had to trust his senses. He knew full well that hikers and hunters who trusted their senses rather than their compasses sometimes walked in circles, but he banished that thought from his mind. Will didn't have a compass.

But he knew he wasn't that far from people. Way off to his left (to the west, he thought), he heard barking.

Will took a deep breath and pressed on.

* * *

The boy was awake. The hermit could tell from the stirring on the sled.

"I want to go home and see my father and mother."

"I know, Jason. I know."

"My name is Jamie, and I don't want to go with you anymore. *I don't*!"

"The men chasing us are bad. They set fires, just to be mean."

"Are they with the men who took me?"

He thought about that. It was getting harder for him to keep things straight, and he didn't have an answer for the boy.

"Can you find my father?"

"I'll try. I promise."

Wolf growled, barked once. The dogs were closer.

He stopped to rest, ate a piece of meat and some bread, tried to quiet his pounding heart. He didn't want Wolf to smell his fear.

He had to choose: He could keep going, knowing that the terrain continued to climb, and that before it started down again he'd have to cross an open stretch, or he could angle off about thirty degrees, taking a low route along a meandering stream. The high road would expose him to view from the helicopters, while the stream route would bring him closer to the men and the dogs but give him a chance of slipping through them into Deer County.

Why was it important that he get to Deer County? What if he just stopped and let the men find him? He touched the burn scars on his face, closed his eyes. As if in a dream, he saw the flames and smoke in a valley. The old sadness weighed on his shoulders, and in his memory he heard shouts and screams, his own among them. He put his hands to his ears, shook his head violently to get rid of the echoes, felt his knees buckle.

He should do it now: put the muzzle of the carbine in his mouth and—

No. Not in front of Jason. What would happen to him? What would he remember?

He opened his eyes, but the shouts and screams did not go away. The sounds were from the boy on the sled. He was crying.

"No, no, no. Don't, Jason. Don't!"

He hadn't meant to shout at the boy. Now the child screamed and sobbed louder than ever. Wolf barked, changed to a howl, and wouldn't stop.

"Shut up! Shut up, god damn you. It wasn't my fault."

He heard other dogs. Getting closer. He started to run, tugging the sled behind him.

"Hold on, Jason. Hold on, boy."

Wolf dashed ahead of him along the stream bank, leaping like a gazelle over fallen limbs. The dog stopped, looked back at his master, and ran like a comet back to him.

The ground along the stream was smooth, but he had to zigzag to pull the sled around dead trees. He could hear the boy. Still crying.

He heard shouts, dogs. Closer now. Too close.

He came to the rotting hulk of a tree, close to two feet thick and stretching from the stream's edge to where the land sloped up. He could rest there, and hide.

But it was too late: As he stood by the fallen tree, he saw the man with the rifle, standing on the other side of the stream about a hundred yards away. The hunter from before? Same size, same look.

The hunter was looking right at him, kneeling slowly, now getting into a prone position to shoot at him. The hunter was shouting something, but the hermit couldn't make it out. His heartbeat seemed about to burst his eardrums.

"Get down, Jason. . . . Wolf, here by me . . . ."

He got behind the dead tree, peeked over it, and saw the hunter, who was worming sideways to take cover behind a rock.

"We'll be okay, Jason. I promise—" As he turned to comfort him, he saw that the boy was no longer there. The boy had climbed over the tree hulk, tumbled in the snow, and now he was waddling like a duck through the snow toward the hunter.

"Jason, no! Don't leave me! Jason!"

The hermit put his rifle to his shoulder, aimed toward the rock the hunter was behind, and squeezed the trigger.

The bullet hit the rock, and the sound of the ricochet echoed

through the woods. The hermit chambered another cartridge
even as he ran toward the boy. Now he saw the hunter,
looking up over the rock, getting ready to shoot at him.

The hermit overtook the boy, wrapped his left arm around
the child, pulled him up to him. With his right arm, he kept
the carbine trained toward the hunter's rock.

"All right, Jason. Don't cry. All right. Don't kick."

The hermit backed up, toward the dead tree. He kept his
eyes on the rock; he could see the hunter's face. His lips were
moving, as though he was talking to someone.

The hermit dropped the boy on the other side of the dead
tree hulk, then rolled over to the other side himself. Where
was Wolf? Here he was, hunkered down next to him. The
dog was growling, its ears back.

Shouts. Other dogs. Very close.

Trying to gulp enough air, the hermit looked up over the
log. Other men, other hunters. Two, no three more, coming
up behind the first one. Taking cover behind trees and
mounds, aiming at him. Wanting to take everything.

"I'll make it right, Jason. I will this time."

He looked to his side. Again, the boy was gone, only now
he was stumbling through the snow going the other way.

"Jason, don't leave—"

Still holding his rifle in one hand, he got up and ran toward
the boy, away from the hunters but in their line of fire.

"Jason!"

And then he saw the last hunter, only fifty yards away on
the same side of the creek bank.

Trapped now. All over. Where was Jo?

As if in a dream, he watched the last hunter kneel down
and aim at him, heard the hunter shout, "Drop it *now*!"

The hermit let go of the rifle just as a bullet hit him from
behind, smashing into his back near his right shoulder and
knocking him off his feet.

The sky stopped spinning, and he realized he was lying on
his back. His shoulder was hot and wet, and it hurt him to
breathe. The rifle was still in his hands. Jason was screaming.
The hermit heard Wolf barking, heard the other dogs coming.
Heard another shot, heard Wolf yelp in pain.

Was he dreaming? No.

As his heartbeat quieted, he could hear the gurgling of the nearby stream.

Will had fallen way behind Raines, he guessed by a few hundred yards. His legs were tired from trudging through the snow. At one point, he had stepped into a deep snow-covered puddle. His right foot had broken the ice with a crack that would have been heard by anyone close by. His sock and foot were still dry inside the boot, but some water had gotten splashed onto his leg at knee level, so that part of his pant leg was soon frozen as hard as cast iron.

For some time, he had been hearing dogs. Now, he thought he heard shouts and screams; he wasn't sure, because the woods played tricks with sounds, and he was no outdoorsman.

When he heard the shots, he ran toward them as fast as he could. He tried to run in a straight line, hoping he hadn't been fooled by the echoes. He picked up the sound of voices coming out of a radio. Cops, he thought. The cops are up this way. Maybe Jerry is there. He owes me.

Will tried to adjust his breathing so that his chest wouldn't get exhausted. He would push himself to the limit; there was no better time.

He heard more radio squawks—he was close to the sounds, no doubt about it—and then a helicopter coming in low.

Now Will was inhaling the cold air in great gulps—he couldn't help it—and praying his heart was in fine shape, as the doctor had said just last spring, because he knew there was a big commotion up ahead, and he was going to get to it, no matter what the cost in pain, and it was quite a big cost, because he was on a long upward slope.

And now he was at a point where the terrain went up even more steeply in one direction, but off to an angle it sloped down and followed a little stream. The low route was the one to take, because Will could tell that the noises were that way.

His legs hurt terribly now, and his back ached, but it didn't matter. He was almost there.

Down a little slope, fresh tracks in the snow to guide him, tracks of men and dogs, and now he was almost at stream level, and there was sky above him (still snow coming out of it), and the sound of a helicopter filling the universe as it came in right over his head, stirring a great cloud of snow.

Just a few yards farther, around a little outcropping, and Will saw where the shouts and radio sounds were coming from.

"God Almighty," he said. "God Almighty."

The helicopter hovered deafeningly. A stretcher was being lowered by cable from it. A man lay on his back, his blood on the snow like spilled port on a linen tablecloth.

Almost collapsing, Will sat on a mound and watched several lawmen lift the body and lay it on the stretcher, efficiently wrapping the man in blankets and lashing him in place. Spinning as it was raised, the stretcher was hoisted into the copter. The scene reminded Will of television footage from the Vietnam War.

There was no need for him to take notes; there was no way he'd forget any of this.

Perhaps twenty lawmen were standing in groups in the snowy clearing. Several held German shepherds on leashes, and two or three were talking into hand-held radios.

And then Jerry Graham emerged from one of the groups, and Will saw at once that he was tenderly holding a little boy.

"God Almighty," Will heard himself say again. "God Almighty."

Will stood up, stumbled momentarily on rubbery legs, and walked toward the men.

"Shafer! What the hell . . . I thought I told you to stay back there." It was Raines.

"I misunderstood," Will said.

Raines stood threateningly before him, but Will was beyond being afraid, and he was in no mood to be pushed around.

"Jerry," Will shouted. "Jerry!"

"Will!" Still holding the boy, Graham broke away from the others and came over to him. "He's all right, Will."

A powerfully built man in a parka trotted over to Graham and Will and started to take the child from the agent. Will recognized him as the police chief. The boy let out a cry and wrapped his arms around Jerry Graham's neck.

"He doesn't want to go with you," Will said to the chief. "Why don't you leave well enough alone."

"Open your mouth again, and you're under—"

"All right! It's all right," Graham said. "This is a good newsman here, Chief. I'll vouch for him. Will, we're all tired here." Then to the boy: "All right, Jamie. I'll hold you. All right."

"Jerry, tell me what you can."

"I can't tell you much. I'm still trying to piece it together, Will."

Will took out his notepad, tried to keep the snowflakes off it, scribbled in a trembling hand. A Deer County deputy had spotted an armed man tugging a sled with a boy on it, had shouted at the man to put down the weapon and surrender. The man had fired from behind a log, the deputy had radioed for help, and reinforcements had arrived. The man was shot when he didn't drop his rifle in time, and after deputies and police officers concluded that the boy's life was in danger.

"That's all we know for now, Will. Except that the boy is alive and seems to be in good health, all things considered. Isn't that right, Jamie?"

Jamie was still in shock from everything he'd heard and seen. But he knew that he was in strong, gentle arms. And he knew something else, and this above all. "I want to see my mother and father," he said.

"You know what?" Graham said. "We're going to send you there right now. Have you ever ridden in a helicopter?"

"No."

"Well, we're going to fix that right now, my friend."

Even as the agent spoke, another helicopter was hovering loudly overhead. As snow flew like cold sparks, Will saw a chair lift being lowered by cable.

"You know what?" Graham said. "There're nice people up there with hot chocolate. Doesn't that sound great? That nice big helicopter will take you to meet your father."

Jamie would have been afraid because of all the noise and the wind, but the man holding him seemed like a nice man.

Then Jamie saw the funny chair dangling from the copter, and he was afraid. But not for long.

"This is better than any carnival ride, Jamie. I bet none of your friends ever rode in one of these chairs."

Jamie felt big, strong hands strapping him into the chair, then the ground was falling away under him, and he was going up toward the big noise of the helicopter, and he was spinning around and around in the chair, up through the wind and snow. But he wasn't afraid anymore, because even though he was dizzy he could see the nice man smiling and waving at him. Jamie laughed.

All of a sudden, he was inside another tin place, and hands were unbuckling him from the chair, and he was being laid onto something soft and warm, and his head was on a pillow. A pretty woman and a nice man were smiling at him, and hot chocolate was in front of his face. Jamie swallowed some and put his head back and closed his eyes. He tried to say that he wanted to go home, but he couldn't make the words come out right.

He could feel the helicopter go up, up, up. He couldn't keep his eyes open. It was all like a dream. A good dream.

"So," Jerry Graham said as the sound of the copter faded, "how the hell did you get here, Will?"

"I walked."

"You bastard. And what do I do with you now?"

Will thought for only a moment. "You trust me. I've kept some stuff off the record."

"So you have."

"And now I get my payback."

"Fair enough. The pool reporters are being briefed right about now. They'll be brought up here in a while to have a look. I don't want them to see you."

"Oh, they'll find out I was here."

"And be jealous."

"I hope so."

"Hmmm. Wait here, Will."

Graham went to talk to a group of lawmen: the Long Creek police chief, two men wearing Sheriff's Department badges, a couple of men Will didn't recognize, and Raines. As Will watched, there seemed to be an argument: Graham against everyone else.

Will looked all around. Blood on the snow was fading to pink where the man had fallen wounded. Then Will noticed a second, smaller spot of blood some yards away.

Graham was on his way back.

"It's settled, Will. You'll come with me. Ready for a hike?"

"Where, Jerry?"

Graham pointed. "That way. We think the screwball came from that direction. We're going to backtrack for a while, using dogs, and see if we can find where the boy was kept. Stick to me like glue, Will. I just told my buddies that we'd have better control over you if you were with me."

"Thanks, Jerry."

Just then, two deputies with German shepherds came by. Will was reminded of something. "Jerry, I thought the guy who had the boy was supposed to have had a dog with him."

"A deputy thought the dog might be going for the child, Will. So he shot him."

The other spot of blood, Will thought. "Where's the animal?"

"Crawled away. Gut-shot, probably. Crawled away to die."

That almost made Will sick. "Couldn't one of those fat-ass deputies take a few minutes to find him, for Christ's sake?"

Graham looked at him sadly, and for the first time Will saw that the agent was exhausted. "We can't plan everything, Will. A lot of shooting, a lot of chaos. The dog's gone, and there's not a goddamn thing I can do about it. This case has taken everything I have. More."

"What now?"

Graham said that he and several other investigators would try to retrace the tracks for clues as to where the boy had been kept. Will could accompany them, observe everything, if he agreed to keep some details out of his stories.

"What kind of details, Jerry?"

"I don't know yet. Things that might be crucial at the trial. Or trials. Don't forget, we're still looking for at least one other kidnapper."

Something about that didn't wash. "Don't bullshit me,

Jerry. You just have the traditional FBI man's approach of wanting to control everything.''

"I could send you back to Long Creek right now.''

He means it. Will knew from the voice. "I'll do it your way if I have to, Jerry.''

"Let's go.'' Graham put his hand on Will's shoulder. It was a conciliatory gesture. "You know how the bureau works, Will.''

"Yeah, I do. After all, J. Edgar Hoover's only been dead about twenty years.''

Twenty-three

■ ■ ■

Will lost track of time and distance as he and Graham walked through the woods. They were a little behind the main group of trackers, and Graham kept in touch with them by radio. They could hear the deep barking up ahead.

In places, the ruts left by the sled, the man's tracks, and his dog's tracks were unmistakable. In other places, depending on the contour of the land and its exposure to the wind, the trail was all but obscured.

The agent's radio squawked. "Graham here. . . . Roger. I'm coming. Something up ahead, Will."

The FBI man and Will caught up to the trackers, who stood in a small semicircle around a spot on a slope where the snow beneath the freshly fallen flakes was packed down. The dogs sniffed constantly and tugged at their leashes.

"They must have spent the night here," Graham said. "Lucky they didn't freeze to death."

Will and Graham stood back a few yards as an officer took photographs from several angles and another jotted notes on a clipboard.

When they were done, they pressed on, led now as much by the dogs as by the tracks, which were getting harder to spot. It was almost midafternoon, and Will was functioning on adrenaline. But Jerry Graham was his age; if he could still move, so could Will. All of Will's mental and emotional circuits were going: As a man, he was elated that the boy had been rescued; as a newsman, he was elated over a big story. He absorbed new details even as he arranged the old ones in his mind.

He was starting to worry a little about time. At some point, he would try to get to a telephone—*any* phone, if he didn't get back to Long Creek in time. He would talk his way into a farmhouse if he had to. He would file a story for the first edition of the next day's paper even if he had to stand dripping from melting snow in a stranger's kitchen and dictate it off the top of his head.

"How're you holding up, Will?"

"I'm making it. So far."

"The next time someone says you have to get out of the Northeast to find really rugged country, I'll shoot him."

"Jerry, what about the other kidnappers? There's at least one more."

"That's why I'm praying that our screwball friend doesn't die, Will. We need to talk to him."

"How bad is he?"

"Bad enough."

"What do you know about him?"

"Not a lot. Average height and build, in his forties. Looks and smells like he lives in the woods. And he has burn scars."

"Burn scars?"

"All around his face, Will. Something bad happened to him. A long time ago."

"Thanks for taking care of me, Jerry. I mean, not shutting me out."

"Hey, I owed you. We're both old enough to know the manual doesn't cover everything. In your job or mine."

"God no, it doesn't."

The snow had stopped altogether, and the clouds were breaking up. Graham's radio squawked again. Will couldn't decipher the message, but Graham's eyes went wide in astonishment.

"Roger, I'm coming as fast as I can. Rope it off. Oh, and get a canopy over it in case the snow starts again." Graham shook his head. "You'll find this hard to believe, Will."

The lawmen stood around the grave-size pit, studying the rusting hot-water tank that lay within. Judging by the dimensions and depth of the hole, the tank had been buried with some care, then dug up again in haste. The snow had covered much of the dirt, and the big clumps of earth that remained visible stood out like chocolate against a pristine white.

The tank had been equipped with a door, really a metal hatch with hinges and a lock. While somewhat crude, the hatch looked efficient enough. The cutting and refastening had obviously been done by someone used to working with metal—or so it seemed to Will, who was totally unhandy with tools and never could remember the difference between soldering and welding. The hatch and its lock had been broken off, probably with a shovel or crowbar, and lay next to the tank. Will found it odd that the hatch, obviously fashioned with such care, had been ripped off in haste. Had the kidnappers lost the key?

"Will, it looks like this is where Jamie Brokaw was kept. Can you believe this?"

As unobtrusively as he could, Will took out his notebook and began to jot down what he saw. The snow covering had been brushed away. Visible through the opening where the hatch cover had been were two woolen blankets, their folds frozen not just with snow but what looked like urine and feces; pieces of waxed paper and several chunks of bread, some frozen and with the peck marks of birds who had discovered them after the hatch was open; several candy wrappers; a jug of now-frozen water; and a flashlight.

Will made notes on all of it, in a hand that trembled from cold, fatigue, and emotion.

"Don't this beat all," one lawman said quietly.

Will wrote that remark in his notepad, wrote down the time of day, wrote how a somber hush had fallen over the gathering. Then he saw something that stunned him, and he knew he would have to include it in his story. He even knew what he would say, word for word:

A veteran FBI agent cried as he stood in the woods beside the frozen pit that had been the hiding place of a kidnapped boy, a pit that almost became a grave.

Will waited until he thought Graham had composed himself. Then he approached him and said quietly, "Do you have any comment, Jerry?"

To Will's surprise, the agent did. "You can say that this is one of the cruelest, rottenest things I've seen in twenty-plus years of law enforcement," Graham said. "Write that down and quote me on it."

The agent turned to walk away, stopped, looked Will in the face. "Another thing," Graham said, almost shouting. "We're going to find everyone responsible for this, and I personally will do all I can to see that they fry in the chair. One way or another."

With that, Graham stomped off through the snow. Will watched him take the Long Creek police chief aside. The two conferred for a minute or more; then Graham came back to Will. "We're trying to decide how much longer to look. It won't be daylight forever."

"Jerry, do you know who actually shot the guy?"

"A Deer County deputy, we think."

Will didn't feel like pressing him for the name just then.

"Sir, isn't it likely that the suspect lived right nearby? I mean, if he had the little boy in the ground here, he must have chosen a place with easy access. . . ."

It was Raines. Will could tell that the cop rubbed Graham the wrong way.

"As long as the dogs are still interested, sir, I think we should continue. We might be very close."

"Okay, Raines. You might be right. A while longer, then."

A small group of investigators stayed by the pit, taking measurements and pictures. The dogs led the rest of the searchers through the snowy woods. Will stayed near the rear of the group. He hoped something would happen before time got really critical for him to make first-edition deadline. Overhead, there was the sound of helicopters. Will heard the squawk of radios.

A little while later, Will heard excitement up ahead. Then he saw Graham coming back to get him. "We found a cabin, Will."

It stood in a small clearing and had been assembled partly from logs, partly from discarded building materials. The tin cans jingled as the men stooped to get under the twine strung around the structure.

The dogs sniffed intently, then growled as they strained on their leashes.

"Hold on, everybody!" Graham shouted. "We've got footprints."

Will stood on tiptoes to see over the shoulders of the deputies in front of him. Beneath the overhang of the crude roof, Will saw man-size footprints and several much smaller ones—clearly a boy's. They had been frozen in the early snow and because of the overhang and the wind direction had not been obscured by the later snowfall.

Will heard the click of camera shutters, saw Graham make some notes, saw a deputy cordon off the section with the prints.

Some yards away, at the edge of a clearing, Will saw the beginnings of a snowman. How crazy. . . .

Graham pushed the door open, peered inside, and said, "Son of a bitch. Someone's been living here, all right."

Will watched the agent step across the threshold, then kneel down and laboriously take off his boots. Then he stood up and took off his heavy jacket. "Please note for the record that I have removed my footwear prior to a preliminary search of these premises. Just so some smart-ass defense lawyer can't say later that I introduced foreign material. That last is off the record."

For several minutes, Graham was inside. As inconspicuously as he could, Will pushed his way to the front of the crowd gathered around the door. He caught a glimpse of the interior—dim light, crude wooden furniture, crammed shelves—and the odor of old wood smoke. And Will thought there was something else: a smell of dog, and of a man who lived alone.

Graham put his boots on again, said something to a couple of men near him, and stepped outside.

"Any sign of any ransom money?" Will said.

"Negative," Graham said. "But I didn't do a thorough search. We'll take this place apart."

"Are you sure the boy was held here?" Will said.

"I'm not sure of very much right now," Graham said. "But I think our strange friend lived here. There's dog food inside, and there're some blankets and some cushions near the fireplace. Some dirty dishes and food leftovers."

"Should we get a warrant before we toss the place?" It was Raines, standing off to the side.

Graham looked to the Long Creek police chief and said, "What do you think?"

"We could seal it off and wait," the chief said. "Warrant's no problem."

Graham seemed to think about that for a moment. "Let's do it that way. I think we have probable cause anyhow, but we'll leave no loopholes."

"All right," the chief said. "I want a couple of men to stay here for a while."

Off to the side, Will saw Raines put up his hand. "I'm available, Chief." Raines's face sagged in disappointment as the chief ignored him and pointed to two older cops close by.

Graham came over to Will. The agent's face was drawn. "I have to go back and give a briefing to your competitors, Will. They'll get a look at the shooting scene and the hole and the cabin. I won't give them anything you don't have."

"I know. And thanks."

But Graham had already turned and walked back to the police chief, with whom he conferred in nods and whispers. If Will got the chance, he would tell his old friend how grateful he was: If Will had had to wait with the pool reporters to see everything—or, far worse, if he had had to wait back in Long Creek with the main pack of journalists waiting to be briefed by the pool reporters—he wouldn't have been able to do much for the *Gazette*'s early edition. Now he could.

But first he had to get back to Long Creek, or at least get to a phone. Ideally, he would get a ride back to town and use the time in the car to study his notes and do a rough outline.

It was no time to be shy. Will went up to Graham and said, "Jerry, I need your help one more time."

"A ride back to town, right?"

"How'd you know?"

"They train us in press relations." Graham chuckled ruefully. "Chief, do you have a chauffeur you can spare?"

Will winced at that, but embarrassment was a luxury he couldn't afford right now.

The chief looked at Will as though he was a nuisance. "What's wrong with the guy you rode out with?"

"I didn't say there was anything wrong with him," Will heard himself say. "I'll take a ride from anyone who's willing."

"Raines? Give our journalist friend here a ride back to town. Okay?"

"Whatever you say," Raines said, scowling.

"I appreciate it," Will said. He needn't have bothered with the thanks, because Raines had already started walking.

The way back to the snowmobile was shorter than Will had expected. Long before he thought he would, Will spotted the clearing. Of course: Raines had had no need to be cautious on the walk back; he'd been able to take the most direct route.

Raines started the machine, put on his amber glasses, and motioned for Will to get on.

There was a lot less activity back at the Rod and Gun Club that had been the base of operations. Will looked for the food truck but couldn't find it.

"What's wrong, Shafer?" Raines said impatiently.

"I was hoping to get a doughnut or roll to eat in the car. I'm famished."

"You're out of luck."

Prick, Will thought.

But when they got in the car, Raines said, "Want half a roast beef sandwich?"

"God, yes."

"I got a thermos of coffee in the backseat. Extra cups in the glove compartment."

They stayed put for a few minutes as Raines warmed up the engine. Will ate and drank as the heater kicked in. He'd been even more hungry than he'd realized. "I owe you," he said.

"So buy me a beer sometime."

"You got it." It might be a chance to pick his brains about the police department.

The ride back was quick. The snow had been cleared from most of the main roads, and the salt spreaders had been out. Raines didn't say much for a while, and Will used the quiet to arrange his thoughts and his notes. High in the story, he would have to say something about the unanswered questions.

"A crazy case," Will said. "What the hell would he want with a little kid?"

Raines snorted. "The old man is rich."

"Right." But Will wondered: How would this screwball woods hermit have known that? And what about the different postmarks on the ransom note? And where was the money?

"Do you have any theories?" Will asked.

"Off the record? Who the hell knows. People who do things like this don't think and act like real people, you know."

"Why do you suppose he dug the boy up?"

"Got softhearted, maybe. Or needed the company. Or went soft in the head."

"In the head?"

"Sure. Best thing to do would have been to leave the kid there. If he didn't want to get caught."

"That's another thing," Will said. "The FBI and cops had said no more money would be delivered until there was a sure sign the boy was safe."

"So?"

"So doesn't it seem that if the kidnappers went to the trouble of digging the boy up, they would have taken his picture and mailed it in?"

Raines said nothing for a long moment, then replied, "Okay, suppose this guy in the woods was taking the kid somewhere for that very thing. To a new hideout, I mean."

Will had no answer for that, but he couldn't help thinking that the hole in the ground was about the best hiding place imaginable. As he relaxed in the warm car, he thought about the research he'd done in the *Long Creek Eagle*'s library. He thought about the two kidnappings in which the victims had been buried underground, how one of those cases had ended in rescue and the other in death. He thought about the 1950s kidnapping in the Midwest, in which a little boy had been killed and some of the ransom had disappeared. And he thought of two other cases from years before, one in central Pennsylvania, the other in Montana. Young women had been seized in the wilds by crazed men who lived in the woods and mountains. Both had been rescued.

Finally, he thought of two other kidnappings, one of a little boy in New York, the other of a youth somewhere in the South. The boy had been taken off the street, the youth dragged out of his home by a gunman as his parents watched. No ransom demand had been made in either case. Neither victim had ever been seen again.

It was true: The only "professional" kidnappers were full-time terrorists. But the amateurs were just as cold-blooded. God only knew what their motives were. And nothing was too strange or too horrible to be imagined.

All the same, when he got a chance he would corner Jerry Graham and ask him point-blank how he felt about this case. Too many things made too little sense.

Twenty-four

...

By the time they neared the outskirts of Long Creek, Will had changed his feelings about John Raines entirely. The cop apologized for having been curt—"It's just the pressure of the case, plus the bullshit of the department," Raines said— and said again that maybe he and Will could have a beer.

Will sensed an opening. "Are you really that unhappy with the department?"

"Yup. Run by political hacks and brothers of political hacks, if you get my drift."

Will did: the chief and his detective brother. "Why do you stay?"

"I don't plan to forever, believe me. That's off the record."

"Of course."

"I came to Long Creek because I wanted to get into police work. When I was first trying to break in, the state police weren't hiring because of the budget problems. So I figured, okay, I'd get a job in a small town while I waited for an opening with the state."

"And you did."

"And I did. That was a couple years ago, and I don't mind telling you it's been disillusioning. Nepotism, ticket fixing for politicians, you name it. Bastards . . ."

"I suspect that stuff goes on in most police departments." Will paused. "Did you ever think it might go beyond ticket fixing?"

"Meaning?"

"Bigger corruption."

"Such as?"

"Fixing accident reports."

Raines looked straight ahead through the amber glasses. "You've been doing some digging," he said quietly.

"A little. More than a little."

"What got you started?"

Without getting specific, Will told him he was suspicious about Fran Spicer's accident, about the drunk-driving charge and the blood test. He told him about the confrontation with Carmine Luna and finding Luna dead in his apartment.

"Yeah, I heard the scuttlebutt about that Luna guy," Raines said. "Goddamn junkie. Working for a hospital, too. And you think he framed your friend."

"Let's just say I have my strong suspicions."

"Why would he do that?"

"I was afraid you'd ask that. I don't really know. Maybe so someone else who flunked his DWI test that night wouldn't get hit with a charge." Will offered that as an opener, knowing full well that it didn't explain what had happened to Fran in the first place.

"What kind of driver was your friend?" Raines asked. "I mean, do you have any notion why he cracked his car up if he wasn't loaded?"

"No. Not yet."

"Not yet. You're not done looking, I take it."

"I don't think so." Will told Raines as matter-of-factly as he could about Spicer, how their relationship had changed over the years: first, Spicer the seasoned newsman and Will the cub reporter learning from him; later, Will the assistant city editor dealing with Spicer as an equal; later still, Will the executive editor, taking care to be respectful and solicitous toward his aging and not altogether reliable subordinate.

"And then you wind up making his funeral arrangements,"
Raines said.

"Yes."

"Sad. But was he ever DWI before?"

"Yes." Will thought back to a night in Bessemer several
years before, when Fran had clunked three parked cars and
registered .19 for blood alcohol. Will had been relieved when
the publisher, worried about the paper's being ashamed, had
ordered him not to run the story, even though holding it out
of the paper had gone against Will's ethics.

"So he might have done it again," Raines suggested.

"I don't know." Now Will told him some of what he'd
found out about Fran's stop at the liquor store, the time of
the accident, what a doctor had said about the blood-alcohol
level.

Raines seemed to digest all of it before saying, "You may
be dealing with more than just a crooked hospital technician.
You know that."

"It occurred to me."

"So watch your ass while you're around here."

"I'm doing my best."

"You seem to have the FBI on your side."

"I told you, Jerry Graham and I go way back. I think he'll
solve this kidnapping before he's through. Solve the rest of it."

"The other kidnapper?"

"Yes."

They pulled up to Will's hotel. Just before he got out, Will
said, "As long as we've been talking off the record, isn't
there something that smells about this whole hermit thing?"

"In what way?"

Will told him the thoughts he'd been turning over: The
newspaper-pasteup ransom demands, the different postmarks,
and the abduction of the boy by a pair of shotgun-toting thugs
on the highway didn't seem to fit in with a strange duck who
lived alone in the woods.

"Okay, Shafer," Raines said grudgingly. "But how did he
wind up with the boy? And if he didn't have something to hide,
why did he take a shot at that hunter who first spotted him?"

"I admit, those are good questions. Here's another:
Where's the ransom money?"

"With the other kidnapper, no doubt. Assuming there's only one more."

"Maybe. I'm assuming Jerry Graham has you guys keeping your eyes and ears open for anyone departing the area in a hurry without a good reason."

"I'm not at liberty to say."

Will dashed inside, changed into dry socks and shirt, called his office, and told the city desk that he had story material no one else had, that he would write about fifteen hundred words for the first edition (he had about two hours to do it), and that he'd polish it up in time for the second edition, which was distributed in the immediate Bessemer vicinity.

"Will," a fretting Tom Ryan said, "are you sure you can do it, or should I get together a wire story in case?"

Count to ten, Will told himself. "I'll do what I said I would, Ry, and I'll do it on time. I'm going to police headquarters now." He picked up his portable computer and dashed out the door.

As Will got back in the car, Raines said, "You look pissed off."

"Office bullshit."

"Sounds familiar. We'll have to talk some more."

"It'll be off the record."

"Your word's good enough for the FBI, so it's good enough for me."

"Thanks. I think."

"I mean, I assume Graham's been talking to you, confidential-like, about whatever hunches he has."

Will's warning light went on. "Jerry's pretty cautious, actually."

Raines just nodded. "Okay. I respect a man who keeps his confidences."

Ignoring the flattery, Will let a little time pass. Then he said, "Let's be hypothetical for a minute, as well as off the record. Okay?"

"Okay."

"Hypothetically, if there was a cop or two who were fixing accident reports, would you have any notion at all who they might be?"

"And would I find out who investigated the accident your friend was in?"

"You're way ahead of me."

"I'm not stupid, after all. Tell me, Shafer, have you asked anyone else in the department who it was?"

"Not yet."

"My advice is, don't. The reports aren't kept too carefully, if you get my drift. You wouldn't get a straight answer, anyhow. Why don't I nose around."

"I appreciate it."

"Nothing to appreciate. Because we never had this little chat."

There was pandemonium at the police station as reporters, photographers, and camera crews shouted questions at police officers and insults at one another. Several Long Creek officers tried to herd the gathering into the briefing room.

"I heard that someone who wasn't picked for the pool got to go along, anyhow!" one angry young reporter shouted.

"I know nothing about that. Talk to the chief."

"I'm going to, believe me!"

Will could barely suppress a smug smile. At the same time, the commotion embarrassed him. He recalled what a politician of yesteryear had said about reporters: "They're like children—easily fascinated by color and motion, but not to be taken seriously."

A police whistle echoed loudly in the corridor, producing a stunned silence. "Listen, folks," a policeman said. "It won't do any good to push and shout. Please go to the briefing room and wait for Chief Howe and Special Agent Graham. They'll be along shortly. We'll have coffee and doughnuts sent in to you."

"Cold and stale, probably. . . ."

Will hung around the fringes of the gathering. Then he approached the officer and said quietly, "Can you help me? I'm too old to compete with these jerks. If you can give me a place—any place—to plug in my computer and think, I'd greatly appreciate it."

The officer studied Will for a second. Like Will, he was on the wrong side of forty. "In there, behind that empty desk.

If anyone asks, I didn't give you permission. You just sat there on your own.''

"Bless you."

Will composed the top several paragraphs of his story, trying to convey the emotion without slopping it on with a paintbrush. But as he wrote, he found himself focusing again and again on the unknown.

He could hardly wait to question Jerry Graham—alone, if possible. The more Will thought about it, the less sense it made. The stunted snowman near the hermit's cabin—didn't that show that the hermit had been playing with the boy? The more Will thought, the less sure he was about anything—except that Jamie Brokaw was safe and well.

After a while, Will heard more commotion outside. Graham had returned, and the briefing was about to start. Will looked at his watch; he had time to get some answers.

He took a seat near the rear, listened to Jerry Graham review the basic facts, then sat bolt upright as Graham said, "I'll be turning the case over to Chief Howe at this point, since my presence is no longer needed now that the victim has been recovered safely."

Without thinking, Will stood up. "Agent Graham, what about all the loose ends here? The other kidnapper, the overall conspiracy. . . . How can you say you're done here?"

Graham's face was tight and hard. Then he flashed his teeth and said, "I appreciate your pointers on how I should do my job." That brought snickers at Will's expense. "The FBI is called in on cases like this when a kidnapping victim is missing for more than a day. Our job is to secure the victim's safe return. This we have done. And since it's clear that the victim was not taken across state lines, there really is no need for the FBI to be here any longer."

"But—?"

"Of course," Graham went on, "we'll be happy to assist the Long Creek and Hill County authorities if they call on us in their pursuit of suspects besides the one, as-yet-unidentified, white male. Thank you, ladies and gentlemen. It's been nice working with you."

Graham smiled, gave a half wave, and exited. Will wondered whether he was the only one in the room who was puzzled. More than that: He was disappointed in his old friend.

For a few minutes, Will listened to the police chief parry questions. Satisfied that he had all the essentials, Will left the room through a back door. He didn't have much time to spare now, but there was something he had to do.

The door to Graham's office was open. "Will! Don't you have a paper to write for?"

"In a minute. What the hell's going on?"

"I don't follow."

"Bullshit. Come on, Jerry. I played your game. . . ."

"It was no game."

"You know what I mean, damn it. I helped you. Or I tried to. Be straight with me."

"What do you want to know?"

"Why are you bugging out?"

Graham leaned into the hall, looked both ways, and closed the door. "I've been called off the case. That's off the record."

"It is only if I agree. By whom?"

The nerves in Graham's face did a dance. "Can't say."

"Washington?"

Graham seemed about to say something, then backed off.

"Someone around here?"

"I can't, Will. I won't. People with more clout than I. That's all I'll say. Can we just leave it?"

"Maybe I'll call FBI headquarters."

"Don't."

"Just to rattle the cage, if nothing else. It's a stupid decision."

"Not mine to make, Will. Or yours." Graham's face was tired and sad. More than that: He looked old.

Will was tired of arguing, and he was getting short on time. "I have to go file my story, Jerry. I guess I should thank you for your help." Will did owe his old friend.

"One last time I'll trust you, Will. My remark to that reporter about his 'indecent lack of compassion' cost me with my superiors. That and the breakdown in surveillance on the ransom drop. That's between us. Please."

"Ah, Jerry. Go public with that crap, for God's sake. Get the press on your side. Hell, you already have me on your side."

"I can't, Will. I wish I could. Sorry we're not going to get a chance to visit more. I'm out of here."

"Maybe next time."

"For sure. My best to Karen."

Will couldn't remember Graham's wife's name. He shook hands numbly with him, went back to the briefing room, and saw that reporters were jostling to get at the telephones. Will knew he had all the facts he needed—or at least all he would get—and he decided to go back to the hotel to write.

He called Bessemer to soothe the nervous editors. Then, in an act of sheer willpower that he was able to bring off simply because he had to, he suppressed the disappointment he had felt over Graham. Instead, he relived the visceral thrill of the pursuit, the joy of Jamie Brokaw's recovery. Those were the emotions he needed to write his story the way he wanted it. He didn't worry much about the order of events: Organization had always been one of his strengths.

When he was done, he pressed the button to transmit by phone to Bessemer. After a short while, the phone rang. "Just a few questions for now, Will."

"For now?"

"Well, you'll be able to polish a bit for second edition, right?"

"Right. Right." He had forgotten the routine. God, he hoped his energy would hold out.

As the editors in Bessemer went over his story, Will followed on the electronic copy in his computer. Will agreed, mostly, with the changes that were suggested, and he didn't feel like arguing.

"Terrific job, Will."

"Thanks."

He made the changes for second edition, called the hospital to be sure the hermit was still alive, gave the hospital's phone number to the editors in Bessemer and suggested that the hospital be called just before the final deadline.

Belatedly, Will realized that he'd had no dinner other than the half sandwich and coffee Raines had given him. No matter. All he wanted to do was get into bed and close his eyes.

Twenty-five

...

The mood at police headquarters the next morning was quiet and sullen. A notice on the bulletin board said there would be a briefing in about forty-five minutes. Around him, Will heard grumbling. As he downed the coffee and toast he'd grabbed at the diner, he wondered whether any of the grumbling was out of envy for him. He hoped so.

Pretending to be bored, he picked up snippets of talk.

"Guy was still alive when I checked the hospital ten minutes ago, but it's touch and go . . . ."

"Old man's gotta be worth, what, five million? Ten? Cable TV is a gold mine. . . ."

"Would he want to live around here if he's that rich?"

"Hey, man, with money like that, you can live where you want 'cuz you can buy what you want."

Will didn't like the tone of the conversation: too much cynicism, too little compassion from reporters who were too young. It didn't surprise him that most of the reporters were much younger than he was. A lot of papers in small and medium-sized cities liked to keep their staffs young: low payroll, low benefits. Will understood that kind of bottom-line philosophy—had practiced it, in fact, when the publisher decided it was time to economize.

With a little guilt, he realized that if Fran were covering this story, he'd be regarded as an old hack by some of the reporters here. Would he have fallen off the wagon?

". . . including the best shrinks in the world to straighten out the kid's head."

What? Will had heard something that put an idea into his head.

Affecting his best hangdog manner to inspire sympathy, he found the same cop who'd helped him before and once again got permission to use the phone at an out-of-the-way desk.

He dialed the hospital and asked for Heather Casey. "Can you talk for a moment?"

"Hi. Sure, for a minute." She sounded rushed.

"I won't quote you and I won't get you in trouble. Promise."

"How can I help?"

"I heard that the guy from the woods is still with us, but that he might not be for long. Can you verify?"

"That's true. He's very critical. Just a second, Will . . . ." He heard her talking to someone else. ". . . intensive care now; they just wheeled her . . . . Okay, I'm back. Sorry."

"He's under heavy guard, I suppose."

"Yes."

"And the boy."

"He may go home later today. His father is pushing for that, and there seems to be no reason not to discharge him. That's not from me. Okay?"

"The child is all right, then?"

"I haven't seen him myself, but I've heard he is. Children can be very resilient." Her voice sounded a little less rushed. "I know they're trying to keep their questioning as gentle as possible—the investigators."

Keep her talking, he thought. "My wife says kids are amazingly resilient. Did I tell you she does some work with troubled teenagers?" He felt a flash of guilt for talking about his wife—using her, in a sense—with Casey. "So the boy is all right psychologically?"

"That really isn't my area of expertise. But I think so."

Now Will sensed that she wanted to say something. "What is it?"

"I've been thinking about that terrible business with Carmine."

"What about it?"

"It seems odd to me, his dying like that. He had a habit, sure, but . . ."

"But what? Addicts die all the time, unfortunately."

"Granted. But he'd taken a very large dose. If he was used to taking that much, it's hard to imagine his being able to hold down a job. Or do anything except shoot up and scrounge for money."

"Well, maybe he took more than he was used to."

"A lot more, maybe. Which made me wonder."

"Whether someone forcibly gave him a superjolt."

"Yes. It would make sense, wouldn't it? If someone wanted to get rid of him, I mean. This is just me talking. I wouldn't say this to anyone else."

"I appreciate your trust."

"We all have to be so tight-assed and careful around here. Mr. Brokaw is a very powerful man. He's quite rich, he's given money to the hospital, and he's sat on the hospital board. Everyone around here is so . . ."

"Why do you suppose the father is pushing for the boy's release?" A true shot in the dark.

"Why, to have his little boy with him, I'm sure. He's very protective."

"But I thought the mother had custody."

"She's—I hear that she's under heavy medication at home right now. So for the time being, the boy would go with the father."

"Was Richard Brokaw's divorce bitter? Was there a nasty custody fight?"

"I really have to go."

"I appreciate your time."

"What surprised me most—not just me, some of the other

nurses, too—is that the boy, well, he's been asking about the man in the woods. Asking if he can see Mr. Woody, as he calls him. Asking about the dog and whether he can see it again.''

''Asking if he could see the man in the woods . . . does that tell you anything?''

''It makes me wonder. I just don't know.''

''It makes you wonder how bad the guy is. Maybe even whether . . .''

''Of course, that may not mean anything. The child said he was given a furry bear to play with, by the mean men, not the strange one from the woods.''

''Do you have any idea who he is?''

''No. Listen, I wish I could take longer, but I have to go. Take care.'' And she hung up.

Will sat still for a long moment, trying to quiet his mind. Too many things at once: the kidnapping and all the questions that hadn't been answered, and Fran Spicer's death. Ah, Fran. Look at the trouble you're causing me, old friend.

A furry bear. It was a little tidbit he could use in his story, the kind of fact the others wouldn't have. But it might get Casey in trouble. Then I won't use it. I won't even tell the editors. No need for them to strain their intellects . . . .

''Shafer?''

Startled, Will looked up and saw Raines standing by the desk.

''You sly dog, Shafer. Getting your own private desk here.''

''Someone took pity on me.''

''Still want to have a chat?''

''Definitely.''

''Let's have a beer this afternoon.''

After arranging to meet Raines at the same tavern he and Jerry Graham had been to, Will went to the press briefing. He was thankful that it was anticlimactic, and that other reporters asked the big questions, for which there were no answers. The wounded suspect hadn't been identified; the hunt for other suspects was on; the boy was doing fine; and obviously the ransom money was still missing. And no, there was still no explanation how the kidnappers had managed to get away safely with the cash despite the surveillance.

Will called his office, said he'd have a follow-up story that would have as many questions as answers.

No, Will said; there seemed to be no chance for pictures of the boy, and no chance that he would be able to talk to him.

"In that case, Will, maybe you should head home tomorrow."

He had no reason to disagree, yet he felt a sense of disappointment. He seemed to be against a stone wall on Fran Spicer's death. But maybe he could get something from Raines.

Will saw him at a corner table. Raines was wearing khaki pants and a green flannel outdoor shirt.

"I almost didn't recognize you out of uniform," Will said.

"This'll be my uniform when I leave this hole. Soon, I hope."

"You have plans?" Will signaled for two beers.

"Nothing definite," Raines said. "Except to get out of Long Creek. Go out west, maybe."

"I'm glad we got a chance to talk. I'm going back to Bessemer tomorrow." Raines looked surprised, so Will went on. "The kidnapping story is winding down, so it doesn't pay to have me here. And my paper is watching the bottom line. I've been trying to eat cheap. But this beer is on the *Gazette*."

"Good. So you don't really have any time left to pursue that stuff about your friend."

"No. And maybe there's nothing there. Fran was an alcoholic, after all. But damn it, it doesn't add up." He paused.

"What you say stays at this table," Raines said quietly.

"Ditto." So Will went over it again, step by step: the timing of Fran's stop at the liquor store and the accident, what the doctor had said regarding the blood-alcohol level in Fran's system, what Heather Casey had said about Fran's being drenched with beer.

"So," Raines said. "But suppose, just suppose the liquor

store owner and the lady in the accident are each a few minutes off on what happened when. Maybe there was time enough for him to get drunk. One body doesn't always absorb alcohol the same way as another.''

Will had no answer to that. Then he wondered whether to tell Raines all that he knew of Fran's drinking history and his fondness for schnapps. He decided not to and said instead, "Isn't it a strange coincidence what happened to Carmine Luna?"

Raines thought that over. "He was a junkie, remember. You saw how he lived. He was a needle freak waiting to die."

"Maybe. But he was uneasy when I talked to him. Hostile, even."

"At the hospital?"

"Yes."

"What'd he say?"

"Nothing much. But he was worried."

Raines waited a long time before speaking. "How many people have you told about what you suspect?"

"Just—" Will stopped himself as he was about to mention Casey; she wouldn't want her name used. "Just my old FBI friend. He's heard some of it. And he's gone."

"So he is. Tell you what. Let me nose around and see what I can turn up. Maybe I can find out about the accident investigation. Discreetly."

"I'd owe you."

"No problem. But you're leaving tomorrow. I don't know if I can do anything by then."

"I'd come back, if I had to. Or hire someone."

"You might not have to hire anyone if you had me looking. Some of the things that happen in that department make me sick to my stomach, Shafer."

Sooner than he wanted, because he liked Raines's company, Will had to leave. He didn't want to wait until the last minute to write; he'd had enough deadline pressure for a while.

Will had walked to the tavern. It was dark out and getting colder, and he gladly accepted Raines's offer of a ride.

"So your FBI friend was no help," Raines said as he stopped in front of the hotel.

"No. But what troubles me just as much is that he left town with all those loose ends. I didn't think he . . ." Will almost said he didn't think Graham was the kind to buckle to outside pressure.

Raines snorted. "The FBI is a great big public relations creation, if you ask me. I thought of joining them once. Then I heard what that outfit is really like."

Will didn't feel much like defending Jerry Graham, so he said nothing.

"I'll tell you this, Shafer. A lot of criminal cases—maybe most—don't end as neatly as they do in the movies. There're always going to be questions about this one."

"Especially if it's up to the locals to find the answers." Will was a little surprised how the beer had loosened his tongue.

"The kid's back, Shafer. That's the important thing."

Will shook hands with Raines and wished him well, in case he didn't see him before he left for Bessemer.

Twenty-six

■ ■ ■

From the top of the hill, he could see the cabin burning. The orange flames and swirling gray smoke were as lovely as flowers against the snow.

Where was Jo? Where was the dog? He started to draw a deep breath so he could call out to them, but his chest hurt too much. Why was that?

Suddenly, he knew why. He was lying perfectly still, on his back. It was cold beneath him, cold as snow. He remembered now: He was lying on the snow. He had to get up, had to grab the boy and run for the cabin.

No, that wasn't right. He was mixing things up. The cabin on fire, and Jo—that had happened a long time ago. Hadn't it? Now he was lying on his back in the snow, because the bullet had spun him around and knocked him down. If he opened his eyes, he would see the sky. But he couldn't open his eyes.

The creek. He could hear the creek. He held his breath to hear the water rushing over the rocks.

No. He was hearing something else. The hum of a machine, a thing that went *beep, beep, beep*. . . .

It was hard to keep things straight. It was hard to tell what was real and happening right now.

That was the way with dreams; you could never be sure what was real until you woke up.

He went round and round, from the hill to the creek back to the . . . bed? Bed.

It was when he knew he was in the bed that the pain was the worst. He sensed that the bed was real, too, but as he went round and round, from hill to creek to bed, he wanted more and more just to let go and spin free. Spin free, so he could be on the hill. He wanted to go back there, back then.

If he let himself go, he could stand on the hill again (he knew he had been there before), and this time he would see Jo and the dog standing nearby, safe. He and Jo could build another cabin, fill it with laughter and the smells of bread and wood smoke.

Round and round he went, getting dizzy. It hurt to hold on to the bed. He sensed that if he let go, he could not come back. But it hurt to hold on. Why not let go?

Round and round. There was the hill again, pure white in the snow. Down there, happy and safe, was Jo. She was smiling and waving to him. The dog was next to her. They could build again, be together again.

He knew where he wanted to be. He let go.

Will was almost done writing his story; in fact, he had done everything but the beginning.

He didn't know quite how to start. He hated stories that began, "Investigators intensified their search today. . . ." Openings like that meant there wasn't much new. Well, there wasn't.

He was about to make a last-minute call to police headquarters when the phone rang.

"Will? Don't say my name over the telephone." It was Heather Casey.

"Hello."

"Do you have a few minutes? I have something to tell you."

"I'm a little pressed, but for you I have time."

"The man died, Will. The man from the woods died."

"Oh. I'm sorry." What a thing for me to say, he thought. But he was.

"The powers that be are preparing a statement right now. Officially, the man is still unidentified."

"Yes?"

"But I can tell you who he is. Or might be."

Will listened, spellbound, as she gave her account.

"Lord," he said when she was done. "And nobody knows yet?"

"Just you. Not even the *Long Creek Eagle* is supposed to know until tomorrow, at the earliest. Even if the *Eagle* did know, it would probably hold off if the right people asked them."

Damn, Will thought.

"You can see why everyone's so nervous," she went on. "It's still a source of embarrassment to the police department, that long-ago thing."

"I'll bet. But why is the hospital being so cautious?"

"Because the hospital wants to stay on city hall's good side for any number of reasons, and city hall and the police department go hand in hand sometimes. So the hospital is giving the police brass extra time. . . ."

"To try to put the right spin on things. Or maybe they hope to keep it quiet until a lot more reporters have gone home. Keep the secret even if they do have to announce the guy's death."

"Yes. You understand such things."

"Oh, yes indeed." Will thought fast. "How many people at the hospital know?"

"Only a very few. Myself and a couple of other nurses who have been here for a while. Is this useful to you?"

"God, yes." Will would have someone in the *Gazette*'s morgue get out the clippings and microfilm from a long time ago. He didn't have much time to verify what he thought he remembered.

In any event, he had enough to go on. The cops thought they knew who the man was. Will would have the story in his paper a full half day before any other paper or TV station reached its main audience. It was a major exclusive.

Will deliberately dampened his exhilaration. He had a lot to do before he could celebrate. "Look, I'm going to need to get a comment from the police chief."

"You won't use my name?"

"No, I promise. If you're not the only nurse who knows, you'll be safe." At least I think she will, he thought. "I'm going to wait until the last possible minute. Then I'll call him."

Will sensed from the silence that Casey didn't understand, so he went on. "See, I absolutely need to give the chief a chance to comment. But by waiting until the last minute to call him, I pretty much guarantee that I beat everyone else on the story. At least I beat the other papers; the TV people can always get on the air faster than I get into print, if they want to. And my guess is that the chief won't be eager to blab about this to many people tonight."

"I see."

"So the only thing being announced at this moment is that the man is dead? That's all?"

"Yes."

"Wonderful." Then Will thought of something else; he asked her to hold while he checked the phone book. Just as he figured. Well, sometimes a newsman had to impose on people. "The chief's home number isn't listed. Do you think you could get it for me, in case he's not hanging around the station?"

"Oh. I know it would be on the administrator's Rolodex. Yes, I'll get it and call you back."

"You're wonderful."

He wondered whether he was shamelessly using Heather Casey. But he had no time to worry about anyone's feelings, including his own. He called his office to brief the editors. Tom Ryan was in charge.

"Ry? Here's what I have. Right now, it's exclusive, and I expect it to stay that way." Speaking as soothingly as he could, Will summarized the story and assured Ryan that he would have his facts nailed down, that the story wouldn't libel anyone, and that if anyone lost his job over it, it would be Will Shafer.

"Ah, this isn't official, then?" Ryan said.

Will could almost hear Ryan sweating. "No, not official. But I have it, and it's right." He took a deep breath, went on as calmly as he could. "If I were back in the office and a reporter I trusted came up with this story, it would be my judgment to use it, Ry. It'll be my ass if it's wrong. But it isn't.''

"Um, should we bring Mr. Glanford in on this?"

"No, God . . . no. Don't bother the publisher. My story will be right, and that's that. I know what the hell I'm doing, and I've been on your end, and the paper sent me to this place to cover this story. . . .'' I was also sent to clean up the mess about Fran that you helped to create, Will thought.

"Okay, Will. It's your call, I guess."

"Trust me, Ry."

Will hung up, cursed to himself. No wonder the reporters complained about Ryan's spine of jelly.

The phone rang.

"Here's the chief's number, Will."

Will wrote it down. "I owe you a drink."

"You're welcome. I have to say good-bye now."

Then she was gone, and it occurred to Will that he might be running out of chances to see her. Was that for the best? Or would the *Gazette* want him to stay in Long Creek another day in view of the story he was about to write?

He began to write (Please, God, don't let the computer break down now), swiftly and surely at first, then with a little hesitation as he came to parts that were trickier on attribution. He would wait until the last possible minute to talk to the police chief.

And if he couldn't reach him?

Then I guess the story can't run, Will said to himself.

If one of your reporters had a story like this and it didn't have a comment from the police chief, would you let it get in the paper?

No.

Then pray that the police chief answers the phone.

"Chief? It's Will Shafer from the *Bessemer Gazette*. Sorry to bother you at home. Look, I know that the kidnapping suspect just died. I want to give you a chance to comment on something. . . .''

The chief swore, sputtered about Will's having gotten his home phone number, made a few vaguely threatening remarks, then went dead quiet as Will delivered his questions. "I promise you a fair shake, Chief."

The chief gave him what he needed and hung up. For a moment, Will wondered, Are the Long Creek cops going to hassle me before I get out of town?

Will plugged in the hole in his story, read it over quickly, and transmitted it to his office. Then he held his breath.

After a while, the phone rang. Tom Ryan had a few questions, and not altogether stupid ones.

"Will, I didn't call the publisher."

"Good, Ry. You won't regret it. We won't."

"Like you say, Will. It's your call. . . ."

It was a long time before Will got to sleep. The death of the hermit made him sad in a way he couldn't define. And there were still too many questions about the kidnapping—questions his old friend from the FBI had not faced, to Will's disappointment.

But overriding the other feelings was elation. He couldn't wait until morning, when the *Bessemer Gazette* would have a story no one else had. Will imagined the looks on the faces of his competitors. He hoped Heather Casey would be proud of him.

When he finally did fall asleep, he was smiling.

BROKAW KIDNAPPING SUSPECT DIES;
TENTATIVE I.D. IS ESTABLISHED

By Will Shafer
Special to the *Bessemer Gazette*

LONG CREEK—The strange, scarred man who was a suspect in the kidnapping of Jamie Brokaw died here last night, shortly before the *Gazette* learned exclusively that the authorities have tentatively identified him as a former member of a "hippie" colony who was badly burned in a 1970 police raid.

The suspect died in Long Creek Regional Hospital of a wound suffered in a shoot-out with lawmen who had cornered him in a remote area of forest near the border of Hill and Deer counties, not far from Pennsylvania. He had never regained consciousness.

The *Gazette* has learned that investigators believe

the man was Steven Sewell, and that the mysterious burn scars on his face were suffered in a controversial 1970 raid by Long Creek police on the "hippie" colony in the woods a half mile outside of Long Creek.

Long Creek Police Chief Robert Howe, reached at his home last night, would neither confirm nor deny that the bizarre woods hermit had been identified. "We may have an announcement soon," he said before cutting short a telephone conversation.

The man tentatively identified as Sewell, believed to have been in his early to mid-forties, is thought to have been burned critically when flames consumed several shacks and tents at the colony the night of May 7, 1970, just three days after Ohio National Guardsmen fired on students at Kent State University.

The fires, the cause of which was never established conclusively, killed three inhabitants of the colony, including a young woman who was living with Sewell. The woman, Jo Stryker, perished in the flames, despite repeated efforts by Sewell and others to save her. She was later found to have been pregnant.

The raid, carried out after repeated complaints from conservative residents of Hill County about the freewheeling lifestyle of the colony's members, prompted a special state investigation. No police officers were ever indicted, although a special grand jury criticized "the conduct of a few officers who were not adequately supervised."

The police who carried out the raid defended it as a legitimate attempt to root out drug traffickers and users. Members of the colony did not dispute that there was widespread drug use—some were boastful of their marijuana-growing ability—but they insisted that some raiders deliberately torched their tents and shacks.

Autopsies confirmed that the three who were killed in the raid had been using drugs a short time before. Several of the injured were also believed to have been using drugs. At the time, police officials linked the inability of some shack and tent residents to escape the flames to drug-induced lethargy.

Despite the lack of indictments against police officers, the raid was a major embarrassment to the Long Creek police and the Hill County Sheriff's Department, which also took part in the operation.

There were reports last night, from sources familiar with events of the still-unfolding kidnapping case, that hospital officials were acquiescing to the police department in delaying an announcement of the tentative identification of the suspect. The police are said to believe that a delay of even a day would mean less intensive publicity. Indeed, the small army of print and electronic journalists that descended on this normally quiet town has already begun to thin.

Identification of the suspect would still leave several major questions unanswered, notably the whereabouts of the ransom money and the other kidnapper or kidnappers. Nor would identification of the suspect who died last night begin to explain his supposed role in the abduction and burial of Jamie Brokaw and the elaborate ransom demands.

Special Agent Gerald Graham of the FBI had been working closely on the case, but he left Long Creek shortly after the victim was recovered. He explained his somewhat puzzling departure by saying that his mission was essentially accomplished with the recovery of the missing boy.

The tentative identification of the suspect as Steven Sewell reportedly came about because several longtime aides at Long Creek Hospital who recalled treating the injured from the 1970 raid took note of his disfiguring facial burn scars.

It was not known why the man believed to be Sewell chose to live in isolation in a remote forest area with only a dog for company. But he did it without attracting much attention, perhaps partly because of a sad fact of life in rural Hill and Deer counties, where the sight of poorly dressed men, women, and children is commonplace. Poverty is as old as the hills there, and as enduring.

Twenty-seven

▪▪▪

Will tried not to smirk as he walked into the briefing room. Reporters were filing in, taking their seats in the folding metal chairs. Some ignored him, or pretended to. A couple glanced at him and looked away quickly. One came up, poked him playfully in the ribs, and said, "Congrats."

Will smiled and said thanks.

The chief came in, and the room went quiet. Frowning, the chief read a statement (hastily prepared after the telephone interview of the night before, Will was sure), which said that his department was still trying to establish the identity of the suspect, who had died the previous night.

"Contrary to published reports, which are premature, we have not ascertained the subject's identity," the chief said woodenly. "At this time, I can confirm that we are trying to determine if the subject was one Steven Sewell. We are still trying to establish that fact."

"Chief, will you be able to make the I.D. through computerized fingerprint records, assuming that the guy might have had an arrest record for drugs?"

"Maybe, maybe not," the chief said. "The subject had some burn scars on his hands."

"Chief, you are not saying that the published report was incorrect, are you?" asked a reporter in the front row.

"Not at this time," the chief said.

Will allowed himself to feel smug. His story had been on target. No, a bull's-eye. Hands down. Damn, he thought, this is more fun than watching over an office and tiptoeing around the publisher all the time.

The rest of the briefing was short and routine. There were no other surprises, no more answers to the nagging riddles.

So he probably would go home tomorrow. He was looking forward to that, yet he was sad, too. Covering a big story could be . . . fun. There was no better word for it. It was why he had gone into the newspaper business.

Will would do some more reporting and writing—on his own, if need be. This time, he meant it.

He had time to spare before filing his story. Energy to spare, too. There was something he wanted to check into, just for the hell of it.

He found the same editor he had seen before at the *Long Creek Eagle*. The editor sportingly congratulated Will on his exclusive story and said sure, no problem, he could have access again to the *Eagle*'s clips and microfilm.

There was no way Will could keep secret what—rather, whom—he was interested in. Although he had become somewhat familiar with the *Eagle*'s information-storage system on his last visit, he would still need help. The morgue clerk, a middle-aged man with a limp, reacted courteously enough, but Will thought he saw a flicker of doubt on his face as Will asked him for the clips on Richard Brokaw.

But the clerk retrieved the clips, arranged more or less in order in an inch-thick manila envelope, and Will began to sift through them. They told the story of a young man from Hill County who succeeded at just about everything he tried: class president and football star in high school, football star and engineering major at Cornell, cable-television entrepreneur back home in Long Creek.

Clearly, Richard Brokaw had never meant to be limited by

the isolation and decay of his hometown. In fact, he had used that very isolation to make himself wealthy, by bringing cable television into the region. Apparently, a lot of people who couldn't afford decent clothes or dental work could afford cable.

But there was something missing from the story of Richard Brokaw's life, and Will wandered out to the tiny newsroom to ask about it.

"Tell me," Will said to the same helpful editor, "where are all the clippings on Richard Brokaw's divorce?"

The editor smiled sheepishly. "There aren't any."

Will was surprised: a bitter divorce involving a prominent local citizen, and no coverage? "No clips at all?" Will said. "Not even when the divorce decree was handed down?"

The editor continued to smile. "Richard Brokaw is a very big man around here. I mean *very*. He didn't want his divorce covered, so it wasn't."

Of course. Will had been momentarily naïve. If there was anything he was familiar with, it was the care and feeding of sacred cows—and how often they succeeded in keeping things out of the paper.

Will thanked the editor for his help and left.

He didn't know what he was looking for—nothing important, probably—but having struck out at the *Long Creek Eagle* made him all the more determined. When he had first driven into Long Creek, he had noted the location of the county courthouse. That was his next stop.

The courthouse had been built in the same era as the Long Creek Hospital. The inside smelled of old marble, wood, and cigar smoke. After a couple of bum steers, he found the right office—really, a corner of a corner of an office.

He waited at an ancient wooden desk for a minute or more until an old man appeared from a warren of filing shelves. He was short, froglike, with white hair and skin. Will wondered whether he ever got any sunshine.

The man looked at Will through glasses as thick as storm windows and said, "Help you?"

"I understand this is where divorce decrees are filed."

"Yep."

"I'd like to see the paperwork in the case of *Brokaw, Richard* versus *Celeste*."

"Nope."

"Excuse me?"

"I said nope."

"It's public record, isn't it?"

"Yep."

"Then I demand to see it."

"Nope."

Will felt his head spinning. This is like Alice in Wonderland, he thought. "Let me get this straight. You agree that it's public record, but you won't let me see it."

"Mister, you're just a stranger standing in front of me. You got no control over what happens in this courthouse. Now, Richard Brokaw has a lot of say in who gets elected county commissioner. . . ."

"And who around here gets to keep their jobs."

"You got it. That's why you don't get to see them divorce papers."

Will started to say something about filing a freedom-of-information suit, or getting a court order (a court order! He was standing powerless in the courthouse, where he was a total stranger!), then thought the better of it.

Ears burning with anger and humiliation, he turned and walked away without saying anything. From now on, he'd have to be more understanding when his reporters couldn't get information. He'd just had a stinging reminder: whether something was public record or not, you couldn't get it—when you wanted it, at least—unless someone gave it to you.

He stopped again at the police station to see whether there was anything new (there wasn't), then decided to stop at the same diner where he and Casey had gone. That reminded him: He had to say good-bye to Casey. He didn't know whether he was sad or relieved, or both.

He ordered coffee and chili, which went well with the cold, gray midday. Still smarting over being defeated by Richard Brokaw—that was how he thought of it—he wondered whether his pride was getting in the way of his judgment. Did the details of Richard Brokaw's divorce really matter if they had nothing to do with the kidnapping?

Okay, Will thought. Suppose, just suppose, Brokaw arranged to have his own kid snatched. My God, could that be? But Brokaw had looked so heartbroken at the press conference. Sure, and he could have made his eyes red by chopping onions. But why kidnap his own son?

Will left a generous tip, complimented the cook for his four-alarm chili, and headed out into the cold. Earlier, he had heard something that stuck with him. Now what the hell was it? He has the best shrinks in the world to straighten out the kid's head.

A reporter had said that about Brokaw. It was true. He could hire a lot of shrinks, get them to straighten out his traumatized son, maybe fix it so the boy wanted his father all the time. . . .

Will, Will. Give it up. That's too fantastic. Isn't it? Is it? So what's the big secret about the Brokaw divorce? And how does that forest freak fit into it? Or maybe he was never supposed to fit into it at all. . . .

He was still wondering when he pulled into the hotel's tiny parking lot. As he got out of his car, a bigger car pulled in right alongside his.

Two men got out and confronted him.

"You're Will Shafer?" one said.

"That's right." Cops, Will thought. I have to keep my head. Can't give them a chance to use their authority. Something familiar about one of them. Had Will seen him at the police station? He wasn't sure.

Twenty-eight

■ ■ ■

"**M**r. Brokaw would very much like to see you. Right away."

Will was flabbergasted. "Sure. Should I follow you?"

"We'll take you and bring you back."

A rear door was held open, and Will settled into the back of a Lincoln Continental. Soon, the car was in one of the few sections of Long Creek that didn't look shabby. The driver turned into a driveway that led to a low gray-modern structure with an edifice as much glass as stone. The car kept going, all the way to the rear, where it made a ninety-degree turn, then another, and proceeded down a short ramp. At the bottom, a metal door rolled open automatically, and the car entered the bay.

"Welcome to the home of Twin Counties Cablevision, Mr. Shafer." It was Richard Brokaw, standing next to the car in a thousand-dollar gray suit and looking totally in charge despite the lines of fatigue and worry that creased his face. "Tony, you'll take Mr. Shafer back when he's ready."

"Yes, sir."

Now, from the newspaper pictures, Will recognized the smaller man as Tony, the chauffeur who had been driving Jamie Brokaw home the night of the kidnapping.

"Hello," Will said, shaking hands with Brokaw and trying not to betray his intense curiosity: What did the guy want?

Brokaw smiled ever so slightly. "Please, Mr. Shafer. Won't you come with me? Thanks, guys."

Will followed Brokaw through a metal door and into a long carpeted corridor. Brokaw's shoulders were wide, and he moved like an athlete. Which he was, Will recalled.

Brokaw stopped at a wood-panel door, which he opened with a key. He gestured for Will to enter first.

The room had a giant desk with an easy chair behind it, a sofa and table along one wall, and several television sets with videocassette recorders. A window behind the desk faced onto the road.

Brokaw took off his coat, draped it over the easy chair, and invited Will to sit on the sofa. Then he reached into a bottom desk drawer and took out a bottle and two glasses.

"I have ice if you prefer," Brokaw said. "But I suggest you drink it straight." He poured into both glasses. "Glenlivet, Mr. Shafer. In my opinion, there is no better single-malt scotch. Do you agree?"

"On my salary, I wouldn't know."

Brokaw smiled and paused. "My prayers were answered when my son was returned to me. Your reporting has consistently been a step out in front of everyone else's." Brokaw saluted with his glass and sipped.

Will drank. Brokaw was right: Will had never tasted better scotch.

"But what's your interest in my divorce, Mr. Shafer? Why are my personal troubles any concern of yours or your readers?"

Of course, Will thought. "How did you know I was checking?"

Brokaw smiled as if to say, Aw, come on. Then the smile vanished. "Small town, Mr. Shafer. As you've no doubt noticed. I know your publisher. I could call Lyle Glanford right now."

Will knew Brokaw was serious. He also knew there was

only one way to handle a threat like that, so he said, "Do it. It's your phone."

Brokaw waved off the challenge. "So what if I keep something out of your paper by calling Lyle. That wouldn't tell me what's in your head."

For a moment, Will didn't know how he felt about this rich, arrogant man who didn't mind throwing his weight around, this powerful man who had seemed, *seemed* to have suffered terribly when his child was stolen.

Will felt at a terrible disadvantage. He was on Brokaw's turf, and drinking his scotch. Finally, Will said, "I wanted to know as much as I could about you. There are a lot of questions about the kidnapping that are still hanging in the air. I'd heard that your divorce was bitter. That caused me to wonder . . ."

Brokaw's eyes flashed in sudden comprehension. "You thought I might have . . . Jesus Christ!" He drained his glass and set it on the table.

"I hadn't come to any conclusions," Will said. "I mean . . ."

Brokaw shook his head in disgust. "Do you believe I could have done such a thing?" Brokaw's face was unchanged, but there was no hiding the pain in his eyes.

"Not now, I don't. I hadn't met you before. I'm sorry."

"Sorry," Brokaw repeated. "Sorry. That word works sometimes. Other times . . . There are things I can't undo, things I wish I hadn't . . ." He shook his head. "My son is back. I thought that was all I wanted in the world. But being human, I want more still. To have things the way they were."

Will finished his drink. "Your divorce, your personal troubles are your business, and they'll remain so. You don't have to call Lyle Glanford. I'm sorry." He stood to leave.

"I'll buzz Tony."

"Is your son all right? I'm not asking as a newsman."

"He is, thank you. A wonderful boy. Making wonderful progress." Brokaw seemed to want to say more.

"Best scotch I ever had," Will said to mark time.

"The divorce papers aren't that interesting, you know. They contain allegations that I fooled around. And I'm ashamed to say . . ."

"It's not my business."

"I travel a lot. I've always felt at ease around women. Sometimes it seemed inevitable. Have you ever been tempted?"

Will felt his face warm. He thought of Heather Casey, and nodded.

"I've promised her I'll stop. I'm going to try very hard."

"Good luck. On everything, I mean."

"And to you."

On the way back to the hotel, Will said nothing to Tony. Will knew he might be passing up a great story opportunity, if Tony would say anything at all about the night of the kidnapping, but he didn't feel like trying.

He wrote a simple, straightforward story, patting himself on the back only slightly when he referred to the chief's grudging near confirmation of the kidnapping suspect's identity. He called his wife and told her to expect him the following night. He told her only a little about his meeting with Brokaw. She thought Will sounded cold, and said so. He apologized, said he was just tired. That was a lie.

As he lay in bed, he thought of his early suspicions about Brokaw. He thought about Heather Casey, how he had used her to get information, how he was attracted to her. He thought of the proverb about no pillow being as soft as a clean conscience.

He slept fitfully.

Twenty-nine

...

In the morning, Will called Heather Casey. "I'm out of here in a little while. I wanted to thank you for everything, wish you well, and . . ." And what?

"As they say, Will, it's been real. Good luck to you, too."

He wanted to say more. No, not just say more; he wanted to be with her and . . .

"So it's home to Bessemer," she went on. "Do you think you'll get back this way soon?"

"No telling." And what if he did? The spell might be broken.

"Well, then. I hope things go well for you, newspaperwise. Am I saying that right? Newspaperwise?"

"You're saying it just fine."

"I'll keep my ears open. That man from the woods, I mean. And everything else."

"Good. Thanks." His words, his voice sounded wooden to him. He would not have this chance again, the chance . . .

"Drive carefully."

"I will." The chance to say . . .

"Bye, then."

"So long." The chance to say that he thought of her as a special woman, a lovely woman, and that any man who—
Click.

And the chance was lost.

He had a cup of coffee and a doughnut at the diner and bought another coffee and two doughnuts for the road. He was eager to get started. But first, one last stop.

The police station had ceased being the command post in a major crime investigation and had become once again the dirty, drab storefront of law enforcement in a broken-down town.

Will parked at a corner, pulled up his collar against the cold, and walked the half block to headquarters. *I owe you this much, Frannie.*

The owlish sergeant at the front desk looked at Will over his half-rim glasses and raised his eyebrows. He was curious but not friendly.

"Good morning," Will said. "I'm with the *Bessemer Gazette*, and I wanted—"

"You got a name, mister?"

Fuck you, Will thought. "My name is Shafer."

"Oh, right. You're the one who knows what we're doing even before *we* do."

"That one, yes. Before I leave your fair city, I wanted to check one more time to see if I'm missing any last-minute reports on the kidnapping case."

"Any information comes from the chief."

"And how might I find him?"

"You might find him plenty pissed off."

"Touché. Can he spare a moment for me?"

"I doubt it."

Steady, Will thought. "Sergeant, I would very much appreciate it if you would inquire if Chief Howe can spare a moment. As long as everything has to come from him."

The sergeant muttered something and left Will standing alone. Will hadn't expected much cooperation, so the little confrontation was partly charade. What he hoped to do was get a feeling about what they might be hiding. Perhaps he could do that by seeing what questions annoyed the chief the most. As Will waited, he idly flicked the big metal-shaving paperweight with his thumbnail.

"Yes?" Chief Howe had appeared at the desk with the sergeant at his side.

"Good day to you, Chief."

"I have nothing whatever to report," Howe said.

"Are you still pursuing—?"

"I have nothing whatever to report." Louder this time.

Will had an idea. It wasn't the best time for an idea, with a dozen pairs of eyes on him, but it was worth a try. In for a dime, in for a dollar. "Chief, would there be anything new on the Luna homicide?"

"My detectives haven't reported to me yet." A light of recognition in the chief's eyes. "And I never said we were calling it a homicide."

"So you're not ruling out—"

Too late, Will realized that in his nervousness, and without thinking, he had kept on flicking the paperweight. He saw the chief's eyes, and he knew at once that Howe saw the gesture as contemptuous.

"Chief, if you could check with your detectives, I'll try not to bother you anymore."

"Mister, I don't run this department for you or anyone else."

Steady, steady. "I know that, Chief. I'm only asking you to ask your brother . . ."

A hush in the room. Will was appalled at his own blunder. He should never have said "ask your brother."

In two seconds, the chief had come to the other side of the counter. He was two inches taller than Will, and forty pounds heavier.

"Mister, all I want to hear from you now is good-bye. You've had all of my time you're entitled to. I've seen the car you drive, and I think I could find a dozen equipment problems on it. Care to try my patience?"

"Nope." Will managed to keep his voice from cracking. He held himself together long enough to walk more or less steadily to the exit. Outside, he breathed the cold air in great gulps. His knees were knocking so badly that the hearty slap on his back almost made him stumble.

"Shafer, you are one cool head," Raines said.

Will laughed, letting the tension flow out of him. "You saw?"

"From a safe distance. Sort of like watching a volcano. You won't get anywhere like that."

"Yeah, I know," Will said more seriously. "I put my foot in it real good."

"Let's walk over here." Raines led Will around a corner of the building. "That's your car up the block, isn't it?"

"The one with the rust spots, yes."

"Okay, two things. When you pull out, I'll watch for a while. It's not much, but it's something I can do. Just in case someone wants to tail."

"I appreciate that."

"I'm a cop, remember? Even here. Second thing is this: I hear tell the cop who investigated your friend's accident is due back. Name's Ted Pickert. Maybe I can get something from him."

"Terrific." It was the first break Will had had on Fran's death since the death of Carmine Luna. "Do you think this Pickert might have . . . you know?"

Raines shrugged. "I'm not close to him or anything, but he doesn't have any reason not to trust me. If he does know anything about Luna, I might be able to tell something just from his reaction."

"I'd love to know if he ever busted Carmine Luna for anything."

"You're thinking the right way, Shafer. Listen, get going and don't shake hands. I know how to reach you."

"All right. And thanks."

"Don't try to call me at the station. I'll be in touch with you."

With that, Raines was gone.

As he headed up the two-lane toward the expressway, Will felt paranoid at first. He kept checking his rearview mirror for police cars. Seeing none, he relaxed a little. He ate the doughnuts, then sipped his coffee, resting the cup in a recess on the dashboard. He would make Bessemer by dark probably, assuming he didn't stop for lunch and didn't hit a snowstorm.

Once he got on the expressway, he'd let go of the hermit and his dog and Heather Casey and Luna and Fran and his stupid accident—he'd let go of all of it, let it fall away with the miles.

Bullshit.

Will pulled off the road. He was near where it had started to happen to Fran. No, he would not let it go. He was a better friend than that. "And a better newsman, too," he whispered.

He started up again, slowly, and soon he came to the gouges in the earth where Fran had crashed. Just past the top of the hill, he saw a house, a two-story frame a decade overdue for a coat of paint. What's to lose?

He drove up the hill and pulled into the driveway, stopping behind a pickup truck that had last been in good condition when the house had been.

Will went to the door and knocked. He waited a long time and knocked again. It was a long shot but worth the attempt. Come to think of it, it wasn't such a long shot. The accident had been followed by the sounds of sirens, and if anyone had been home here that night . . .

Just as Will was turning to leave, the door opened. In the doorway stood a woman, white-haired, eightyish, face as wrinkled as the skin of a chicken's feet.

"I'm sorry to bother you, but I was wondering if you might know anything about a bad accident down the hill there several nights ago."

"Crazy bastard slammed into a woman and almost killed her. Yeah, I called the cops. They got here quick."

"Ah. Do you, I mean, can you tell me. . . ?"

"Who're you and what's your interest?"

"A friend of mine was involved. He died of his injuries, and I'm just checking on what happened."

"Can't say I'm too sorry, the way that crazy son of a bitch was driving."

"I know the accident was my friend's fault, legally anyhow. But is that hill more dangerous than it looks for any reason?"

"Hell no. Just gotta use common sense. There's a sign and an arrow. Tells people there's a hill and they gotta slow down. That goddam fool didn't."

"How do you know that?"

"Christ sake, I heard the son of a bitch coming. First one way, then the other."

"One way and then the other?"

"You hard of hearing, sonny? I was standing right near that window there. Had it cracked open, 'cuz I had the Franklin stove going that night—it was cold out—and it made so much heat inside, I needed air."

"And what did you hear?"

"Heard the engine revving, heard the tires squeal. Like he was having a hard time holding the road. Heard the engine going like a son of a bitch. Thought it was teenagers."

"And then?" Will was shivering on the porch.

"Went by like a son of a bitch. Up that way." She pointed toward the expressway. "Then all the screech and gravel sounds when he turned around. Zoom, back this way. Then a crash down the hill."

"I see. Is there anything else? Could there have been two cars?"

The woman shrugged. "What do you care about all this? He was a friend of yours, you say?"

"Yes. Actually, he . . . Never mind."

"Probably drunk, he was."

"Thank you for your trouble." But Will's thanks were to a closed door.

Why were you going so fast, Frannie? You weren't that drunk, were you? No, you weren't. Not if you were at the liquor store at seven and in a wreck at seven-thirty. So what happened, Frannie?

Will drove slowly, back toward Long Creek, the way Fran Spicer had driven to his death. He was looking for—what? He had no idea what or, for that matter, why. But there was something; there had to be. Fran stops to buy schnapps and beer, his favorite poison, at seven. A half-hour later, he cracks his car up, but he's only come a short way. And how drunk was he?

Just past the crest of the hill, Will saw the abandoned box-shaped concrete building he'd seen earlier. Looks like a little machine shop or something, Will thought. As he drove past, he saw the faded sign over the big metal door—BODY SHOP— and, in his rearview mirror, a driveway along the side leading to the back. From the boards on the windows, he figured the building had been idle awhile.

Will had passed the liquor store again, and something clicked in his mind. Will thought hard. I'm Fran Spicer. I've just driven from Bessemer. I'm stressed out because in my heart I wonder if I can handle this kidnapping story. It's dark out, and I see the liquor store there. Ah, me. I buy schnapps and beer, figuring it'll help me relax once I get where I'm going. But I'm an alcoholic. I want—

No, Will thought. If I'm an alcoholic, I don't want a drink, I *need* one. I can't wait. And I'm driving along just after leaving the liquor store, and I see that abandoned body shop right there, and my headlights catch the driveway along the side of the building.

And I'm slowing down, going to turn left into the driveway. And I'm going to drive around the back of this building. And here I am, and I'm shaking and anxious and struggling with myself, wanting to drink so bad, so bad, and yet not wanting to.

Did you park right here, Frannie? Seems like you might have. It was dark, and you were alone with your demons. You figure what safer place than a boarded-up garage—

Finally, it registered: the soot around the plywood in the window holes and where a rear door had been. This was no long-abandoned garage; there had been a fire here, and not that long ago. God Almighty. Now Will remembered the item in the Long Creek paper: two men killed in a garage fire.

Will got out, shivered from excitement as well as from cold. He walked toward the rear door, which was above a low set of cement steps. Now he saw: the stray scraps of metal and charred wood, junk strewn around the building's perimeter, the half-burned tires lying in the weeds—all left-overs from the blaze.

"And the fire hadn't yet happened when you came this way, Fran. This was still a working garage. Now isn't that a coincidence."

No, not a coincidence. In the corner formed by the low stone steps and the rear wall of the building, Will saw the bits of bottle glass where the fire hoses had driven them. He even recognized the red, white, and blue label of Fran's brand of schnapps.

Will knelt by the steps, looked at the glass. With sad satisfaction, he saw that the cap was still on over the broken neck. "So did you win the most important battle, after all, Fran?"

Will stood up, tried to give himself up to his intuition. You were here, Fran, and then you left in a big hurry. Didn't even buckle your seat belt. You were afraid, terribly afraid.

Without knowing what he was looking for, Will walked slowly up the driveway toward the road. He scanned the side of the burned-out building. The corners were still intact, and there were no spotlights where one might have expected them to be. So it would have been pitch-dark that night.

Will was at the edge of the road now. The cold seemed to clear his mind. Okay: What happened next is easy. Fran turned to the right, then headed up that way, back toward the expressway. No doubt about that; the old woman had heard him. Why right? Because a right turn is almost always easier; it would have been easier here because the driveway is banked a little for a right turn. And if Fran had the choice, for sure he'd head back toward the expressway, back where he'd come from rather than deeper into strange territory.

You were afraid, Fran. Driving like a bat out of hell. Or trying to; that clunker of yours didn't always accelerate that great, did it? Any good car, any car with pickup, could have overtaken you in the short haul.

Will drove to the nearest phone booth, the one in front of the liquor store. Using his credit card, he reached the FBI in Pittsburgh. Jerry Graham was not in. Would Will like to leave a message?

"Tell him I think he should get back to Long Creek as fast as he can," Will said. "I think I've got something. I'll be in touch later."

He dialed the Long Creek police, tried to disguise his voice as he asked for Raines. Raines was out on patrol, and Will could leave a message.

"No thanks," Will said.

He dialed the *Long Creek Eagle*, asked for the clipping morgue. Then he was told that the paper didn't do research for outsiders. He got his call switched to the city desk, told an editor who he was, got switched back to the clipping morgue, and finally got cooperation.

"Your paper had a story on a fire recently on the road up to the expressway," Will said. "Couple guys got burned up. I'd appreciate anything you can tell me."

"Sure, I knew those guys. Not the first story we had on them."

"No?"

"This ain't that big a town. Few years ago, they got probation for breaking and entering. Before that, they were regulars in juvie court. That wasn't written up, but everyone around here knew. Just like they knew they dealt in stolen auto parts."

"Tell me more."

Chuckle. "What's to tell? Every town has a couple of eight balls like the Santos brothers. Bill and Ron, about a year or so apart. Mid, late twenties. Screwups from grade school on. Always wanting to get rich quick, and never mind how."

"Eight balls who grew up to be crooks, probably."

"Nothing you could print, but sure. Cops used to roust them once in a while, but there was never anything they could prove. Terrible thing, though, getting burned up like that. Should have known better than to try to clean up with gasoline. Them being mechanics and all."

In for a dime, in for a dollar. Will drove back to the garage and parked in the same spot. He tried to remember the technical definition for trespassing. Well, he wasn't on private property with the intention of committing a crime (exactly), so that should count for something.

It was snowing lightly. His car tires left faint tracks on the driveway. He was wearing a good windbreaker and hoped it wouldn't get dirty.

The door was solid plywood—no way to knock it in with his shoulder. Aware that he was taking a perilous extra step, he opened his trunk and fished out the jack handle. He found enough space to cram the end of the handle between plywood and door frame and pushed hard. He heard a shriek of splintering wood, and some soot fell onto his jacket sleeves.

The plywood swung in, and a blast of foul air assaulted his nostrils. Smells of burned grease and rubber and (only his imagination?) flesh.

Will stepped into the darkness, felt the jack handle bump against something. Another step, and his feet almost went out from under him. "Jesus . . ."

Ice, all over the floor. He could see the interior now, from the light coming through the burned-out roof. Snowflakes fell gently through the hole above, as though into an old cathedral, coating the grease and grime and God only knew what.

He paused to collect himself. He was still near enough to the door to see his car, and now he could see the area just inside the garage well enough to make out ruined welding masks and a blackened tangle of hoses and cutting torches in a corner.

Something else: lying on the floor, a piece of sheet metal, about the size of a dinner tray and curved. Will drew the rest of the curve in his imagination, and for an instant his mind's eye saw the hot-water tank where Jamie Brokaw had lain.

"My God Almighty." His whisper was swallowed by the silence.

Stepping cautiously (he felt grit in the ice now; the footing was better), he moved into the interior. It would all make sense, wouldn't it? The fire was before Jamie Brokaw was found, so no one connected the metal here with the hot-water tank. Hell, why would they?

"But you saw, Fran. We'll never know just how or what, but you saw."

Off to one side, he saw a long, narrow room, spotted the blackened commode buried under ashes and ice. Something drew him to the door—intuition, instinct. Providence. He saw something frozen in the ice on the bathroom floor. At first glance, it looked like part of a brush, or a mechanic's rag. Then Will saw the little tail.

A child's toy bear.

Will nudged it with the jack handle. You were here, Fran; you were here. And Will remembered what Fran Spicer had said on his deathbed: "The story of my life." Ah, Fran. I thought you were feeling sorry for yourself, getting ready to die, and here you were trying to tell me something.

"It was the last, best story of your life, Fran. The last, best story, and you never got to write it. Son of a bitch!"

Furious, Will jammed the jack handle into the ice surrounding the bear. Again and again, he poked it, feeling the ice chips fly into his face, but the bear would not come loose.

Will let his shoulders slump, rested one arm on the jack handle. He had to reach Jerry Graham, had to make him get his ass back to Long Creek. The garage had to be turned inside out. The money might be here.

The hermit in the woods—God Almighty, he had saved the boy! He wasn't a kidnapper, for Christ's sake!

But it still didn't add up, Will thought as he stood under the hole again, feeling snowflakes settle onto his ears. What didn't add up? The Santos brothers didn't. It sounds like those two didn't have a full deck between them. Just a couple of nickle-and-dime crooks, trying to make some big money in a stupid, amateurish—

All kidnappers were amateurs. Hadn't Jerry Graham said that? Both the Santos brothers had been stupid: Wasn't that what the guy from the *Long Creek Eagle* had said? Then where had the brains come from, the brains to raise the ransom demand? The cleverness to mail the ransom notes from scattered post offices?

An outsider, a smart outsider, had taken over the whole thing.

"You guys were in over your heads, weren't you?" Will said. "You should have stuck to what you knew best, nickle-and-dime shit. Well, you paid for what you did. This fire was no accident, was it?"

Wind swirled over the hole in the roof, and more snow and soot fell. Then Will realized that the gust was part of another sound. The sound of a car pulling around to the back of the garage.

He tiptoed toward the rear door, saw his own car through the crack, glimpsed the second set of tire tracks. He couldn't see the other car, but he heard the door slam.

Will slipped into the darkness behind the door, wondered at once whether it was the right place to be, knew it was too late to change his mind. He gripped the jack handle tightly, swallowed hard, and tried to breathe evenly.

Will heard the soft scuffing on the steps outside, then nothing. Whoever it was was standing right outside. A long, long silence followed. Will breathed slowly, ready to use all his animal strength to smash the first hand or head that came through the door. If he could strike first, he could get out. Never mind his car; he would run, run, run. . . .

Will saw the flashlight beam, saw the wafer of light playing in the shadows along the floor. The light darted into the garage, then back toward the door opening, then deep into the garage again. More silence, and Will didn't see the light anymore. But he knew the intruder was still there, on the other side of the door.

Will wondered where the flashlight beam was. Then something made him look down, and he saw the light sweeping back and forth under the door, back and forth over his feet. For a long, absurd moment, Will's terror was suspended. Had the man outside seen his feet? Should he stand on tiptoes?

"Shafer, are you there? It's Raines."

"Raines! Oh, Jesus Christ!"

Will came out from behind the door, saw the smiling face behind the amber shooting glasses. Still holding the jack handle, he put his other arm around the cop's shoulder. "Jesus, Raines. I was scared half to death."

"You and me both, Shafer." Raines exhaled deeply, holstered his service revolver, and stepped inside. "Listen, Shafer, I called the FBI in Pittsburgh and left an urgent message for Graham."

"But you didn't reach him?"

"No. I left word for him to get back here fast."

"You did? So did I."

"What'd you find?"

"I don't know everything, but I know Jamie Brokaw was here, right here, just before he was stuck in the ground. The tank he was buried in—it was outfitted right here. Look at that curved metal there, and those torches."

"Jesus, Shafer. The two guys who ran this garage."

"Yes, but not just them. Someone else was involved. Took over the whole thing, maybe, and then killed these two."

"Jesus."

"Listen, my friend Fran was here. He was here, Raines. The night he died."

"My God. The guy who cracked up his car?"

"No. He didn't crack it up. He was run off the road. Then he was soaked with beer, wetted down as he was lying in the wreckage. Something had to be done with him, because he was here. He saw!"

"How do you know?"

"Because right out there, at the base of the steps, there's what's left of a schnapps bottle. Schnapps was Fran's favorite starter drink. I found out he bought schnapps and beer at the liquor store right up the road. And today, just now, I put myself in his place. I could do that, because I knew him so long, knew how he must have felt that night, when he was fighting with his demons. . . ."

"Shafer, you're more than a sly dog, but we've got to get out of here. . . ."

"And the sad thing, or the terrible thing, is that he beat his demons that night. And look over there, frozen in the ice on the floor. That kid's bear? They gave that to Jamie Brokaw to play with. I know they did. It happened here. Right here!"

"We've got to get out of here, Shafer. You especially. Away from this place, away from this town. I know that Pickert has been talking to the chief today, and I know the chief's been following you. The chief saw you in the phone booth just now—I'm sure of it."

"Pickert and the chief?"

"That's why I called the FBI, Shafer. Neither one of us is safe around here."

"The chief's connected with the guys who ran this garage?"

"He was, sure. The Santoses and the chief's brother, they

all belonged to the same metalworkers' union a while back. Until these two Santos fumble-fucks went into business on their own. I told you, all the people in this town know one another.''

"Carmine Luna?''

"Let's get out of here, Shafer.'' Raines took Will by the arm and steered him outside. ''Luna was one of Pickert's snitches. They washed each other's hands. Don't you see?''

"Sure. When Fran had to be framed, there was someone in the hospital all set to do it. They weren't going to let him live afterward, I'll bet, because of all he knew. But his body was so weak, they didn't have to do anything.''

Will followed Raines down the steps, over to Will's car. Will's teeth were chattering, from excitement and the cold. "Raines, you've got to get away, too.''

"Don't worry about me. I've still got a uniform. It's tough to kill a good cop. But you won't be safe until you're back on the expressway, where it's all state police.''

"God Almighty,'' Will said, opening his trunk to toss in the jack handle. "Where the hell is the FBI?''

"Screw 'em. Just get moving, Shafer. I'm going to be right behind you until you're on the entrance ramp. Then I'll be in touch. Maybe your brilliant FBI buddy will get here in time to help.''

Will started to say something in defense of Graham, but nothing came out. Graham wasn't here.

Just as Will was opening his car door, he saw Raines looking up the driveway toward the road. Then Raines's face went hard. "Shafer! No time to go out the front way. Forget your car.''

"What?''

"They're here, Shafer! Here! The chief and . . . Christ!''

Will watched as though hypnotized as Raines opened his car door and pulled out a high-powered rifle equipped with sling and telescopic sight. In one smooth motion, Raines had the weapon draped across his back and was running toward the outskirts of the woods behind the garage.

"Run fast, Shafer! Follow me. I know what I'm doing.''

Will obeyed, half-stumbling at first on rubbery legs through the junk-strewn grass around the garage, then to the brush just beyond.

"Raines!" The voice of Chief Robert Howe, bellowing from the driveway along the side of the building.

The boom of a shotgun—there was no mistaking it—from the driveway and the clatter of the pellets through the brush and branches.

"Here, Shafer. Here."

Will was within the protection of the brush now, and a few stumbling steps beyond that within the trees' embrace. He could see Raines up ahead of him, running faster than Will could run but holding back for him, waiting.

"Raines!" The chief's voice farther back, followed by the metallic *click-clack* sound of a fresh cartridge going into the shotgun. But Will knew he and Raines had a chance now—a good chance!— because while a shotgun would blast through a man's flesh at short range it was all but useless half a football field away.

With every step, heedless of the thorns and vines and branches that slapped at his cheeks and forehead and gripped his ankles, Will was gaining on Raines. He was almost even with him now. Raines had a rifle, a much longer-range weapon than a shotgun. They were going to make it, going to make it.

"You hit?" Raines said as Will drew even.

"No. No. No."

"You're sure?"

"Yes. Yes."

"Stick to me like glue, Shafer. I didn't come this far to let you get killed. To get killed myself, for that matter."

"Do you have any plan?"

"Just to stay cool and get out of this. We're both in better shape than that lard-ass and his partner."

"Who's his partner?"

"Not sure who, besides Pickert."

Farther back now, right behind the garage, the sound of car doors and trunks opening and closing. Will heard two voices. No, three.

"Don't stop to look back yet, Shafer. We're putting distance between us and them. And I'm a better shot, if it comes to that.''

''The chief had a shotgun. Are there any rifles with them?''

''Don't know. Doesn't matter. I can shoot better than any of those assholes.''

Will found Raines's bravado reassuring. Then he had a dark thought. ''You know where you're going? I mean, can they take a shortcut somewhere and be in front of us?''

''I'm not going to let that happen, Shafer. Trust me. I know these woods better than that. If it comes down to it, I'll make the straightest line I can toward the expressway. It's quite a trek, but we can do it.''

Will settled into a fast jog behind Raines. He forced himself to breathe as evenly and deeply as he could, knowing that if he had to push himself beyond what he had ever had to do before in his life, his chest would last longer that way.

Raines bounded easily through the woods, despite the added weight of the rifle over his shoulder. Yes, he was in shape, in great shape. He moved like a running machine, half-glancing over his shoulder every twenty yards or so.

''I'm right with you,'' Will said.

Raines seemed to nod. At one point, he made a fist of encouragement.

They were into the deep woods now. The air was cold, but the ground still had some sponge in it. Several birds flew from under an evergreen.

''Here, Shafer.'' Raines led him into a protected gulley. ''Kneel down and breathe deep through your mouth.''

''I'm okay. I am.'' But this was worse than a neighborhood jog.

''You're doing fine, Shafer, but I'm a little younger than you. Just rest easy. I have a good view of back where we came from. We'll take a minute to get fresh. Then put more distance between us.''

Will was in no mood to argue. ''What will they do if they catch us?''

''They know what they have to do if they catch us. That's not going to happen.'' Almost affectionately, Raines slapped the stock of his rifle. Then he brought it to his shoulder—

"Relax, Shafer, I'm just looking"—and trained it back the way they had come. At least Will thought it was the way they had come; he could no longer be sure.

"Ready, Shafer?"

"I'm ready to do whatever it takes." To stay alive, Will thought.

"Good. Come on." Raines put his strong hand on Will's shoulder. "Like I said, they know I'm a better shot—"

Dogs.

Raines and Will heard the sounds at the same time. Absurdly, Will thought, German shepherds can run faster than I can. He felt sick to his stomach, especially when he saw Raines's eyes behind his amber shooting glasses. Will saw fear in the eyes.

"Shafer, you've got to keep up with me. Those dogs will tear us apart."

"No. I won't let that happen to me. I won't."

"Just keep up, then. Stay right with me."

"As long as I can breathe, I'm with you. All right?"

"Let's go, then. It doesn't matter how fast the dogs can run, because they're still attached to their handlers. I'm still better than any goddamn cop around here."

I hope so, Will thought. I really do hope so.

Raines led the way in a half trot into deeper woods, where decades-old evergreens shaded the forest floor. Will lost track of time and distance. Now and then, he heard dogs behind them, but they did not seem to be gaining. He knew there was a long time to go before dark. Was that good or not? Would night offer safety? Probably, assuming that Raines knew his way around. And he certainly seemed to.

When they rested again, Will realized he was hungry as well as tired. The one time in his life he could have used a big breakfast for the energy, he'd settled for doughnuts and coffee. . . .

Will looked around him. He couldn't be sure, but the terrain seemed like the area where the hermit had lived and died, where Jamie Brokaw had been buried. "Are we close to where the boy was in the ground?"

"Relatively speaking. Couple, few miles."

"Does it make any difference to us what county we're in? It might make a difference. I mean, they can't just cross into another county and kill us, can they?"

Raines didn't answer.

Far off in the distance, Will heard a helicopter. For long, long seconds, the sound hovered at the very edge of hearing. Raines seemed not to be aware of it. Then the sound was gone.

"Raines, listen. You're better at this than I am, but it makes sense to me to get into another county as fast as we can. It has to make them think twice, if we can do that."

"It makes no difference to me."

"No?"

"No."

Will didn't understand, but he was as much an amateur as the kidnappers had been. And they were dead. The Santos brothers were dead. Now, Will had to trust Raines to keep him alive. "Jerry Graham, where are you when I need you?"

"What?"

"My FBI friend. If he got here, we'd be safe."

Raines snorted. "The FBI screwed up, Shafer. They screwed up the case. Believe me."

"I guess. I guess they never put any stock in what I found out about Carmine Luna."

"The FBI figures that's local police business, Shafer. Dealing with scum like that. Fag scum."

"You knew Luna, too?"

"Not really."

Not really? No, that couldn't be right. What had Raines said about Luna: "You saw how he lived." Hadn't Raines said that? Will was sure he had, as though Raines had seen Luna's place.

A terrible, chill calm settled over Will. He'd been able to imagine that the Long Creek police chief and maybe someone else in the department could have been involved in the kidnapping. He'd just never thought of Raines.

Now he remembered the Kansas City kidnapping case from his boyhood, the case he'd read about in the *Long Creek Eagle* morgue. Son of a wealthy car dealer, kidnapped and killed, thrown in a lime pit.

And a crooked cop assigned to deliver the ransom money had stolen some of it. Terrible evil followed by terrible greed.

And here I stand, Will thought, a naïve fool. Standing under a tree with Raines, listening for the dogs and the good guys. I'm just his insurance, as long as I'm alive.

The dogs were closer.

Will was afraid to look Raines in the eye, afraid of what he would see behind the amber shooting glasses.

Raines hadn't known Luna, but he talked as if he'd been to his apartment. No doubt he had. And Raines had never hunted or fished with the other Long Creek cops, but he knew these woods very well. Of course, he did.

The ransom notes had been mailed from all over the place. A cop—not the chief, but a cop—could routinely drive all over the place and mail stuff wherever he wanted to.

It was Raines who'd always seemed to be there, right on the edge of the case, willing to help, to share information. No! Not to share, but to find out what Will knew, about Fran's death, and what kind of investigator Jerry Graham was.

Raines had been able to lift the ransom money, because he'd known all along how the drop would be made, about the surveillance, when the money could be lifted safely. Raines, with the big plans about leaving Long Creek and never coming back. Always the helpful Raines.

No, it didn't matter to Raines whether he and Will got into another county or not. Just a few minutes before, he'd said, "It makes no difference to me."

Raines had followed him to the garage, wanting to see what Will had found out. And now Raines knew that even Will Shafer couldn't be naïve forever, that even Will Shafer could add two and two. Eventually, anyhow.

I'm his insurance, Will reminded himself. As long as I'm alive, I'm his insurance.

Helicopter sounds, closer than before. People were hunting for them. Raines heard it. And the dogs, closer now.

"Get down low, Shafer. Stay down." Raines's voice was cold and hard.

Will obeyed, lying flat against the cold leaves, able to feel his own heartbeat, closing his eyes against the terror. Could it be that Raines didn't yet know that Will had figured it out?

Will could think of nothing to do, nothing. He kept his eyes closed, listening to his heart over the sounds of the copters and the dogs. Maybe if he could just stay calm, stay calm. He knew he didn't deserve the chance after being such a fool, didn't deserve the chance after what Fran and Jamie and the hermit had suffered. But he wanted the chance, anyhow. Our Father . . .

"Shafer! Get up."

Who art in heaven . . .

"You okay, Shafer? We gotta move. . . ."

Will felt Raines's hand on his arm, lifting him up.

"Stay with me, Shafer. I need—"

Will could not resist looking into Raines's eyes, and he saw the glint of recognition behind the amber glasses. And then Will saw the flash of fury, and panic, behind the glasses. For just an instant, as he stood chest-to-chest with Raines, Will had the advantage of surprise.

What happened next was heaven-sent. Raines started to grab Will, who stepped back. Then Raines was caught in indecision: He could either grab Will physically and try to wrestle him to the ground or he could cover Will with his rifle. But Raines had the rifle slung over his shoulder, and in his anxiety he made a clumsy motion instead of what should have been a simple deft one.

Still looking right at Will, Raines tried to get the rifle into position. But his footing wasn't right, and in his awkwardness he arched his back as the sling caught on his coat for just a moment, and in that moment Will stepped forward and pushed as hard as he could on Raines's chest. And Raines's feet slipped on the leaves and went out from under him, and Will could see the surprise in the eyes behind the amber glasses as Raines took a hard fall on his back.

The fall was made harder by the rifle getting in the way. Will rejoiced in the *whoof!* that came out of Raines's chest, a sound Will heard as he bolted and ran back the way they had come, or at least the way he thought they had come—it was so hard to tell in the woods. Not that it mattered, because Will was running, running. . . .

"Shafer? Shafer!"

The voice told Will that Raines would have trouble getting his wind back. The sound of branches snapping back there and Raines's curses meant he was even having trouble getting back on his feet. Will wasn't sure where he was going, but he was running, running. . . .

"If you don't stop, I'll shoot you in the leg, Shafer. Then you'll stop. . . ."

Will was running, running, even as he heard the explosion from Raines's deer rifle. He would not stop, would not stop, no matter what. He would not let Raines get him.

Another shot from behind, and this time Will heard a bullet go *splat* into the ground, but way off to one side. Raines didn't really know where he was shooting.

"Shafer! If you don't come with me, I'll shoot you so your wife won't love you anymore. I can do that, Shafer. I'm that good a shot. Trust me."

Thorns, vines, leaves, twigs went slap, slap, slap at Will's face. He didn't care; he would let all the skin on his face and his hands be ripped away if he could keep on running—

Rock, log, it didn't matter. For an instant, Will felt something hard and slippery under his left foot before he went down like a large, slow stag. His right arm came under him, but instead of breaking his fall it came up into his chest, knocking all the breath out of him and filling him with a blinding pain.

"Shafer? Don't move, Shafer."

Will tried to crawl. He moaned in pain, then tried not to moan. Raines was coming up on him.

"If you come with me, we'll both walk out of these woods, Shafer. I promise."

Will got to his knees, supported himself on his good arm, crawled a few yards. He was dizzy-sick from nausea but he would not pass out, would not. He thought he heard dogs, shouts of men, helicopters. Or were they just the sounds a man hears before he faints? He crawled.

"I know I'm close, Shafer. They're no match for me, and neither are you. I can leave you so your wife will love you, or I can . . . you know. Let me find you."

Will got his good arm around a tree, managed to stand up.

He didn't think Raines could see him yet, and he didn't hear footsteps. He did hear the dogs and the helicopters and the shouts; there was no mistaking them.

"Still your choice, Shafer. I'll do what I need to do. You know that. I can kill. You know that. Whatever I need. They'll never execute me. Shafer?"

Raines's voice was from a different direction now, and closer. Slowly, Will maneuvered himself around the tree, away from where he thought the voice had been.

"There's still time, Shafer. I can tell you where the money is, tie you up, and be on my way. They'll never know, Shafer. I offered your friend a deal. I did. He said yes, but he was a lousy actor. Ran away. Come on, Shafer. Let's be a sly dog."

Sure, Will thought. Fran ran away because he knew you'd kill him. He wasn't stupid, wasn't drunk.

"John Raines! John Raines! We have you surrounded. Lay down your weapon at once. We have you surrounded."

"Shafer? I can see you, Shafer. . . ."

Raines's voice was much closer, and Will could hear his steps. But a tremor in the voice told Will that Raines was lying, desperate, that he couldn't see him yet.

"John Raines, we have you surrounded!" A voice through a loudspeaker. A familiar voice?

"Please, Shafer. We can be partners. We're both better than they are. Don't you see that, Shafer?"

Will slid around the tree a little more.

"These people aren't even professional cops, Shafer. Don't you see that, you sly dog? Where are you?"

Something made Will turn his head slowly around the tree. Raines was standing about fifty feet away but looking away from him.

"Raines, drop your weapon." The loudspeaker voice was familiar.

The sensation was like watching a movie. Will saw Raines drop to one knee, saw him bring the rifle to his shoulder, this time in a sure, deft shooter's motion, and begin to aim in the direction of the voice.

Another rifle shot, and Raines was knocked back. His head rolled to the side, toward Will, who turned away when he saw the steam rising from the brains on the wet leaves.

* * *

"Will? It's all right, Will."

Something cool and wet being held to the side of his face. Still in the woods.

"It's all right, Will. You're safe. You just fainted, that's all. You're going to be fine."

Will was aware of blankets across his back and gentle hands on his shoulders. He tried to say something.

"Relax, Will. It's all right."

Will recognized the voice, and he summoned all his strength to say, "Thanks for coming back."

"I never left," Jerry Graham said.

Thirty

···

Will thought he was dreaming. Then he felt the bruises from the fall, and he knew that the noises were those of the hospital waking up. Then he remembered everything that had happened, and he wished he could go back to sleep.

"Mr. Shafer? Mr. Shafer, good morning."

Reluctantly, he opened his eyes and looked into one of the loveliest faces he could remember. Copper skin, crow black hair, eyes deep and dark, like ponds. From India or Pakistan, he thought dully.

"Mr. Shafer," she said. "I need you to wake up for me, please. I need to draw a few bloods."

Damn; he hated needles. "I was just here for the night," he said. "I should be going home today."

"I still need a few bloods, please."

He lay on his back, endured the needle with his eyes closed, relaxed.

"You can sleep again if you want to, please."

"You're lovely. Do you know that?"

She was gone. Had she heard him? Lord, what kind of

drugs did they give me to loosen my inhibitions? Am I going home?

He closed his eyes again, and when he next opened them a tray was on the table next to his bed.

Breakfast.

He sat upright, saw that he was alone in the room, although there was an empty bed on the other side. He wheeled the table arm around so that the tray was over his lap, then removed the plastic covers from the dishes. Coffee, orange juice, bacon, soggy pancakes. He was famished. After a couple of painful starts, he figured out what moves not to make with his sore arm. He ate everything.

"Good morning. How're you feeling?" The doctor was no more than thirty, at least six four, powerfully built.

"Linebacker?" Will said.

The doctor chuckled. "Tight end. Holy Cross. Tore my knee up senior year. Nothing wrong with your appetite."

"Am I going home?"

"We'll see. Probably. Do you hurt much?"

"Here and there. Guess I'm lucky to have a room to myself."

"The guy who was in it died just before you got here."

"I hope that isn't bad luck."

"He was eighty-six. Your blood pressure and heart are fine. You're up to having some company."

The doctor went out. A moment later, Jerry Graham came in. He was wearing casual slacks and a sweater. "How are you, Will?"

"Alive. Lucky to be, I guess. You?"

"Hanging in there. I needed a heavy sedative last night, though. I wanted to thank you again, Will."

"For what?" Feelings had welled up inside him; Will was surprised at the anger he felt toward the FBI man.

"Everything. For being honest. For being such a digger and helping us get at the truth."

"Sometimes we get lucky, Jerry. Even when we're groping in the dark. Which I was. Far more than I realized."

"Right. Right. I'm sorry, Will, but I didn't have a choice. Or I didn't think I did. Maybe we can square things."

Will tried to empty his face of emotion. He felt like a fool, and the presence of the man who had made him feel that way didn't help.

"Will, would you like me to lay it all out for you?"

Ah, the big test. Will's pride wanted to say, Shove it, Jerry. His curiosity said something else.

"Will?"

"Only if you give it all to me, Jerry. Otherwise, screw it. I don't want to be treated like a kid again. If you can't give it to me straight, I don't want it."

"Understood. So here's the whole thing. All of it."

Graham told him that suspicion had focused early on the chauffeur, Tony Musso, despite official denials to the contrary. But an exhaustive check of Musso's background had turned up nothing unsavory.

Still, Graham had continued to interview the chauffeur, on the theory that the kidnappers had ooviously known a good deal about the boy's going back and forth between father and mother. After tentatively ruling out other present and former employees of the Brokaw household, Graham theorized that the chauffeur had somehow brushed against the men who would become the kidnappers.

"At some point, Will, we learned that Musso had stopped one day at the Santos brothers' garage. It was almost by chance. He needed a fuse in the car replaced."

The Santos brothers had engaged Musso in friendly conversation, finding out soon enough whom Musso worked for—"There aren't that many chauffeurs around here, Will"—and more than a little about Richard Brokaw, his ex-wife, and their son.

"When I told Chief Howe that the chauffeur had stopped at the Santos brothers' garage not long before the kidnapping, he suspected them at once. The chief doesn't pretend to be a genius, but he does know the community, and the brothers had a bad rep."

"Why weren't they arrested right away, Jerry?"

"Because we didn't know where in God's name the boy was. Then came the fire at the Santos brothers' garage. We didn't know what was going down, still didn't know where the boy was and whether he was alive or dead."

"But it was too much of a coincidence that the Santos

brothers would get killed like that after you'd begun to suspect them.''

"Way too much of a coincidence, Will. Especially after I got some expert advice. From you.''

"Me?''

"I didn't have time to bring in a semanticist or an outside expert on newspaper typefaces, Will. I had to go with what I had. Someone I could trust totally. You, Will.''

Will closed his eyes and suppressed a laugh. Ah, yes; Jerry Graham could still charm.

"Your instincts about the ransom notes were dead-on, Will. About their having been written by different people, and what that meant.''

"That was so obvious.''

"To you, maybe. You're a word person. But have you ever digested a sheaf of police reports? Anyhow, the chief and his detective brother figured the Santos brothers didn't have a full deck of cards between them. So if there was a so-called 'brain' involved in the kidnapping, it had to be a third party.''

Graham paused while Will adjusted the height of his bed.

"Another thing, Will. The first ransom demand, fifty thousand, was such peanuts. I mean, why kidnap a millionaire's son and ask for fifty grand?''

"Unless you're a petty nickle-and-dime kind of crook to start with.''

"Exactly. The kind of crook who burglarizes a place and steals the coins from the vending machines. Which the Long Creek cops think the Santos brothers did now and then.''

Will asked him why he began to think that a cop might be the third party in the kidnapping. Graham said the ease with which someone had picked up the ransom money from the drop site along the road at the edge of the woods had made him think the "smart" kidnapper might be someone on the inside of law enforcement, someone who knew who would be where, and when, on the stakeout—including which cops would be most likely to be careless.

"In a way, Raines had already drawn attention to himself, Will. From his first day as a Long Creek cop, just about everyone found him a pain in the ass. Show me a person who can't make friends with anybody—anybody—and I'll show you a nut.''

"He was making friends with me, Jerry. Or I thought he was.''

"Now you know better. I'm sure a psychiatrist could explain it in fancy language, but the bottom line is that Raines was totally amoral, incapable of compassion or empathy, absolutely self-centered and selfish. Everything he said—everything—was for effect, to gain something for himself. And damn everybody else.''

"It sounds like you knew him.''

"In a way, I did.'' Graham said he'd spent a lot of time on the phone with the bureau's experts on criminal behavior, particularly sociopaths and psychopaths. ''Will, are you up to hearing all this right now? I can come back.''

"I like to take bad medicine in one gulp, Jerry.''

"I've got some good medicine, too, Will.''

"How did you zero in on Raines?''

"I didn't, Will. At least not by myself.'' Graham explained that another cop had noticed that Raines was putting more mileage than usual on his patrol car, and that his daily activity log didn't account for it. So Graham and Howe had begun to wonder why Raines would have been driving all over the county when he wasn't handing out that many traffic tickets.

Around that time, the ransom notes were being mailed from different corners of the county. ''And that's where you were a big help, Will. When you noticed that funny newspaper typeface. . . .''

"Latin Condensed.''

"Whatever. When you noticed that funny lettering from the *New York Times*, and then you told me that the *Times* used in the ransom notes must have been bought right here in Long Creek. That really made us focus on Raines. Especially since the chief remembered seeing Raines reading the *Times* now and then.''

"So you didn't really dismiss what I pointed out about the lettering on the ransom notes?''

"Lord no. Quite the contrary. I was just putting on an act.''

Yes, Will thought. So much of it had been an act. Was I anything more than a prop? "Why did you have to put on an act, Jerry?"

"So you'd be in the dark, Will. I thought it might help in getting Raines to rise to the bait. Maybe you remember how I made a show of closing the door whenever I talked to you and I thought Raines was around."

"Now I do. Twenty-twenty hindsight."

"It's that way for all of us. So when Raines started pumping you, trying to learn what you knew about me—"

Lightning flashed in Will's mind. "You had his car bugged, you bastard!"

"—trying to learn what you knew about me," Graham went on evenly, "we knew we were closing the ring."

"And you couldn't just grab him?"

"No. Certainly not when the boy's fate was up in the air. And the involvement of Steven Sewell—a one-in-a-million accident—really had us scratching our heads. We didn't know how many kidnappers there were. So we had to let things take their course."

Graham said the tape recording of the call to the Deer County Sheriff's Department by the "hunter" who reported spotting a man and boy in the woods had been analyzed. The analysis had indicated a strong probability, based on comparisons with recordings of Raines's voice from routine police calls, that the "hunter" and Raines were the same man. Raines had only partly succeeded in disguising his voice; Graham's remark to Will that the "hunter" sounded like an old man with bad dentures had been a lie for Raines's benefit.

"You already know about the poor pathetic hermit and his dog," Graham went on. "He saved that boy, Will. It's my theory that Raines was going to kill that boy. Maybe take his picture first to get more ransom money. Then kill him, one way or the other."

"Unbelievable."

"For people like you and me, yes. Not for someone like Raines, who doesn't—didn't—function like a human being."

Graham was red-eyed and looked tired. He poured himself

some water from the pitcher on the little table. "We didn't know what to make of your friend's auto accident, Will. How it tied into the kidnapping, I mean. Or even whether it did. But the Long Creek cop who investigated it, Ted Pickert, was suspicious early on. He got to the scene quickly, and he thought he saw another car making haste out of the area."

"Raines."

"We think so. We know so. But it wasn't until you found the schnapps bottle—"

"When did I tell you about finding the bottle?"

"Last night, when you were drifting in and out after being sedated. It wasn't until then, when we knew about the schnapps bottle being there, that we surmised that your friend had stumbled on the kidnappers and the boy in the garage. Under hypnosis, the boy gave us an almost dreamlike account of a strange man coming into the garage, scuffling with some other men, knocking over a green tank and a red tank as he ran out. But we, well . . ."

"You didn't know how much to believe him."

"No, we didn't know how much to believe the child," Graham said. "Especially considering what he'd been through."

Will sat up and poured himself some water. He felt tugged from two directions: He wanted to hear what Graham had to say, yet he was eager to get out of the hospital. After a long moment, he said, "I've wondered what Fran went through."

"That's another thing. Early on, the chief picked up on the fact that Raines was showing a lot of interest in the accident involving your friend."

Graham said Howe had seen Raines sneaking a look at the accident report, perhaps to see if the investigating officer had indicated any doubt that Spicer had been drunk. The chief had then made sure the investigating officer was unavailable, to Raines or anyone else.

"I feel badly about misjudging Howe," Will said. "He's not as dumb as I thought. Worse than that, he's a better man than I thought."

The agent shrugged. "We make mistakes. Go see him before you leave town."

Will pressed the buzzer on his bed, told the nurse he wanted to leave, so if any doctor needed to check him out, now was the time.

"Hmmm," the nurse said. "Your blood work isn't back, and you had quite a stressful experience. A man your age, it might be best if you stayed another night."

"No," Will said.

As Will got dressed, he and Graham talked about the things that would never be known: how and at what stage Raines had found out about the kidnapping and muscled in on the Santos brothers; when and why he had decided to do away with them, and exactly how he had done it; why Raines had decided to eliminate Carmine Luna, and whether Luna might be alive if Will hadn't gone after him.

"Don't dwell, Will. I'm trying not to. I killed a man, after all."

Will felt badly for him, but there was nothing he could say to help. Then he remembered something. "You told me you never left town, Jerry. Where the hell were you?"

"At the chief's house. His wife is a hell of a cook."

"The money, Jerry. What about the ransom money?"

The agent shrugged. "We tossed Raines's apartment and his car. Nothing." He went on to explain that Raines had been watched when the hermit's cabin had been discovered. Graham reminded Will that Raines had seemed eager to stay there. "It occurred to us that he might have had a small amount of the ransom money with him, maybe tucked in a boot—"

"And might have intended to plant it in the cabin to make it look like the hermit was part of the kidnapping."

"Right. That's all conjecture. We'll probably never know."

"I just remembered. Near the cabin, it looked like someone had started to build a snowman. . . ."

"And Raines stepped on it. Howe and I noticed that, Will. Of course, that made us wonder all the more if the hermit was just an innocent outsider. But we, we . . ."

Graham paused, shook his head. His eyes filled, and suddenly Will understood. He waited for his old friend to go on.

"We thought about trying to pass the word among the search party that this strange guy with the kid might be innocent. But we weren't a hundred percent sure. And how would we have passed the word without tipping off Raines? How, Will?'' The agent held out his hands, palms up, in a gesture of helplessness.

"Jerry, you just told me not to dwell. You had to make a life-or-death decision. This guy Sewell, he was probably paranoid, and he might have had some leftover problems from his days as a heavy drug user. And he had a gun.''

"Which he used, unfortunately. Which made it easier for Raines to shoot him.''

"Raines?''

"The ballistics tests on Raines's weapon aren't final yet, but we're pretty sure it was him. We interviewed the others who had him in range, and none of them fired the fatal shot. Or so they said.''

"It would make sense, Raines shooting him.''

"It's perfect. Raines kills him, and it's all legal and kosher. The hermit never gets to tell his story.'' Graham paused; Will had never seen him look sadder.

"Wait, Jerry. If Raines shot the guy legally—I mean, if he thought it was all legal—why didn't he come forward and say he'd shot him?''

"Oh, I set a little trap after the hermit was shot, Will. I spread the word it was a deputy who had nailed him—I told you that, remember—and waited to see if Raines would correct me. The kind of man he was, if he'd had nothing to hide, he would have wanted credit for shooting him.''

They talked for a while longer, agreeing that they'd get together sometime, somewhere just to visit. After Graham said good-bye, Will called the hotel and said he'd be over in a while to settle his bill.

After hanging up, he remembered that he had left his car behind the burned-out garage. When the panic subsided, he called the Long Creek police and was told that his car had been towed to the department's lot, where he could pick it up whenever he wanted.

"Did you find any equipment violations?'' Will said.

"Huh?'' The officer seemed nonplussed. "Tell you what, you want us to look for any, we'll be glad to write up a ticket.''

"No thanks. Say, if the chief is in, I'd like to come by and see him a little later."

"I'll pass the message."

So he did have one last chance, after all. What would he make of it?

He spotted Heather Casey coming out of the intensive-care unit. "Don't you ever take a day off?"

"Oh! Hello. I'm here on overtime, as a matter of fact. How are you feeling?"

"A little tired and sore, but okay."

"So, then, you've been given permission to leave."

"I told them I was leaving, yes."

She smiled at the nuance. "Men. You're all alike." She said it as a joke, but the words reminded both of them of what they had talked about, and what he knew about her. He saw it in her face, and he was sure she saw it in his.

Will remembered how it had been a long, long time ago when he broke up with a girl: Nothing either of them said sounded quite right. "Anyhow," Will said, "I'm glad I got a chance to say good-bye in person."

"I'm just going on a break. Would you like some coffee?"

Say yes, he told himself. "No thanks. I have a couple of stops to make before heading home. I just wanted to tell you . . ."

She waited.

". . . to tell you . . ."

Still she waited.

And he took one of her hands in his, kissed it, and held on. "To tell you what a lovely person you are. What a lovely woman."

There was no mistaking the sadness behind her smile, or that it was a farewell. "Have a good life, Will."

He gave her hand one last squeeze before letting go. Then he walked to the elevator without looking back.

The chief's office had a big window overlooking the parking lot.

"Hey! Good to see you up and about," Howe said, standing to shake hands. His smile was friendly.

"Thanks. I would have gotten here sooner, but I got the slowest cab in town."

"Probably the last one," Howe said, offering a cushioned chair next to the desk.

"Thanks for retrieving my car."

"We won't even charge for the tow."

"That's nice of you. Especially since I've been wrong about so many things."

Howe smiled and waved his hand as if to dismiss Will's concerns. "You a baseball fan, Shafer?"

"I follow it a little."

"Then you know that a great hitter is one who succeeds one out of three times. One in three! If I'm right more than half the time, I think I'm doing good."

"I try to remember that myself. Sometimes I think that if I could only put out yesterday's paper again, I could make it perfect."

Howe chuckled. Then Will felt almost faint. He had forgotten all about his newspaper. My God, were the editors in Bessemer expecting him to file a story today for tomorrow's paper? And what had they done for this day's paper, with him out of commission?

"Chief, can I use your phone?"

Tom Ryan answered. "Will! Great to hear your voice. How are you?"

"Good, Ry. I know I've been out of touch, and I was wondering how you folks made out for today's paper? And do you want me to do anything for tomorrow?"

"That's what I call dedication, Will." Ryan affected a good-natured tone, but it didn't fly. Then he told him the *Gazette* had run a wire-service story on the shooting of Raines for the first edition, followed by a staff-written article for later editions.

Will waited; he knew from Ryan's voice that there was more to come.

"Will, we sort of, you know, downplayed your being there and all. We thought, or the publisher did, that we should be careful about becoming part of the news ourselves, if you get my drift."

"I get your drift."

"Same thing for tomorrow's paper, Will. We figured we'd
. . . we'd do a staff piece from here, using the wires and
whatever we can get by phone."

"Sounds good, Ry. You don't need anything from me,
then?"

"I guess we're all set, Will. Maybe you can start thinking
about writing a piece for this Sunday. Sort of a wrap-up,
putting it all in perspective."

"Sure, Ry." He hung up before Ryan could change his
mind.

"Everything under control?" Howe said.

"If it isn't, I don't care."

"That's the spirit. Say, I have a present for you."

Howe opened a desk drawer and took out a metal shaving
mounted on a block; it was just like the one Will had seen on
the station desk.

"You don't have to use it as a paperweight," Howe said.
"It can be an effective weapon."

"I know just what to do with it." What he would do would
be to leave it in his office. He didn't think Karen would like
it.

"My brother, he made a bunch of these," Howe said.
"Just before he shipped out."

"Shipped out?"

"To Vietnam."

"So he joined the force right after he got back?"

The chief looked surprised for a moment. "Oh, no. Different brother. The one who went to Nam was Billie. Bubba,
we called him, 'cause he was the baby of the family. Yep."

The chief paused, cleared his throat, and went on. "Hell,
I remember when we saw him off. He says to us, 'Want me
to bring you a set of Charlie's ears?' Charlie meaning Viet-
cong. And I says to Bubba, 'Just come back.' But he didn't."

Will felt ashamed. He had assumed too many things, big
and small, and for the wrong reasons—or no reason.

Howe picked up the shaving, ran a finger lovingly along
the curl. "He used to watch for these big shavings to roll off
the lathe, Bubba did. Then he'd wait for 'em to cool and fish
'em out of the scrap bin right under the machine. I have a
bunch at home. So does my brother. My other brother."

For an instant, Howe's face showed his sadness. The instant passed, and he was all business again. "There's a couple of things you might be interested in, Shafer."

Howe said he'd heard that a woman from Wisconsin had called the hospital to ask whether anyone had claimed Steven Sewell's body. Told that no one had, she hemmed and hawed, finally saying that she might want to make funeral arrangements.

"Thing is, Shafer, this guy Sewell didn't have much of a family even before he became a wood nymph. Then everyone disowned him because of the drug scene and all that."

"So who is this woman from Wisconsin?" After Howe told him, Will said, "I'll be damned. That's sort of nice, isn't it?"

"Yeah. I think money's a problem, though."

Will had an idea but said nothing.

"You know, Shafer, I was only a rookie cop way back then. At the time of that raid, I mean. Sure, I wanted to kick ass, and I didn't much care for all that long hair and flag-burning stuff, especially with Bubba and all, but I personally never set fire to anyone's cabin. I mean, I would never go that far, no matter how I felt."

"I believe that, Chief."

"I just wanted you to know. I was on that raid, but I never struck a match. I couldn't live with myself if I'd done something like that. Most cops, Shafer, you'd be surprised, they've got feelings like anyone else. Most of my people are decent cops. A little rough around the edges, some of them, I admit. . . ."

"I know you have some good people working for you, Chief."

"Damn right. Now this guy Raines, he helped tip himself off. All that crap about how he was gonna join the state police, how he didn't think the FBI was so hot . . ." Howe snorted derisively. "It was all bullshit, Shafer. That arrogant bastard. I knew there was something wrong with him as soon as I met him. I just sensed that he was a bullshit artist."

Which is more than I can say, Will thought. "Chief, I have to get going. Thanks for everything."

"Come see us sometime."

"I will."

"Shafer, I almost forgot. There's something else you'll be interested in."

Will was shown into a huge living room, where the fireplace glowed a fierce orange. He stood before it, warming the legs his temperamental car heater had left chilly, and allowed himself to daydream. The living room had enough furniture to fill Will's entire house.

"Hello." Brokaw tossed his windbreaker over a sofa and offered his hand. It was cold, and his face was flushed from the outdoors.

"I called your office," Will said. "They told me you were home this afternoon."

"It seems like the best possible time to give a lot of attention to Jamie. His mother is coming over later. Just for a low-key kind of visit. What brings you by here?"

"Oh, I just wanted to wish you luck before—" Will stopped himself before he got too deeply into the lie. "There's a woman in Wisconsin who wants to claim Steven Sewell's body and give him a decent burial. She doesn't have a lot of money."

"Who is she?"

"The younger sister of the woman Sewell lived with years ago. The one who was killed in the fire."

"I'll be damned."

"Seems her family was all torn apart back then, first because the older sister was living with this guy and they weren't married, and they were doing drugs, all of that. Then she got killed. Anyhow, looking back after all this time, realizing that the older sister seemed happy, the family wants to bring Sewell's body to Wisconsin. To bury him next to his girlfriend."

"Can we cut to the chase, Mr. Shafer?"

"I was hoping you might want to help."

Brokaw's eyes sparkled, then softened. "Provide a good burial for the man who probably saved my son's life . . . Done! I'll see to it right away."

"That's terrific."

"I'm paying a debt. I have a lot of debts to pay. Now, I

think I'd better bring Jamie inside. The doctors told me to
not let him overdo it for a while.''

"He's okay, then?''

"If he was any more okay, I couldn't handle it.'' Brokaw
laughed, then seemed to size Will up. "Come see for yourself.''

Brokaw put his windbreaker back on. Will grabbed his coat
and followed him through the huge kitchen, out through an
attached garage, through a door to the outside.

"A beautiful place,'' Will said as soon as he saw the rolling
snow-covered hills.

"Thank you. It's lovely in the summer. I own about a
hundred acres. Over to that hill. That pond is mine, too. You
can't see it so well now.''

Brokaw led him along the side of the house. Even before
they got to the back, Will could hear the boy's laughter. Then
they were at the rear of the house, standing on a windswept
patio, looking down a long slope toward a small barn a hundred yards away and next to it a fenced area about half the
size of a football field.

Standing just outside the fence and obviously keeping an
eye on the boy inside was a parka-clad man whom Will
recognized as one of those who had picked him up at the
hotel. The man waved at Brokaw, then waved again, to Will,
and Will waved back.

"Just a little while longer,'' Brokaw shouted. "Then bring
him in. Okay? He's supposed to take a nap.''

The man smiled and nodded.

"I want him to be rested when his mom gets here,'' Brokaw
said.

Through the slats of the fence, Will saw the boy. Jamie
Brokaw was running (no, waddling like a duck) in a blue
parka and leggings, kicking up powdery snow. The pony ran
around him in wide circles, tossing its head in delight, its
nostrils sending steam into the air. Then Will saw the dog,
which barked as it dashed headlong between the pony and the
boy.

"This may sound crazy in view of everything else, but I
was so damn happy when the police chief told me about the
dog,'' Will said.

"It doesn't sound crazy," Brokaw said quietly. "The vet says the dog has a great constitution and should be with us for a while. I love the damn animal, but he's really Jamie's dog all the way. Hell, I'd gladly spend ten times what I did to make the dog better. I owe him something, for God's sake."

As they watched, Jamie Brokaw somersaulted in the snow, then lay still. The big German shepherd, slowed only a little by the bandage around its midsection, pawed at the child, as though trying to turn him over.

"Jamie!" Brokaw shouted. "Don't get the puppy too tired now. Remember what the vet said." Then to Will: "Did I say puppy? The damn thing eats more than the pony does. Jamie calls him a puppy."

"Every kid should have a puppy," Will said.

"Funny you say that. I'm thinking of getting a puppy. It'd be good for Jamie. Good company for the big dog."

"Nice."

"Say, I'd appreciate it if your paper wouldn't write about this. At least until things quiet down."

"I understand. Not to worry."

It's the kind of story that writes itself, Will thought. Wounded dog that helped rescue kidnapped boy is adopted by child's father after being found by farmer and taken to animal shelter.

"Tell you what," Will said. "Maybe we can talk to you a month or so from now."

"Fine. Or do you just want me to call Lyle Glanford when I'm willing to have a reporter and photographer here?"

"Frankly," Will said, "you're better off dealing with me. The publisher has his good points, but he sometimes confuses things."

Brokaw chuckled. Then he said, "You don't, Shafer. You're good at sizing up people, at cutting to the chase."

Will knew what was coming next.

"Not everybody has that knack, Shafer—Will. We might have a place for you in our organization. Unless you're an incurable newspaperman."

"I appreciate the flattery, but I'm afraid that's just what I am. This, all of this, reminded me of that. And right now,

I'm going to get going while the weather holds out. I'm happy for you, Mr. Brokaw. Happy for your son, too.''

Will resolved to phone Jerry Graham as soon as he could and tell him about the hermit's dog.

Jamie stood up and brushed the snow off. It was time for Jake the pony to go back to the barn.

Wolf's eyes were wild and happy. The dog shook, and snow flew off his fur into Jamie's face. Jamie laughed, and Wolf made a funny noise like he was laughing, too.

Jamie knew it was time for his nap. He was getting tired, and he knew his mother was coming to visit later. She would be there when he woke up. He liked going to sleep in his room with the dog next to the bed.